# SYNCHRONY

## ANTHONY S. BUONI

TRANSMUNDANE PRESS

ISBN-13:978-0692526149
ISBN: 0692526145

*"Death, the only immortal who treats us all alike, whose pity and whose peace and whose refuge are for all -- the soiled and the pure, the rich and the poor, the loved and the unloved."*
Samuel Langhorne Clemens (Mark Twain)


*"I'm not afraid of death because I don't believe in it. It's just getting out of one car, and into another."*
John Lennon


*"When his wife was at his side, she was also in front of him, marking out the horizon of his life. Now the horizon is empty: the view has changed."*
Milan Kundera, *Encounter*


*"Life dies but forever will there be music. Always."*
Nicholas A. McGirr, *The Growing Dim Project*

This book evolved over many years, but I owe special thanks to:

Adelle Davis
Alisha Costanzo Chambers
Aaron Bearden
Michael Lister
Bethany Hildebrand
Lynn Wallace
Mark Boss
Joni Scott
Tony Vicjo ll
Conrad Young
Rob Blanchette
Nicholas Jordan
Shannon Rose Leahy
Larry Martin
Mom, Dad, Fallon, Steven, & Elise

# A-SIDE

♪

ANTHONY S. BUONI

Daydreaming in the backseat, Vanian noticed Lake Powell's choppy dark waters spilling into the emerald Gulf of Mexico as Bad Apple's minivan crossed the Phillips Inlet Bridge. A sign announcing "The World's Most Beautiful Beaches" framed between arched palm trees was the first thing with enough power to draw Vanian's mind from the mysterious, redheaded woman he'd seen at the past three shows.

With the tour nearing completion, the singer needed a break from labyrinthine highways and smoky barrooms where miles blurred and strangers congregated with scaring, overfriendly grins. One final event—a homecoming on the first stage the band ever played—and they could rest.

Vanian welcomed familiar faces, though suspected his had changed.

"Home again," Dar said, snuggling in Kitty's arms on the middle bench.

His voice brought Vanian's attention to his road weary band mates. Isolating, wandering thoughts were not uncommon for him, and though the group knew and accepted his eccentricities, how often did the band travel in silence?

Dar chewed at the calluses on his fingertips, the result of his frantic handling of his bass guitar. Kitty grabbed his hand and rested it on her breast.

"In high school," Dar said, "getting away from Panama City was all I thought about. I can't believe how happy I am seeing this shithole again. We weren't even gone that long."

Carter, thumb-drumming the steering wheel, glanced at the bassist and his pregnant girlfriend in the rearview.

3

"The condos look smaller now that I've seen real cities and skyscrapers," he said before returning to his finger rhythms.

"Yeah," Vanian said, drifting away again.

Had he really missed their hometown?

The road curved as Vanian looked up and squinted at the angry sun rising over towering billboards advertising overpriced seafood restaurants and gaudy tourist attractions.

Don't forget to visit the gift shop filled with t-shirts and magnets before you leave. Make sure you buy a plastic alligator for the little ones so they'll always remember the trip. Did you try the Beach Burger?

Just like everywhere else.

Always the same big box prisons and strip malls, the same tired faces desperately seeking respite from their cog-and-gear lives. Now, coming home after spending serious time floating through strange lands, he toiled with a deep emptiness.

"I never realized how close to the ground clouds look here," Carter said.

"Close clouds, my ass," hissed Astro, chipping nail polish from his midnight black fingernails with a pocket knife in the passenger seat. "I bet it pours before we get to the club. We'll be unloading in the goddamned rain again, just like Asheville. It's a wonder one of us didn't get electrocuted during that gig."

Vanian sighed. During tour something inside the guitarist changed. Lately it seemed he'd complaining and drinking hard, even by Bad Apple's rowdy and decadent standards. Vanian worried Astro needed reeling in before trouble swallowed him in one greedy gulp and patted the corner of its lips with a fancy napkin. Alongside Bad Apple's growing reputation, Astro, too, was budding, rapidly mutating from an obnoxious buddy to something darker.

Regardless of Vanian's reservations, the band was sliding across home plate with troves of interesting stories and more money than planned thanks to Kitty's business savvy.

"It was one of the better shows," Vanian said, glancing at a protection charm constructed from intersecting eastern hemlock twigs. Presented by an Appalachian witches' coven, its safeguarding powers rippled up his left arm as he traced the bindings with his fingertips. "The venue kicked ass, and once the rain let up, the view was incredible. I couldn't differentiate between the stars and the mountain lights."

4

"That was a good merch show," Kitty said, stroking a harp tattoo on Dar's shaved head. "A lot of CDs and shirts found homes there. A few buttons too. I wouldn't mind having a house on one of those hills." She pinched Dar's earlobe. "What do you say, lover? Can we retire in the Smokies?"

Dar pulled his ear from her fingers and looked up at her. "I don't care where I'm at as long as you're near."

Astro snorted. "Gross. I can't wait till we're out of this limping, cramped turd. We're not a droopy dick garage band anymore. When are we tightening up and getting a real tour bus?"

"Hey," Carter said, his voice dripping with hurt. He stroked the dashboard. "Don't knock the Badmobile. She's gotten us around just fine. There was hardly any trouble with her this tour."

Vanian knew Carter's attachment towards the vessel was intimate, like a lover. The minivan and trailer filled with Bad Apple's equipment and luggage were technically his, paid for with his parent's good fortune. Over the years he'd spent hours under the hood keeping the aging machine running, transplanting her robotic organs whenever they sputtered or seized.

"Hardly?" Astro folded up the knife and tucked it in his favorite torn black jeans.

"Overheating in Indiana and Texas aside, we saved a lot of money touring this way. I have no trouble fixing anything on her."

"It's fucking embarrassing pulling up in this piece of shit."

Carter protested, but Vanian interrupted.

"Easy. We've been working hard. Eating grease morning, noon, and night while living like sweaty nomads is not sane, but it's almost over."

Using the hemlock charm's energy, he released empathetic vibrations into the Badmobile. A simple, but effective, cleansing spell.

"We're ahead of schedule, so we'll unload at the Mozzy early. I spoke with Henry, and he said if he's not there, Steve will help set up." Vanian yawned, basking in the spell. "Should buy us decompression time."

"Hmm," Astro said. "I'll hit up Dirty Janessa, take her to Ms. Newby's later, get her drunk, and then split her in two with my rock star cock. You were right, Dar. Guess it ain't so bad being home."

"Calm down, Romeo." Kitty leaned between Carter and Astro. "I heard her and Hunter moved down to Miami."

Astro huffed. "Hunter? Miami? Bet those junkies went down there for the easy pills. Fucking losers."

"Besides," Dar chimed, "didn't you pull enough trail pussy? I swear, you poked a different groupie in damn near every town. Next tour there will be a few hungry mouths calling you daddy."

"Quit studying me and focus on your own loins, buddy. I know monogamy has you crazy jealous of my godlike sexual prowess, but you'll be investing in diapers and sippy cups soon. Told your parents she's carrying your devil spawn yet?"

Kitty's hand traveled to her stomach. Not showing physically, her emotions and appetite were the first clue she was with child before an over-the-counter pregnancy test confirmed it. She often vocalized how much she hated feeling like she was a drain on the group or in the way their progress. Was motherhood also threatening her independent nature?

Dar placed his hand over hers, rubbing her stomach together. "I told mine when we were in Austin. They're happy for us. Kitty's don't know yet."

Kitty kissed Dar's neck. "They're kind of old-fashioned, so I thought it would be better telling them in person."

"I'm sure they'll be thrilled, especially when you describe puking in the morning. You know how bad that shit smells coming off a whiskey drunk?"

"Enough, Astro." Vanian hated discord. He played peacekeeper, lighting pale yellow candles and casting serenity spells with his alone time. "They've done nothing wrong."

"What about you, Van?" Astro asked, pointing a chipped black nail at Van. "Telling Cali how famous we are?"

Vanian fell quiet as he pulled back his long black hair. Standing up left room for return jabs, and Astro always aimed his assault at Vanian's alcoholic mom. Parents were a sore spot for both men.

"No, probably not," Vanian said. "It turns out bad. I told you last time mom threw an empty quart bottle at me because I didn't bring her cigarettes."

"What a shitty world. Right, man? Your mom's a welfare case drunk, and my folks are in the islands ignoring my existence. Life's a whore."

"Life is beautiful." Vanian sent out more positive energy.

Astro squinted. "What?"

Locked in Astro's pinprick gaze, Vanian did not break eye contact.

"Dude," he said, "I'm with my best friends, working my dream job, and traveling the country. How can it get any better?"

"Gospel, brother." Carter chuckled. "Ya know, for a card-carrying witch, you sure do walk with God."

Vanian, thankful for interference, knew the occult bothered Carter. Religious polar opposites, they got along. They respected each other musically, and spiritual discussions never invoked raised voices. Forgetting how deep Carter's Christian roots ran was easy given their pub crawl regime. Vanian would catch himself taking jokes too far and halt, conscious of Carter's sensibilities.

His concentration drifted towards the longleaf pine trees zipping by; their familiar energy tickled his soul. Maybe he'd start a magical herb garden in the spring. A night blooming one filled with Moonflowers, Evening Primrose, and Angel's Trumpets.

"This show means a lot to me," said Vanian. "To be honest, you guys, I'm a little nervous about singing in front of the old crowd, even after those large shows. Henry was there at the beginning. And we haven't played his club in two years. It's like we've come full circle."

Dar leaned back, placing a hand on Vanian's shoulder, squeezing. "We're going to kill it tonight, man. If we sound half as good as we did in New Orleans, Panama City will tell their grandchildren about this one."

"They already will once I whip it out onstage." Astro laughed, wiggling his pointer finger at Carter's cheek and ear. "You'll finally get a glimpse at the legend."

The drummer shot him a glance. "We've all seen enough of that little—and I stress little—fellow between your legs. Pick out another CD before you go blind."

"Now we're talking," Astro said as he rifled through the purple CD book. "Time for real metal, losers."

Astro pushed in a black labeled disc, and cracking speakers filled the Badmobile with distorted electric guitar.

Content they'd sidetracked the guitarist, Vanian looked up at the puffy gray clouds drifting past the light blue Florida sky. His mind wandered back to the redhead in the front row, how she looked into his eyes as they sang the magical words together.

# DISC 1

# HOMECOMING

# ♫ TRACK 1 ♫

Vanian pushed open a side door, unlocked as Henry promised, and stepped from the afternoon sun's bright light into the darkness of a tight hall used for running bar stock. The Mozzy's familiar smells—stale alcohol highlighted with lingering fog machine and cigarette smoke—was not different from other clubs they'd played across the country, but the Gulf of Mexico added a twist of salty air that brought memories flooding back to the singer. He made his way to a heavy black curtain and slipped through, entering the main room as feedback ripped through the empty club. With adjusting eyes, he saw his old friend Steve, laughing and fumbling with the mixing board's knobs in the DJ booth by the front entrance's double glass doors. Across the large chamber, the office door beside the proscenium stage opened. Henry, still sitting in his swivel chair, poked his head out.

"What the hell are you doing?" Henry, always on edge, did not hide the aggravation in his voice.

The club owner's caterpillar eyebrows and bushy moustache always reminded Vanian of a video game villain. The singer suppressed a laugh, amused by the little things you miss about people and places. Vanian hid in the curtain, watching.

"It's Halloween, the season's biggest show, and you're sounding like a fucking intern out there."

Steve scratched his sideburns and fumbled his red ball cap's brim. "Sorry, boss. My fingers slipped."

"There's only one thing your fingers better be slipping into, and I don't see any of that in your booth. Tighten up. If Bad Apple hears you pedaling your pickle, they might pull out."

"This is Vanian we're talking about, Henry," Steve said. "He's not skinning out on the gig. We got history."

"Yeah, but that was before Bad Apple signed to Meow Records, before that single made internet waves. Now there's more at stake than a lousy bar tab."

Steve waved a hand. "Come on. So 'Gypsy Girl' is getting attention. It's not like they're The Rolling Stones or fucking Madonna."

"Noticed and climbing," said Henry, waving a pointed finger in the air. "The internet has spotted them, meaning the world has spotted them. It doesn't matter that they're from Panama City, these boys really have a shot. And if I had a chance to blow this hovel ten thousand miles from my memory, I'd do so without a spaghetti fart."

"I like it here."

"Come on, you'd leave in a heartbeat if the right job or piece of ass beckoned. You know it."

Steve crossed his arms.

"These boys don't have to slum, Steve. They'll be playin' arenas soon. That's when it happens, that second album. Their faces will be all over pop music magazines. Teenage birds across the country will have Bad Apple posters pinned up in their bedrooms beside cute kittens hanging in there and rainbow surfing unicorns."

Steve chuckled. "Cute kittens and unicorns, boss? Bad Apple is kind of dark, remember?"

"I'm talking about a household name, son. And these boys are ours. We're showing them we can run with the big dogs. If we're professional, Bad Apple will come back, putting the Mozzy on the map. We'll be able to book whoever we want. That means a packed venue, and a packed venue means—"

"A happy Henry," Vanian finished, stepping from the curtains. Henry said it when he was riled up, and the expression was a joke among those in the know. "And don't worry. Anytime you want Bad Apple rocking the Mozzy, you got it. So long as your intern stops comparing us to Madonna, that is."

"At least it wasn't some clean cut boy band, fucker." Steve jumped down from the DJ booth and met Vanian halfway across the dance floor for a warm embrace. "And all this time I thought daylight killed your kind. Look at the vampire now, all grown up."

"Aw, come on, Steve. It hasn't been that long since we kicked it."

"Longer than you think, Van. While you guys were picked up by bigger venues, recorded tracks, and started playing out of town gigs, I was hitting books and working for Henry Scrooge over there. Time stands still for a man like me."

Steve's words cut Vanian. It was no secret Panama City was tough. A lot of good people were trapped in dead end cycles of substance abuse, debt, depression, and broken homes. Steve was smart. Vanian hoped one day he would break free from the rusty chains and leaden shackles hidden beneath the white sandy beaches and clear azure-jade water.

Vanian took a step back, arms akimbo, unsure of a response.

"But still it goes on," boomed Henry, now by their side. He shook Vanian's hand then pulled him hard into his beer-swollen belly. "Vanian, baby. How are you? I've been going crazy here. This show's going to be huge. And I mean porn star huge."

Henry grabbed his crotch for emphasis.

"I've been running spots on the radio stations, and there's even a television plug. I've printed up flyers with Kitty's old artwork from the first shows. Remember that one with Nosferatu sinking his fangs into a black apple, blood spilling from fang-holes and spelling out the band's name?"

Vanian nodded. "Yeah, that was the cover of the first garage single we cut."

"I placed them in head shops and coffee houses in town and on the beach. We'll be so busy, I have beer trucks on call."

"Sounds like a party," Vanian said. "We also get a bar tab, right? I am pretty sure it was on the rider."

"Whatever you need. Let me know, and I'll make sure you get it."

"Put Steve's drinks on our tab too. For tight sound, we need him on our side."

Henry and Steve exchanged a glance. "No problem. I don't want him drinking too much before the show. No shots, only beer. Got it? Afterwards, he can have whatever he wants."

"Great. We'll play an extra song or two just for you, Henry."

"Good to have you back, kid. You made it from Pensacola fast. Hey, where are the other guys?"

"Pulling the Badmobile out front for unload. We wanted to make sure things here were ready before hauling the equipment to the door."

"Of course it is. Just like I said." Henry faced the soundman, jabbing him in the chest. "Steve, help Vanian and the boys bring their

13

equipment in. Get them ready so that after we turn and burn the other bands, we can get the main event going."

"No problem, boss."

Henry looked at his watch and rubbed his nose. "It's really good to see you, Van. The beer taps have been losing pressure, so I have to make a few more calls to get them checked before the show. I'll be in the office if you need me."

"Thanks, Henry."

"Steve, if the guys need anything, you hook them up, understand?"

Steve nodded.

"I also want those decorations pulled out of storage. When Jabberwocky, Kristin, and Les get here, I want that shit ready so they can get their bars in the holiday spirit."

When the owner returned behind the office door, Vanian laughed. "Man, he ain't changed a bit."

"You know he's in there right now, sharpening number two pencils and trying to figure out another way to snare a buck. It's still early for his scotch and powder, but who knows? It is Halloween, after all."

"Yes, it is. Happy Samhain."

"You still have that cottage on the West End?"

"Yeah. Haven't dropped by yet." Vanian has seen enough motel rooms and missed his home.

"At least you have a place tonight. I was going to offer mine till you got settled."

"Thanks. Dar and Kitty still have theirs. And Carter has his parents' beach house."

Steve cocked an eyebrow. "I take it their ministry has been good to them."

"Yup. I am not sure about Astro. When we left, he was sofa surfing."

"Dude, I got him. I know to hide my skin mags and pot before he gets there."

"Don't forget your booze and food." Vanian shook his head, wishing they were joking. "Kid has no shame."

"How was he on the road?" Steve asked. "I mean, I've known Astro a long time. I know how he can be. When were kids, he shoved an M-80 down a bullfrog's throat and laughed when it exploded. He was always doing weird shit to the animals around the South Lagoon neighborhood. I know we were just young, but it bothered me."

The thought also troubled Vanian. "Astro has a cruelness he doesn't hide, but I've never seen him hurt another living thing. I wouldn't stand for it. He's a knucklehead, for sure, but his guitar work gives the band an edge that we need."

"Like I said, kid shit. I just..." Steve slapped him on the shoulder then waved Vanian to the main entrance. "Let's get your stuff."

Outside Carter and Dar were handing pieces of the drum kit to Astro while Kitty stood in the building's shadow, chatting on her cellphone. Astro's shaggy brown hair dripped with sweat as he carefully rested a kick drum beside two coffin-shaped guitar cases. He wolf-howled when Steve approached.

"Old Henry must be paying you well. You're fat."

"Good to see you, too, Astro."

When Kitty heard Steve's voice, she walked over and threw her free arm around his neck, phone glued to her ear. She mouthed *hello* before returning to the shade. Dar pinched Steve's ass before grabbing a round leather bag filled with cymbals.

"So, Astro, is what they say about groupies on the road true?"

Astro, filling his arms with drums, laughed. "Man, you wouldn't believe the bitches that want to give you a handy because you pull off a few fret board modes."

"Really?" asked Steve.

"He's been taking full advantage of his musical status," said Carter. "A few years from now, there'll be a VH1 special about his many paternity suits. He probably has multiple STDs, too."

"If I'm lucky," Astro said.

Vanian rolled his eyes and picked up the guitar cases, wondering if the guitarist was serious or if it was more of his endless bull. It annoyed him how his friend communicated. The tough guy act got old fast, but Astro didn't notice.

"What about you, Carter? Still with that woman in Atlanta?" Steve asked, scooping up a green duffel bag filled with costumes. They pushed through the club's main doors and lugged the equipment to the stage. Kitty, still on the phone, held the doors as they filed into lifesaving air conditioning.

Carter cleared his throat. "Yeah, I'm still with Annabelle. We don't see each other. Guess things are fine."

"They're not really together," Astro said. "It's a front—she's just his fag hag because Carter is too chicken shit and Christian to face the truth."

"Really, dude?" Carter asked. "Since when is my love life any of your business?"

Astro started protesting, but Vanian's glare halted his attack.

Steve ran a hand through his short dirty-blonde hair, scratching the thick matching sideburns framing his face. "How is Kitty these days, Dar?"

"Preggers," Dar said.

"No shit?"

"We found out in Chicago. Man, we were on fire that night."

"Jesus, are you two ready for that?"

Dar nodded. "I know it complicates things, but we'll be great. We'll make it work."

Vanian hoped so, too. His bassist and manager were essential components to Bad Apple's success. Losing them would be a deathblow.

"I sure hope so," Steve said. "She's a fine woman. You've done good."

"Thanks."

"Tell me, how was Chitown? I've heard it's fucking crazy up there."

"The devil was restless underneath us. Also happened in New Orleans." Astro shifted the drums in his arms, balancing them and flashing the sign of the goat with his right hand. "Cities of sin, band of darkness. Drove the crowds fucking nuts. I've been seeing ghosts since then."

That piqued Vanian's interest. He'd heard a lot of Astro's trash talk, but never ghosts.

"Wow," said Steve. "Sounds like you guys are really cooking. What about you, Vanian? Taking the Jim Morrison challenge with any bar whores?"

Vanian's cheeks warmed. On tour he'd seen plenty of beautiful women. A few even whispered sweet nothings and hotel room numbers in his ear before and after gigs, but the singer was not putting himself out there. As far as he was concerned, Bad Apple was working, gaining exposure, and pushing their first single, not chasing the affections of random women.

"He's going limp dick on us," Astro said. "Women throw themselves at him, but he's too busy reading and writing. Always got his nose in a damned book. Tell you the truth, I've caught him stealing glances at me during the 'Gypsy Girl' solo."

"Leave him alone," Dar said as he put the cymbals on the stage. "You know he's waiting for the right woman. The only person overcompensating is you, Astro. All those whores you keep hooking up with—we know what that really means."

"Oh, yeah, what's that?" asked Astro.

"It means no snatch will ever fulfill the desire burning inside your heart. You know that aching, that need of a hairy ass rubbing against your bare chest? That means you're gay, dude."

"Fuck you," Astro snapped.

"See?" Dar said, waving his arms around in the air, shaking his head. "Fuck me, you throw rocks at women. There's no denying it, you're a fag."

Astro leapt on Dar, knocking both men to the dance floor.

"Look at 'em go," Carter said to Steve. "Can you imagine what it's like living in that minivan with those two childish animals? Pure madness."

Vanian, arms crossed, looked at the Mozzy's stage. Their first show there had been a fiasco. Dar's amp kept shorting out, Carter broke his kick drum, and Astro was too drunk to maintain time. Vanian was wrestling a cold. Throughout the gig, his voice crackled. Between sickness and stage fright, the singer fought throwing up on the eight sympathetic friends present. After the show, Henry surprised him by inviting Bad Apple to another gig, beginning the band's professional career.

Looking back, Vanian wasn't sure how they'd come so far.

As Dar and Astro wrestled each other, Steve walked beside Vanian.

"Bring back memories?" Steve asked.

"Yeah. Nothing will replace those first shows here. We sounded so bad."

Steve laughed. "You guys were never terrible."

"Come on, Steve. We were kids. No amount of fake blood and H. P. Lovecraft costumes made up for our musical lassitude. We were simply bad."

"Look at where you guys are at now. That album, *Vector 5*, was hot with two Ts, H-O-T-T. You know what's funny?"

"What's that?"

"The first time I heard you on the radio was during Freak's local showcase, *The Middle of Nowhere* about a year before he died. Do you remember that?"

"Yeah." Vanian heard the late radio DJ's laugh, a voice silenced by cancer too soon, too young. "He was a good kid."

"When I heard that, that piece of shit bedroom cassette you guys recorded, I thought it sounded pretty cool. But when I heard a Bad Apple studio recording on Reverb Nation, I knew you cats were looking at this place in the rearview. Couldn't have happened to better kids too."

"I miss the way it was"

"The Mozzy or the band?"

"The band," Vanian said, unaware of his true feelings until the moment he articulated them. The revelation caught him off-guard. "This fire in my chest burned for us to make it, you know, actually go somewhere. Since the nonstop bigger clubs, the fire has…petered out. I miss goofing off around here. I know I've outgrown the place, but I am nostalgic. It's home."

"Well, maybe you can buy land here after the band settles down."

"I belong in New Orleans—I'm lured by the Mississippi's polluted glow. The cobblestones and swamp are calling me. They're magic. I don't know, Steve. Sometimes you can't go home again."

"That's bullshit, and you know it." Steve looked at his shoes.

For the second time that afternoon, a weird pain tugged at Vanian's heart.

"Well, wherever you wind up, you will always have friends here." Steve hugged Vanian. They looked over to Dar, Astro pinned down underneath him squirming. Carter hovered overhead, and all three were laughing and swearing.

"Still the same old crowd," Steve said.

"Peter Pan and the Lost Boys." Vanian sighed, pulling at his hair. He saw split ends that needed trimming. It was time to re-dye his dark brown roots black and fix the white strip running along his bangs again.

"You ready to set up?" asked Steve.

"Yeah. Your PA ready?"

"Yup. Just get Carter to set up his drums. While he's doing that, we'll get the stacks inside and onstage."

Fifteen minutes later, the five men were sweat-soaked and breathing hard. After unloading the amplifiers, Steve dollied them into the building. Carter assembled the hi-hat as Dar ran wires connecting synthesizers to a large amplifier. Vanian adjusted the microphone to match his height, placing a few inches between mouth and windscreen.

Astro, setting up his amp, cussed after pinching his hand under the head.

"People believe this job is glamorous," he said, "like they show on TV. Another fine example between the fine line of reality and fantasy in showbiz, fellows."

"He doesn't get tired of hearing himself talk," said Dar. "We go through this every show."

"I heard that, Dar. Don't make me come down there and mess you up again," Astro called.

"What? Mess me up? I wasn't the one screaming bloody murder for mercy a little while ago, faggot."

Astro tensed up. "Are you steeping to me, boy? If you wanna do the man dance, I'll tango. Say one more thing and I'll—"

"Boys," interrupted Vanian. "This is our homecoming. Let's have a happy one. What have I got to do for your cooperation, sing a lullaby for ya?"

Astro grimaced as the rest of the band laughed.

"No," Dar said. "We're cool."

"I hope so," said Vanian. "I don't want our hometown seeing us piss and moan like a bunch of bitches. This will be the hardest show on the tour. We need to be tight. They see us acting like gromits, and they'll come in like sharks."

"Hey, there's no such thing as bad publicity," Astro said.

"Yes, there is," said Vanian. "And we don't want any of it. Tomorrow, the only thing I want these cats talking about is how they can't wait for the next album. We on the same page, or is there a problem here?"

"Same page," said Astro. "Just fooling around."

"Let's get working. Then we can dick off," said Vanian as he tightened the microphone in place. Fun was fun, but it was business time. "I'm sick of hearing your little love spats."

They finished setting up in silence until sound check. They tested the drums, synths, bass, and guitars, saving the microphones until right before their set. Steve looked over the mixing board one last time and pulled out a cigarette, tucking it behind his right ear. While they were hanging prop skeletons and severed baby doll parts from the lighting rig, Henry came from the office smiling.

"Everything's set. Both radio stations just called, and they've received a great response. They're broadcasting live remotes here tonight. Rockin' Ron and Six Pack want an interview. I'll bet Shortbus and Stroke will also wave a mic under your nose."

"No problem. I'll give a shout out reminding listeners if they bring canned goods for charity, they get a free Bad Apple button," Vanian said. "A lot of memories in this venue, Henry. What you're doing for local music is commendable."

"Thanks," Henry said. "It—it means a lot."

"Smoke break," Steve said. "I'm in need of a delicious cancer stick to poison what's left of my godforsaken lungs. Coffin nail, anyone?"

"Don't smoke, but I'll join you," Vanian said, resting his red guitar on a stand behind his mic. "When are you giving those nasty things up, man?"

"When death is knocking at my door," Steve said. "The same day I accept Jesus."

Carter huffed.

Vanian climbed off the stage and followed Steve into the sweaty and still autumn air. He considered summoning a cool breeze, but decided saving his energy for the show was a better idea.

Steve sparked a plastic red lighter, igniting a square and taking a long drag, letting the smoke slowly escape from his open mouth. Vanian made sure he stood downwind.

"So," said Steve, "what's going on in your life?"

"I've been writing a lot of stuff other than music. I've been dabbling with prose, ya know, gone back to my roots and tinkering with a novel."

Before Vanian ever picked up a guitar, he wanted to be a writer. Growing up with books as companions, it was only natural that one day he'd write his own.

"Really? The Great American Novel. Ever the pessimist, I'd say it's a hard business to get into, but you seem to have a knack for breaking through glass ceilings. You've already built a name for yourself. Might help you sell books."

"If I write a novel that sells, I'm donating proceeds to the homeless or people trying to get off drugs," said Vanian. His eyes drifted. "I saw so much shit on the road, it turns my stomach."

"You're something else. Canned food drives at a goth concert and now this," Steve said. He took another drag, careful not to blow the smoke into Vanian's face. "You weren't much of a loner in high school. How come you're not with a woman, enjoying her company?"

Vanian was bored with friends and strangers meddling in his love life. He wanted more than the white picket dream. Vanian craved the moon.

The redhead's face flashed through his mind.

"It's complex. I just can't bang a random skirt. Kerouac wrote in *The Dharma Bums* that 'pretty girls make graves', and I happen to agree. So many things come with sex. STDs and kids aside, the emotions are intense. So many cats miss the evolutionary express, dragging their knuckles across the ground, looking for a piece. I want more than good looks, and I need someone who feels the same about me. I need a partner."

"A lot of people want that," Steve said. "You have to just roll with it. Once in a while, you're a doormat. Other times, there's mud on your kicks. That's the nature of relationships. Love is like a sore dick. You can't beat it, and when it's hard, it hurts."

"Ha," Vanian said. He wanted to change the conversation but didn't know a spell strong enough.

"I can tell you're looking, but why haven't you settled for at least close to what you want?" Steve asked.

There was no escape. Steve was going all the way.

"Any prospects?"

"This is going to sound crazy." Vanian paused, unsure about revealing his secret crush. He didn't know the girl, and taking interest in an audience member beyond a subtle glance was a page from Astro's playbook, not his.

"Try me."

Vanian noticed an albatross circling the club. "I've been seeing this woman at the shows. The last three. She's always in the front, always alone, looking me in the eyes or singing."

A slow smile crawled across Steve's face. "Ah, so there *is* a groupie you wanna make?"

"No. There's something different about her."

"What a load of shit, man. You want to fuck her. If I was you, I'd be taking full advantage of my status. Look at Astro. He may not possess couth, but that cat has no reservations. He knows this run away carnival ride won't spin forever, and he's fulfilling primal whims. Good or bad, he's at least taking what he wants." Steve took another drag on his cigarette.

"I told you, my body is sacred. I don't sleep around because it's mistreating the divine. I'm looking for the right woman, not the easy one."

"You're setting yourself up for hurt," said Steve. "Let one woman in, and sure enough, she'll topple you."

The Tarot image of the Tower flashed across Vanian's mind. The card's crumbling edifice and falling people represented destruction of achievement; washing away accomplishment before starting anew. Surfacing in his recent readings, Vanian noted the synchronicity.

"What's worth having if there's not work or risk?"

"I don't want to see you hurt."

"I'll deal if it happens."

"Just be careful," Steve said, fumbling the cigarette. "There's a lot more to protect than your heart. Some women only want dollar signs. Now that you're popping, you might look like a mark."

"I see your point, but the right one is out there. I know it."

"I'll never understand you. You feel things so deep and so different. I want to crawl into your head and see what's going on in there."

Steve flipped the cigarette to the ground and twisted it with a pivot of his snakeskin boot. The embers spread in an arc before burning out, and Vanian thought they resembled a fiery river.

"It's a scary place, Steve."

"No shit."

Carter and Astro filed out of the Mozzy.

"Let's go downtown and hit the coffee shops," Astro said. "Maybe we can cause a scene, sign autographs."

"Oh, Binjo's afterwards," said Carter. "I want one of our albums from the place that helped me fall in love with music. That'd be crazy. How long has it been since you've seen Paul, Van?"

Vanian cringed. The indie record shop's owner dated his mother for a few years when Vanian was a preteen. Before Cali sabotaged the relationship with alcohol and other men, Paul and Vanian were close, giving him his first guitar and teaching him chords and tablature, a shorthand version of sheet music. Paul helped Vanian harness his voice, encouraging singing above growling. But his lessons didn't end with music. He also opened Vanian's magical mind, giving him the power to cast spells.

Paul was the closest thing to a father Vanian had ever known. When Paul and Cali separated, his mother made it clear she didn't want him hanging around her son.

The pain still haunted him.

"I'm chilling in the greenroom. Read, or relax. Maybe write."

"What's up with Dar? Anyone know his plans?" asked Steve, pulling out another cigarette.

"We're dropping them off at their apartment so they can pick up Kitty's car. They're visiting her folks for dinner," Astro said. "How would you like to be a fly on that fucking wall?"

"You want to kick it with us, Steve?" Carter asked.

"Can't, man. Sorry. I need to stay here and get the bars stocked. Set up the other bands when they show. I figure you guys will be on before midnight, so get back by nine so Henry doesn't croak."

"Sounds good," said Vanian. "Tell Paul I said hello, and please don't get into trouble."

"We'll try," said Astro as they wandered towards the Badmobile. "But make sure you have bail money just in case."

# ♬ TRACK 2 ♬

E ntering Binjo Records, Astro admired the new coat he'd bought from the thrift shop. Black vinyl, it fell past his ankles, had several silver buckles along the waist, and the red velvet skull pattern interior was reversible. Astro shelled out over two hundred dollars for the coat but knew it would look phenomenal onstage. Image sold the package, and he was giving Bad Apple fans what they wanted.

Behind the counter, Paul Obol put down his pricing gun and smiled. His blue eyes sparkled behind thick glasses, gems in an aging face. A silver pentagram dangled from a chain around his neck.

Astro thought he looked older than ever, wondering if he took pills to get hard. Maybe he could score a handful.

"Howdy, Paul," Carter, entering, waved.

"As I live and breathe, Bad Apple."

After pushing the glasses up his nose's bridge, Paul rose from a wooden stool and came from behind the counter, shaking their hands.

"The show's all over the radio. There's a flyer in the window, and I've been stuffing handbills in bags with each purchase. All my customers have been talking about it. The Mozzy is going to be slammed tonight."

He scanned the guitarist. "Looking fly, Astro."

"Thanks. The coat is new. Probably going to be hot as a whore's left tit onstage, but it should get the panties wet." Astro skimmed the music posters on the ceiling and walls, wondering if Paul would kick him one. "How's the shop going?"

"Tough competing with the internet, but I still know some magic. Having instruments, strings, books, DVDs, and t-shirts in stock keeps them coming around. Then there's my loyals, they see this joint as a vital part of their lives. They meet up here, leave their zines and chapbooks. Younger bands leave demos like you kids did a few years back. They all want to be Bad Apple."

"Poor saps," Astro said, chuckling. Any wannabe garage band hoping they would ever be as good as Bad Apple was absurd.

Carter leaned against the counter. "It's cool we've inspired other artists. Do you have any copies of *Vector 5* in stock now?"

"I make sure I don't run out. They're by the wax." Paul walked to an aisle of 12" vinyl records, stopping before an endcap underneath a sign reading BAD APPLE AND LOCAL. The entire top row of CDs was *Vector 5*. "I have a few also stocked in rock and pop, just to be safe."

"I'd like to buy one," Carter said, scooping a copy off the shelf.

"This guy." Astro jabbed a thumb at Carter. "We got a thousand copies in the trailer."

Paul shook his head. "I'll just give you one, if you want it."

"No, no. I'm supporting your shop."

Paul beamed and headed behind the counter. "Anything else you need?"

"Yeah." Astro began heading to the CD rows. "You have anything with balls? Any Acid Bath or Waltari?" Astro, tiring of the moody Darkwave songs Vanian kept writing, really wanted to push the band in a black metal direction before the singer turned them into pop star clones. He thought he'd learn heavier chops and spring them on the next rehearsal. "Maybe Cradle of Filth?"

"We have all that. They're also in rock and pop."

"Rock and pop? Jesus Butt Pirate Christ, Paul. You really need a metal section so my hands don't touch this pussy music."

Astro deliberated spitting on a nearby poster of a blue-eyed blonde wearing a cowboy hat until his gaze fell on her voluptuous cleavage. He was famous now. She'd agree to a tumble. He'd paint those corn-fed tits with electric, demigod semen.

Maybe cut her.

"It's too hard separating the subgenres now. Organizing it alphabetically was the easiest way." Paul rang up Carter's CD then swiped his debit card.

"Slacker."

Astro scanned the CDs and pulled out a Dimmu Borgir album, flipping it over to read the track listing. Creatures entangling the raised red song titles reminded him of the darkness he'd been seeing, foreboding creatures glimpsed from the corner of his eyes since the Chicago show. He put the album back and shook the thought.

After signing the receipt, Carter unwrapped his CD from its cellophane cocoon and peeled off the tape holding the case together. "Got a felt pen?"

"Uh," Paul said, looking around the cluttered register area. "Yeah, there is a bunch of markers here somewhere. Ah, there they are."

He slid open a drawer and reached in, holding up a few colors. Carter grabbed silver, and nodded in appreciation. Removing the sleeve from the jewel case, Carter signed his name on the bottom left of the album cover. The silver ink popped against the black background. Carter blew on the ink while waving the insert like a paper fan.

"Hey, Astro, come sign this."

"Should be charging for the damned thing. You know how much the signature of the first person they electrocuted is worth?" Astro set his CD on the counter and took the pen from Carter. "Just this, Paul."

After signing across the CD's center image and handing it back to the drummer, Astro fumbled out a twenty and slapped it on the counter. "What are you even doing with that?"

Carter shot him a wink. Astro wanted to slap his smug face. That would teach that faggot a thing or two about flirting.

"I gotta ask," Paul said. "How's Vanian?"

"He sends his regards." Carter reinserted the sleeve into the jewel case, shutting it. "He's writing, as usual. Been a while since you've seen him, huh?"

"Yeah. Cali… Well, that's a dusty story that belongs on another rainy day's shelf. I'm glad he's doing well for himself. He always was a clever boy." Paul looked off in the corner of the shop instead of at the band. "He floats through here once in a while and checks up on me. It's funny seeing him grown up, how fast time passes and all."

"Why don't you come tonight?" Carter asked. "I'm sure he'd love you there."

"Nah." Paul's eyes snapped into reality. "It's way past my bedtime. I have an early mandolin lesson. Besides, it's Samhain, and I won't risk running over trick-or-treaters. I'll catch you guys next time around."

The door opened and a pretty redhead wearing a Pink Floyd tank top entered.

"Hello, nurse," Astro said in a singsong voice.

The way her perky nipples danced, it was obvious she was lacking a bra. Shameless flirt. He could grab her throat, pull her to the ground underneath the country girl poster, and then take her in front of Carter and Paul. Shredding her shirt would take little effort, and Astro imagined biting off one of those nipples and forcing it into her mouth with a prolonged bloody kiss. Afterwards, she'd thank him—after all, how often can you say you've fucked a legend?

"Hey, aren't you two in Bad Apple?" she asked.

"Yeah, and we would like to invite you to the show tonight." Carter handed her the autographed CD.

"Is this for me?"

"It is now. I'm blessed for my life, and I like to pay it forward."

*That selfish little prick,* Astro thought as he coughed twice in the crook of his arm. "Must be nice having Christian money to throw away."

He wasn't jealous of Carter or his privilege. Astro also came from a wealthy background, but his parents opted spending their retirement sailing the Caribbean after Astro's behavior and lifestyle crossed theirs too many times. An older couple, they figured Astro would learn more if they cut him off.

He'd never forgive them for it.

Carter ignored him. "What do you say, coming out tonight?"

"Oh, hell yeah. I wouldn't miss it," she said. "The whole town is going."

"Excellent. We'll see you there."

Astro rubbed his hand along the girl's arm. "Are you old enough to drink?"

She had no idea how powerful he was, how much control he possessed. The choices in their relationship were his.

He loved it.

Carter turned to the shopkeep. "Paul, it's time for us to split."

"You boys break a leg tonight. Tell Van he is in my thoughts."

"Will do. Come on, Astro. Let's grub and get our faces on."

Astro flashed the girl a dangerous smile. "See you around."

## ♫ TRACK 3 ♫

Pushing green beans to one side of the plate, Dar was waiting for the sky to fall.

Kitty's no nonsense Republican parents always made him wary, let alone on the night the bassist planned on confessing he'd knocked up their only daughter. Kitty, adamant un-bagging the cat was her responsibility, had spent the past twenty minutes telling her father about life on the road. Dar dreaded the fallout following the moments after she delivered the good news.

"We ate the best soft pretzels in Philly," she said, cutting the porterhouse steak's filet with opulent silverware. "They had these little kiosks all over downtown, and people were lined up for them. Investing in pretzel stands might be a good idea, Daddy. I've never seen any here, and they would make a killing in Pier Park with those tourist dollars floating around."

"And who would run these stands, Kitty?" her father, Carl, asked as he buttered a potato with olive oil spread. Since his heart attack seven years earlier, the family monitored their salt and cholesterol intake, a diet Kitty maintained even after her and Dar moved in together.

Dar wondered if the news would kill him, feeling guilty afterwards.

"It would be a great job for a high school kid. There's virtually no cost going into making the pretzels, and the darned things smell so good they practically sell themselves. It's money in the bank."

"It sounds wonderful, dear," said Pearl, Kitty's mom.

Dar wondered how she and the former-soldier-turned-businessman became a couple. With her graying hair tied up in a bun and round spectacles on her button nose, she should be putting apple pie in a farmhouse window, not sitting at a dinner table worth more than most people's cars. Something didn't fit about the match, but then he figured her parents must look at him and Kitty and wonder the same. She was a college woman; he was the best at beer pong in the band. She was logical; he was passionate. She was good with money; he loved partying. Dar cut into his steak and laughed to himself, amazed at what mysterious force brought and kept people together.

"What's so funny over there, Dar?" Carl asked, breaking his thoughts.

"Uh, I was just remembering the characters at last night's show. There was this guy who looked like a parrot. His hair was four different colors, and he had tattoos on his face. And I don't mean the side of his head, I mean his face. Real bright ones, too. Like a cake exploded on him."

"No job will hire a man looking like that. Kid is probably a drain on society." Carl poured red wine into a glass. Without ever looking up from his plate, he asked, "So, Dar, speaking of drains, when are you going to drop the rock star nonsense and finish school?"

Dar seized. The conversation was heading for rocky shores with no lighthouses in sight. "We sold a lot of t-shirts and CDs on the road. Kitty is an excellent salesman—"

"Salesperson," she corrected, batting her eyes at him.

Dar hoped the words would just keep flowing. "Salesperson, right, and we were planning on taking money from the tour and recording another album."

"Another album, huh? About that first one, I saw in the liner notes you're calling yourself Kitty Corpse nowadays, honey." Carl wiggled his knife in the air, never taking his arm off the table. "That's pretty morbid, don't you agree? What is Grandma going to say when she sees that?"

"Grandma's blind," Kitty said. "She won't be able to read it."

Carl frowned and turned to Dar. "And you. I suppose you're dragging my daughter along the Oregon Trail again."

"Yes." Dar swallowed a mouthful of biscuit before continuing. "She's indispensable to us. She handles venue owners, manages money, and up-sells the hell out of merch. She's a part of the band." He wouldn't admit it to Kitty, but he got a cheap thrill seeing Carl cringe when he swore.

"Look, Dar, I get the entrepreneurial spirit. I made my first splash selling medical equipment hospital to hospital until I became the big fish and opened my own distribution center, so I understand the desire to build your business, your brand. My main concern is that rock bands are a flavor of the week, and in a few years when Bad Apple becomes yesterday's thing, what are you going to fall back on?"

"Right now I'm focused on writing music. I'm sure I'll bounce when the time comes."

Carl looked right into Dar's eyes, into his soul. "What about marriage and kids? You both don't plan on living in sin forever, do you?"

Dar said nothing, balling his hands under the table. Squeezing hard enough to dig his fingernails in his palm, he held his breath.

"You can have a kid without being married, Dad," Kitty said.

"A bastard? In this family? When that happens, I'll start voting the Communist ticket."

"Well," she said, "you'd better get to the ballots because I'm pregnant."

Pearl dropped her silverware on the plate. They sat in silence, looking at each other as Carl's face turned red, his hands trembling.

"I thought I raised you better than that," he said in a low voice. "In this day and age with all the diseases running around, why would you have sex without a condom?"

"Dad, we've been together five years. It's not like I fucked a stranger behind one of the shows."

Pearl gasped. Carl slammed his hands on the table.

Dar resisted a smile.

"That's it. Get out. Both of you."

"But, Carl, darling," Pearl said, "we're not finished eating."

"Yes, we are."

Dar drained his wine glass before standing up. The first rule of showbiz entailed always leaving the crowd wanting more, a decree now laying shattered over half-eaten meals and cooling pumpkin pie.

"Thanks for having us over," he said. "The food was real tasty."

Pearl nodded.

Carl sat there, staring at the uncorked wine bottle.

Kitty rose, kissing her father on the cheek and hugging her mom before she took Dar's arm and escorted him away from the table.

At their car, Dar opened the driver's side door for her. He was amazed at how beautiful she looked, how she'd stood up for him. She started to get in, but he grabbed her arm and kissed her.

"I'm so sorry that didn't go over well."

"It'll be okay. Dad just needs time to get used to the idea. I'm really happy we're doing this."

"I am too. I really am."

Dar knew his face betrayed him. As reality sunk its fangs into the situation, certain change loomed in the horizon.

"What's wrong? Did they get to you?" Kitty rubbed her hand against his chest.

"Is he right? I mean, we really should have a better plan for the future."

"You're right, we should," she said. She pressed her body against his. "And we will. I was of the mind we bring the little one the road with us. We can homeschool her better than any classroom around here and show her the world at the same time."

"You keep on saying *her*," Dar said. "You know we're having a boy, right?"

"Get in the car, asshole."

Dar looked at Kitty's parents' home, vowing to one day have a nicer place for his family.

# ♫ TRACK 4 ♫

Vanian was in the greenroom as the opening band, Drowsy Rain, took the Mozzy's stage. He'd devoured most of his paperback copy of *The Stranger* before donning his favorite stage clothes: black slacks and a matching long-sleeved shirt flimsy enough Vanian didn't melt under the brutal stage lights. He teased his hair up with styling gel and painted his fingernails black. Playing guitar would chip the nail polish during the night, but he didn't care. Putting on a makeup mask helped him push through another set. He wondered how long he would go on playing rock star. Crucifying his words each night in front of a crowd in love with an image was wearing thin.

He wanted serenity, solace.

Vanian leaned back in an overstuffed sofa and watched condensation roll down the side of a water glass. Wishing he had divining tea leaves, his gaze wandered across the surface of the clear fluid, reflecting the bright vanity lights. As his eyes relaxed, images appeared in the water. The lights melted into lava pouring from the side of a volcano, forming a river. He heard the boiling fluid bubble and pop as fiery fingers stretched outwards, louder and louder until he shook off the scrying spell's trance. Unable to make heads or tails of the omen, Vanian cracked his knuckles, loosening his fingers so they could glide over the fret board.

He heard Drowsy Rain ask the crowd if they were excited Bad Apple was back in town, and a roar filled the greenroom. Vanian smiled at the response, his earlier nervousness fading away.

Those first days playing music were so far away.

Paul and his mom gave him an acoustic guitar for Christmas, the pagan holiday Yule, when he was eleven. It wasn't what he asked for.

Vanian wanted an old typewriter for writing poetry, but his mother told him they were outdated, insisting he use Paul's desktop word processor. The final gift under their faux tree was a misshapen cardboard box. He opened the present and stared at the instrument tucked within soft, white foam paper. Fresh wood wafted across his nose, and he was instantly addicted. Pulling the guitar from the box, he ran his fingers across the six strings—fingers that looked so trivial against the fret board. When plucked, the notes both frightened and excited him.

He had no clue where to start.

Paul gave him lessons. The two spent a lot of time hanging out in Binjo's. Whenever Paul was busy with inventory or helping customers, Vanian picked up licks from older guitarists drifting in and out of the shop, learning licks by bands ranging from The Beatles and Nirvana to poppy rock songs on the radio. Vanian soaked up the lessons. Paul was patient with the boy, and Vanian loved him. Then Cali slipped away into the bottle…

After lighting a candle and charging it with energy, Vanian smeared white theatre base over his face, careful to cover his ears and neck. Once his skin could pass for the back of an index card, he applied black eyeliner and gray eye shadow. He smeared on black lipstick and puckered, smoothing out the uneven job. After a few ashen cheekbone highlights, he resembled a reanimated corpse from a classic horror movie.

Perfect.

He closed his eyes. The rest of his band would be around soon, and they would have to put on one hell of a performance. These shows cut him the deepest.

The greenroom door opened and Dar entered.

Vanian opened his eyes and looked his friend up and down. Dar was dressed like a vampire priest. Fake blood poured from his lower lip's corners into spider-webbed rivulets down his throat.

"I see you rummaged through your apartment. Looks good," Vanian said.

Dar took a seat next to Vanian and kicked his feet up on a rectangular ottoman splattered with random red and yellow paint blotches. "Nothing in here matches," he said. "So close, no matter how far."

"I know," said Vanian. "Did you see Kitty's parents?"

"Yeah. Kitty told them the news."

"How did they take it?"

"They don't think I'm ready. They want me ditching the music and nightlife scene for a real plan."

"Maybe they're wise," said Vanian. His mother's only life advice was don't have kids because they ruin your plans. He wondered what growing up with a real parent would have been like. "You two have been saving, right?"

"Yeah."

"Buy a little house and settle down."

"And do what? This life, the music, it's what I know. This band is not just my bread and butter. It's my passion. I get paid to horse around with my best friends while getting fed free drinks. I leave this, what do I have?"

Vanian rubbed his chin. "You have a family."

"I'm going to have it all. And when we're ready, we'll settle down. Probably plant our roots here, maybe buy in the Cove...kind of spooky back there."

"I like it there, too." Vanian knew the bassist made sane decisions. Dar would tell him when the time to call it quits came. "So, you're straight for another album or two?"

"Yeah," Dar said. "Of course. Got a ways till the lady and I are set."

Vanian extended his fist. Dar pounded it.

Dar looked at the wall clock hanging beside a refrigerator covered in band stickers. "I see the guys are running late as usual. Didn't Steve say nine?"

"What do you expect? If they were on time, I'd be afraid something was wrong."

"You know," Dar said, "I noticed you looking at that chick the past few nights."

Vanian's heart seized. Had he ogled her?

"Yeah?"

"Yeah. She's not a stranger. She's from here, man. I've been seeing her for years. She was at our old shows, back when we were playing free gigs in McKenzie Park."

Vanian was dumbstruck. "For real?"

"Sincerely," said Dar. "I think she's liked you a long time."

"Do you know her name?" Vanian asked.

"No, but I can find out if you want."

"I don't know," Vanian said. First Steve knew about his interest and now Dar. Word was getting around fast. "I'm not good at picking up women."

"You don't have to pick her up," Dar said. "Just talk to her. Find out what she's about. We have a break after this show. Take her out to dinner or see a movie. It's been a long tour."

"Yes, it has."

"Three months and we're back in the studio. Then you'll have to concentrate on the creative stuff. For now, chill. Ease your worried mind and live. Fuck all this tortured artist crap and experience life for a change."

Vanian laughed. "Might just kill me."

"If you're lucky, you'll be the first of the gang to die," said Dar.

"What does that have to do with luck?" asked Vanian.

The greenroom door opened, and Henry poked his head in.

"Howdy, boys. Excited about tonight?"

"Yes, sir," said Vanian. "The others will be here soon."

"Drowsy Rain is almost done," Henry said, the overhead light reflecting on his scalp through his thinning hair. "Danger Shaft next and then you guys. The place is really filling up. They're buying the hell outta your t-shirts and my beer, so this is win-win."

"Good," said Dar. "Let us know if there's anything we can do."

"Just play your hearts out," said Henry before vanishing.

"He's a phony fuck," Dar said once the door closed. "He's about dollar signs nowadays."

Vanian was offended. Henry was good to them over the years.

"It is business," Vanian said. "Besides, if it wasn't Henry, we'd be paying in some other guy's place. At least this is a cat we've known."

"True. I guess you have to pick the best cock from the bouquet of pricks."

Dar sparked a cigarette, rocking his head from side to side and cracking his neck.

"Are you nervous about being a daddy, Dar?" Vanian had sidestepped the question long enough.

"I'd be lying if I said I wasn't. Kitty's a fantastic woman, though, and I couldn't be happier."

"That's what matters."

"You know, it'll be funny showing him pictures of the band and us growing up. I can hear myself now: Here's when we released ten thousand praying mantises at the poetry reading, and here's when we killed thirty men, women, and children onstage."

Vanian laughed. "You said *he.*"

"Damn straight, I did." Dar fell silent. "I didn't think that night we were tripping on acid and shrooms while pounding beats out with our fists on Astro's back porch that we would be standing here."

"Me neither, cat."

Vanian remembered the night Bad Apple officially took their moniker. They tinkered with a few cover songs, playing them around campfires and during long, booze-filled weekends. When Astro expanded their consciousness with psychedelic substances, something cosmic and primal took over. They started making music by grunting and pounding their fists on the concrete slab underneath their crossed legs. Later that night, they wrote down a bunch of ideas for the band's name on an odd amount of ripped paper slips and drew them from a tattered top hat.

The last remaining was Bad Apple.

That week, they began writing original songs…

Dar glanced at himself in the mirror. "You start out wearing t-shirts of the band you love. Meet likeminded people, start jamming in a shed. I fucking loved playing at the sheds. Remember when we said we'd rather be dead than a barroom cover band, that what we had to say was important?"

Vanian cracked his knuckles. "We made the right decision to stick with originals, even if no one showed up at first."

"So…what do you wanna open with?" Dar asked, rubbing his tattoo of a giant plant shoving a screaming man into its mouth on his right leg.

"I say 'Outpatient Therapy', an oldie but goodie. Most of the crowd will recognize it, and it's fun. Since it's kinda loud, it will also give Steve a chance to right the levels for the more intricate tunes."

"Tight," said Dar. "I'm crowd bopping for the familiar faces. Kitty might need a hand at the merch table, and I can catch a swill. Want a beer?"

"Thanks," Vanian said, "but I'm sticking with reading. Maybe after the show I'll get down with ya."

"Suit yourself. See you after Danger Shaft's set."

Vanian nodded. Dar stood up, and started for the door, pausing with his hand on the doorknob. "Thank for the tête-à-tête."

"Any time, brother."

## ♫ TRACK 5 ♫

Henry sat in the office, pouring over a big-buttoned calculator as Drowsy Rain's music filled his club. The numbers were looking good. The best against a slow season. Expensive condos replaced many of the older, reasonable hotels dotting Panama City Beach's Miracle Strip and alienated younger, budget-minded tourists, the same clientele who flocked to Mozzy's underground shows.

Rising gas and food prices also bit into extra cash.

Forced to pay the acts less, the bookings suffered. Young groups eager for exposure and a few cold beers were few and far between. Many understood their talents and wanted cash. Henry considered himself fair, normally offering four hundred dollars for one band that would play three sets totaling four hours. Those acts played a lot of covers and bought in their own following. For instances where younger bands played originals before a headlining act, he would pay each opening band two hundred dollars for an hour set and five to six hundred for the main event. He also added a percent of the door for the musicians to spilt, usually equaling two or three dollars a head.

Even with his generosity, older local acts were delusional about their position on the musical food chain, demanding as much as two thousand dollars for the same performance. Dealing with those assholes was his least favorite part of running the Mozzy. Grabbing them by the ears, knocking them in their smug fucking dicks, and laying down exactly how things are didn't happen in the real world. He was careful not to burn bridges—that was bad business—but it was getting harder and harder meeting the nightclub's cost.

Bad Apple was a class act because they agreed to five hundred for an hour set, kicking their door percentage to the younger bands. Vanian's main concern was that Henry allowed collecting canned goods for the needy. The kid's passion amazed him. Henry wondered how long it would take before the cutthroat record business hardened the singer, before he became a spoiled rock star prick smear like the lot of them.

He'd seen it happen to lesser musicians.

He opened a box of yellow Number two pencils and fed one into an electronic sharpener. The grinding wood relaxed him. After putting a point on the pencil, he rested it atop a day planner covered with blue, black, and red pen scribbles. He opened the desk's top drawer and pulled out a bottle of cheap scotch, uncorking it. A healthy, three-finger shot filled his favorite tumbler before he corked the bottle. From his pocket, he produced a bag of cocaine and dumped a pile on the desk. Without chopping it up, Henry snorted it, chasing the bump with a shot.

Henry loved drugs.

Cocaine, the mark of class and wealth, was his favorite. Beside its numbing and lifting effects, he loved the ceremonious ritual of railing out pinky-sized lines, rolling up a hundred dollar bill into a straw, and sucking the powder into his skull. Even more than the ingestion process, he loved the secrecy behind it. The taboo knowledge becomes power the user has, and choosing whether or not to share that information was part of the trip. Trust can walk you on the moon or to the clink. Though cheap, Henry enjoyed that thrill, it added excitement to rigor.

Henry thought about using blow to supplement the club's shoestring income. His dealer, a rouge apothecary named Lucio, tempted him with quantity, but the game was dangerous, too risky for a mistake. He couldn't tell Steve; the soundman was deeply involved with business operations. One day he would find someone trustworthy enough to play games with, and then they would both be skipping down Easy Street.

Times were tough, and with his habits, this Bad Apple show was a godsend.

# ♫ TRACK 6 ♫

A stro and Carter showed up as Drowsy Rain finished their set, the Badmobile billowing dark gray smoke from the hood.

"Told you this ride was a piece of shit," Astro said.

Carter's brow furrowed. "Shut up. I'll fix it later. We need to get in there."

A security guard watching the parking lot opened the side door for them, and they avoided the line extending from the box office and stretching into the bustling parking lot. They followed the tight hall to the dressing room where Carter brushed his hair. He didn't go all out with makeup and fancy costumes because it wasn't him. It got too hot pounding the drums wearing a hokey Halloween outfit, and behind the drum kit no one really saw what he looked like, a subtle blessing.

When they went out, Vanian, Dar, and Astro were easily spotted. There was no telling how many quiet dinners and late night drinks were interrupted by a fan recognizing them from online videos or live shows. They didn't say much to Carter, hovering around the others like planets trapped hopelessly in their gravity. Carter didn't mind, enjoying the fans' surprise when he revealed himself.

He loved being social, but also liked dodging some of the weirdoes the band attracted. It was a Catch-22. All in all, Carter was proud of what the band had achieved, even if he offered the least amount of input to the group.

One day, he'd ask Vanian if he could write a few songs.

Watching Astro pile on foundation, drawing jagged lines and patterns over his face until he looked like an escaped lunatic, Carter thought it was an improvement. Astro's normal stage attire was leather picked up from bondage boutiques across the U.S.—a French Quarter leather shop was one of his favorite haunts. After donning the skin-tight outfit, he wrapped chains and fake rusty barbwire around his chest and legs. Astro slipped into his new coat, marveling at himself in the mirror.

"I'm bringing a townie home tonight," he said to Carter.

"Oh, yeah?" Carter knew his band mate's narcissism knew no boundaries. He didn't want to start a fight or feed Astro's vanity, so he tried appearing distracted by fumbling with his shoelaces.

"Maybe two of them. Ever bang two broads at once?"

"No," Carter said. He wanted out of this conversation as fast as possible. "One usually keeps my hands full."

"Shit," snorted Astro. "You're doing it wrong, man. That friend of yours in Atlanta, you put too much importance on her. You haven't seen much of each other, and still, you write to her like a goddamned woman."

Carter wasn't ashamed that his relationship with Annabelle was a complicated charade, but the less Astro knew about his personal life, the better.

"I write a lot of people. When you love a person, you'll do anything for them."

"Bullshit. I wouldn't die for vagina. There's no one out there that would. Love is just a garbage marketing stunt the greeting card companies cooked up so you have to buy shit in February."

"Forgive me if I disagree." He didn't want a fight with the moody guitarist, but he believed in love unconditionally. His parents and God filled him with love, and Carter knew exactly how lucky he was.

"What's there to disagree about? Love is what we experience when the chemicals in our heads want us fucking. It's nature, nothing more. We're programmed for procreating so the species can survive. Anything else is fairytales and leprechaun gold. That's why no one stays together anymore. Because we've woken up."

"My parents are still together." Carter rubbed his shoulder. He was ready to beat drums. "Thirty-five years."

"They're sick," Astro said as he darkened his eye shadow. "That's what Christianity does to you."

Carter was officially offended. "No, they're pretty happy. Over the years, I've seen them go through ups and downs, but they always managed to stick it out with each other. They bicker, but that's life. Great love stories are about overcoming adversity. Look at us. We argue all the time, but none of us would trade what we have for anything."

"That's because we're not screwing each other. Once dick goes into vagina, a friendship is doomed. Common knowledge."

Carter grabbed his drumsticks. "Now I'm crying bullshit. There are a lot of good couples out there. Look at Kitty and Dar. They're so happy, they could lay eggs."

"They're worse than anyone else I know," Astro said. "Bring a kid into this world. Fuck, all the war and disease and pain... They'll be lucky if their kid doesn't get filled with bullets at its grade school."

"Now that's sick, man," Carter said. "Where's your faith in God?"

"My god hung himself long ago. All I have is me. That's how I entered this world, that's how I'm going out."

"Sad outlook, man. I have no worries because God will see things through. You've been embracing darkness too much, Astro. It might catch up with you."

"You'd better keep your ass behind the drum set where it belongs, Carter. Let us real musicians do the work. Our darkness is the reason we snared the record deal in the first place. You think we'd be sellin' as many CDs and t-shirts if we were singing hymns about your Christian God?"

Carter did not believe Astro had insulted their band mates, love, his parents, and God in the same conversation. It was a new low for the guitarist. Carter sensed the danger dancing behind his eyes more and more.

"Actually, there's quite a market for praise rock. Bands such as—"

"I don't want to hear it, Carter." Astro snapped the eye shadow's lid shut. "If you don't like what we're about, altar boy, go drum for a Sunday choir. But if you want to make the real bucks, better keep the time for Vanian's satanic poetry."

"There's nothing evil about what he sings." Carter knew he was defeated—there would be no appealing to Astro's brimming hate. "Listen to him. It's romantic."

"Head up your ass," Astro said, jumping up and kicking aside a polka dotted beanbag. "You have no idea what's going on here. I'm grabbing a beer. Get out of your prissy hair so you can pray. Don't ask Him for anything too essential."

Astro squinted his eyes.

"You're going to be waiting a long time."

Astro exited the dressing room, slamming the door behind him. A framed flyer advertising an old Bad Apple show fell from a nail on the wall, landing face-down on the dressing room's dingy red carpet.

"You're missing the point," Carter said under his breath. He looked at the makeup strewn over the counter and sighed, thankful he was the band's obscure member.

# ♫ TRACK 7 ♫

**D**ar weaved through the dense crowd, occasionally stopping and signing a CD insert or flyer. A guy with a diamond tattoo under his right eye flashed a copy of their demo. Most fans wanted a hug or a handshake, gestures he had no problem returning. After all, the fans were why he was traveling and starting a family.

Bellying up to the bar beside a Lazy Susan filled with square napkins and red stir straws, he grabbed football-shaped coaster and rested it in front of him. Water rings on the wood annoyed him. Throwback to the years he spent bartending before music became a serious option, a clean bar was habit.

Dar saw the bartender, Jabberwocky, heading his way. Jabberwocky wore the bar's standard uniform, black Mozzy shirt and black slacks, but he was known for always altering the color of his Mohawk. Tonight, his hair was green.

"Hey, Dar," said Jabberwocky, spinning his shaker in his right palm and flipping it once in the air and catching it behind his back. "Henry said whatever you fellows want is on him, so what are you drinking tonight?"

"Beer. Whiskey and lime shot, shaken." Normally he would open with a Long Island ice tea instead of beer, but Kitty had been grumbling about his drinking since they discovered she was knocked up. Dar knew he'd wind up drunk before the night was over—it was homecoming and therefore unavoidable that old acquaintances would toss numerous cocktails his way—but he would let the process unfold slowly.

"Coming up." Jabberwocky dipped into the reach-in cooler and pulled out a canned beer, popping it open with his shaker. He set the beer on the coaster and started making the shot. Dar pulled out a Lincoln and dropped it into the plastic tip jar when Jabberwocky returned with the shot. Jabberwocky waved a hand. "You don't have to do that. Henry insisted we take care of you."

"Hey, this means a lot to me. If you see me with that thirsty look in my eyes, keep 'em coming. You don't want me drying up on a night like this."

"Sure thing." Jabberwocky rang a brass bell dangling from the wineglass rack overhead, letting the crowd know he'd earned a respectable tip.

Dar knocked back the shot, enjoying its bitter finish. A few drinks before a show loosened him up, but he needed to be careful. If he indulged too much, his fingers would become sluggish and sloppy. Holding up his part of the sound would be impossible. The same held true for the rest of the band. Those wild nights when they drank more than they should have before taking stage always ended in disaster.

Philly was one such instance.

They were playing a gig at the Electric Factory after swilling too many two dollar Mexican beers at O'Neal's. They stumbled from the South Street pub, laughing and joking, but Astro and Dar got into a skirmish about which Tool album was stronger, *Undertow* or *Ænima*, and that fight resurfaced onstage during a song called "Skeletal Horse." Vanian managed breaking up the punches and turning it into a stage gag, but the club owners weren't too thrilled about the ruckus. The band would never play their club again.

He took the beer can and reentered the crowd. The Mozzy was filling up, and the heat from the bodies was suffocating. The air's energy tingled deep in his bones. Dar knew they were going to play their balls off.

Making his way to their t-shirt stand, he managed crossing the dance floor without being stopped. He wasn't the only one dressed up. Seventy percent of the crowd wore face paint and black threads. The Army of the Night was out in full force, showing their goth spirit with black wings and Romantic clothes.

When Bad Apple first started in Panama City, the scene was weak and unorganized. The moment a decent venue sprung up, cops or Bible thumpers were shutting it down.

Bad Apple began the change, gathering and redistributing canned goods and pet food donations to homeless missions and animal shelters. The press ate it up, and the crowds grew. The scene became endorsed by prominent local business names, supporting Bad Apple's humanitarian efforts. Even this far in their career, two cardboard boxes sat next to their t-shirt stand, nearly filled with generosity.

Dar slid behind the table, straightening a pile of their CDs. Kitty smiled when Dar entered, revealing long pointed fangs. She had been a part of the band since their first show, forming Bad Apple's original fan club and sketched their logo. The band liked it, so they let her develop the look of Bad Apple. She designed their first album cover and website. Her money printed up the initial t-shirts for the merch table; her business savvy made the venture profitable.

"I see people are really kicking down the cat and dog food tonight." Dar hugged Kitty, giving her a peck on the lips. He was careful not to smudge her lipstick, a lesson learned early on in their relationship.

"They care more for the animals than the people," Kitty said, adjusting a black velvet cape around her neck. In her Victorian blouse, she looked as if she belonged in a Hammer vampire film. Her ice blue eyes sparkled like Christmas morning. "I can't say I blame them. People hurt each other out of boredom and greed. They have no control over their lusts. Animals are free of that. When they love you, it's for keeps."

"Well, you know I love you, right?"

"I know, Dar. I happen to love you too. Excited about jamming tonight?"

"To tell you the truth, this is the most nervous I've been since we played the Triton Festival in New York. All the people there. It's a good thing you were by my side. You took my mind off the size of the crowd."

Dar paused as a lady in a Crüxshadows shirt bought a poster of the band dressed up as zombies and crawling out of mossy graves, one of his favorites. After Kitty collected the money and tucked it into the cashbox, she turned, tossing her straight black hair over her shoulder.

Dar couldn't believe how lucky he was.

"Tonight it feels like before high school, playing those Surfside Middle School talent shows. Or like having my eighth grade algebra teacher hovering over my shoulder during a test while I try remembering the quadratic equation. Shit. This is way worse than that New York show."

Kitty chuckled. "You will be tremendous, you always are. The band has matured, and the crowd hasn't heard it yet. It's tightest rock I've heard in ages."

"You're biased."

"I am, but I mean it. Don't mistake my opinion as fan boy ass-kissing. Just a friend offering honest opinion."

"I appreciate it, Kitty. I didn't mean it bad. It's just—"

"It's just nothing. And while I'm at it, Astro is getting too big for his shit shoes, and I don't like it. That look he gets in his eyes when he's on a bender scares me. He needs to lay off the sauce and women before something bad happens. Why don't you knock him down a notch or two? You know Vanian won't do it. He's too nice."

"He steps in when he has to," Dar said, not wanting to step on his friend's toes. "He's of the mind that we're grown-ups capable of taking care of ourselves. I happen to agree."

"Most of you are. But Astro...I did a tarot reading on him last week in New Orleans when you boys were drinking at the silver structure, and strife cards kept popping up. So many inverted staffs and swords. That boy's heading for trouble."

Dar hated ill words concerning a friend and band mate, but Astro's uneven temperament was obvious. The guitarist was falling apart, and Dar didn't have an idea where it was leading.

"In Austin, I heard him tell a skirt he wanted her to be his girl and come on the road with us." She'd shouted obscenities through the motel room walls, threatening to cut off Astro's cock and shove it in his ass. Maybe it was an eye for an eye. "There's no telling what happened between them, but I suspect she hates our band now. I see him heading down a rotten path too."

"I just hope you guys get him settled before—" Kitty stopped as another customer walked up to the booth.

Dar recognized her as the woman Vanian noticed in the crowd.

"Hey, Patricia," Kitty said cheerfully. "Good to see you out again." She leaned across the table, embracing her. "You keep on vanishing before we get a chance to talk. I was wondering if you were showing up tonight."

"This is my home, too," she said. Her red hair fell in two braids, framing her face and dangling over a Nick Cave shirt. "I wouldn't miss this. Not for all the tea in China."

"Oh, I'm so scatterbrained sometimes," Kitty said. "This is Dar, Bad Apple's bassist and controlled noise master. Dar, this is Patricia."

"Hi," Dar said. He couldn't believe it—he wished Vanian had agreed to a drink. They shook hands. "So you dig the music?"

"Yes. When I was younger, I would come listen to your McKenzie Park shows. It was a trip seeing you guys in your executioner's masks, chopping off fake limbs and shit."

"Yeah," said Dar. "Those were good times. If you go back that far, how come you didn't talk to us?"

Patricia bit her lower lip. "I guess I'm shy. Social anxiety...I don't know."

"Well," Kitty said, "you're amongst friends. No call for that anymore."

"Indeed," Dar said. "Would you like to come backstage after the show and meet the rest of the band?"

"Y—yeah, I'd like that," Patricia said. Her cheeks flushed.

"Cool. Just hang out while the club thins," said Dar. "Maybe kick it with Kitty until it's just us."

"Excellent," she said. "I guess I'm grabbing a beer. I'll see you later."

"Later, girl," Kitty said.

"Later," said Dar. Patricia waved before disappearing into the moving bodies. He turned to Kitty and said, "Patricia was her name, right?"

"Right."

"I know someone who wants to meet her." Dar bounced up and down, a jig he teased Kitty with when he possessed knowledge she didn't. It drove her nuts, but he couldn't help himself.

"Who?"

"Vanian."

"No way," she exclaimed, bringing a hand over her mouth. "That's crazy."

"He's watched her at the past few shows. He even mentioned her in the greenroom tonight."

"That's so cool. Do you think they'll hit it off?"

"Who knows? Vanian can be strange, especially with women."

"Yeah...I know. I believe he'll like her, she's artsy and quiet too."

Dar paused. Kitty's gears turned. "Don't you go playing matchmaker now."

Kitty batted her eyelashes. "Who me?"

"I'm grabbing another beer. I wanna loosen up."

"Don't get too carried away. I'm not babysitting you tonight."

"Scout's honor." He pecked her lips again before sauntering to the bar.

# ♫ TRACK 8 ♫

After Drowsy Rain's set, Steve ran a quick sound check for Danger Shaft, making sure their guitars and drums were under the red on his mixing board. Too much power would damage the equipment. Over the club's speakers, he flooded the Mozzy with a mix CD featuring Bauhaus, Nine Inch Nails, and Depeche Mode, perfect music for a goth and hardcore show. Once the levels were under control, he entered the sound box and flipped on the house mic.

"All right ghosts and ghouls. Next up we have a terrifying set from those musical maniacs, Danger Shaft." He put a lot of inflection on their name, drawing out the A in both words as if announcing a professional sporting event. The crowd cheered.

He adjusted the knobs on the lighting board. A steady bass drumbeat filled the club, and the onstage fog machines kicked on, a haunted sea flowed off the stage and spilled onto the dance floor.

Distorted bass guitar and drums filled the nightclub. Danger Shaft had no guitarist, and their choppy quality that reminded Steve of a chained pit bull's angry barks. The singer came onstage wearing a scuba mask, and he growled into the microphone as he jammed his right hand down his black cargo pants, simulating ferocious masturbation. Steve liked a more poetic sound, but the band got the crowd moving. Dancing turned into shoving. Before long, a mosh pit formed. Security tightened in on the action, making sure the slam dancing remained friendly.

He couldn't remember the last time he'd seen the Mozzy so busy.

## ♫ TRACK 9 ♫

Backstage, Vanian plugged his acoustic electric guitar into a digital tuner the group shared. He could lock the strings in by ear, but he preferred running them through machines. Using the device eliminated variances between instruments and sounded more professional. Paul always stressed a tight act's importance. He was a patient teacher, and Vanian knew he was reaping the benefits.

Van missed him.

Vanian strummed a few bars. The melody he'd been tinkering with proved difficult; he struggled pinpointing the fabled lost chord of Moody Blues lore. Frustrated, he ran through a Dorian scale, warming up his fingers. Astro was much faster at the modes. Vanian preferred the simplicity of open chords and simple strumming. Less was more, another lesson from Paul.

Lacking the classical crooner pipes, Vanian was insecure about his voice. He was off-key and timid. But the message of the words and the confidence Paul instilled brought Bad Apple's brooding sound together. His mentor once said there's no need to sound perfect, just mean it. Vanian found when he trusted that advice his voice cast a spell on the crowds. Paul had shown him more than a few fret board licks and jazz chords. He'd been taught magic.

As Danger Shaft's edgy sound permeated through the walls, he sighed.

During their late teens, Vanian and Dar ate a lot of LSD. During those trips, he saw the universe's echoing ripples, vibrating physical manifestations of cosmic and psychic energy. An insight to auras, their innermost selves, Vanian discovered people were affected by their surrounding vibrations. If you were always listening to depressing music, your life would fill with sorrow. If you listened to angry music, you would carry those emotions over into your daily life.

Vanian realized that he not only received ripples, he was also capable of broadcasting them. Every thought, each emotion, and all the words he said and sang had the power to alter the external world.

The idea so rattled Vanian, it changed his entire existence. He monitored his words, finding himself quiet in most situations. His songwriting took the change's brunt. The lyrics became positive, more literate. He dropped negative people he hung around, unhealthy food he ate, and changed how he treated others, hoping his efforts would help the world in some way.

It was spiritual awakening, and Bad Apple's music evolved with Vanian. He regretted not being able to tell his mentor how much it mattered, but life left loose ends.

Things were funny that way.

Vanian picked up his copy of *The Stranger*, flipping to a page bookmarked with a Serenity Prayer card given to him by a Louisiana fan. Finding dog eared pages in books killed him, so the card served two purposes. It was the fifth time he'd read Camus's masterpiece, and Vanian felt a connection with the main character's isolation. The paragraphs helped drown out the violent music playing in the other room, and Vanian was peaceful again.

# ♫ TRACK 10 ♫

Astro stood in the corner of the Mozzy, watching Danger Shaft while sipping on a Long Island ice tea. He liked the trio's style. They had a brutal approach to melody, attacking their instruments like lifelong enemies. They were obviously satanic, the bass drum boasted an upside down pentagram, and the lead singer's tattoos were demons and inverted crosses. Between verses, he spit on the crowd, and they fucking loved it. No doubt their set would end with smashed guitars. As they swore like sailors and flipped off the aggressive crowd, a smile tugged at Astro's lips.

Bad Apple was chick rock, too romantic for his blood. They had pull now, and a great image. With more balls, they would be hardcore gods. Wannabe guitarists would throw their lives away learning his licks. It made his cock stir.

Astro, on his third Long Island, didn't care if the three creepy shadows were still following him. The booze relaxed his muscles, putting him in the not-give-a-shit zone. Those ominous, shapeless things were nothing more than a nuisance, like the hangover after a five day designer drug binge. Tonight was his night, and he had returned to take his pedestal among the peons.

He loved standing in front of people and playing guitar. Music was sexual. Sliding his fingers across six strings was public masturbation, without the hassle of police busting his skull for indecent exposure. The women, as well as a few of the men, drooled during his intricate solos. He loved watching them scramble for the cheap, thin picks he'd toss into the audience. They were trying to grab a piece of legend, as if the only way they could be a part of something grand was by making sure it passed through a capable gatekeeper first, a soul already blessed with significance.

Astro didn't mind sharing his power with the serfs.

It was part of the job.

Another swill from his drink. He loved drinking and smoking; they went hand in hand. Knowing bad habits would take him down wasn't a bother—there were worse ways to die. He didn't want to be old anyway. Check out while you're still vital instead of draining the people you gave a fuck about. Needing someone looking after you was weakness.

Astro was strong.

As Danger Shaft finished their set, Astro searched the crowd for a date. He needed to get backstage soon, but narrowing down his marks before the gig wouldn't hurt. The show was a normal townie gathering, a pathetic court held for the hipsters and the lonely. The desperates not worthy of his gilded cock.

Then he saw the redhead wearing a Nick Cave shirt ordering a shot.

She was perfect for a fuck.

It's show time.

## ♫ TRACK 11 ♫

S teve unleashed the fog machines, covering the stage with a thick haze.

The crowd was on edge, silently pushing forward. Steve loved the anxiety before the main groups set. Wisps of marijuana caught Steve's nostrils, but locating the culprit in the dense crowd would be impossible. Halting the show was useless; the night was nearly over. Hitting the toggle again, Steve unleashed another menthol-scented cloud over Bad Apple's instruments, bringing up the black light backdrop.

Carter was already behind his drums when the soft purple illumination from the stage lights came alive. Dar entered from stage left and stood behind his synthesizer, pushing the switch that started an electronic loop of a Theremin's cry, Bad Apple's banshee wail. Vanian and Dar loved classic horror movies, and that passion for old spook shows bled through their music, their look. Next, Astro entered the stage opposite of Dar with his guitar hanging from a studded, leather strap. He hit an A chord, sending an anxious, but brief, cheer through the onlookers. From behind Astro, Vanian slid to his spot on center stage, pulling his axe over his shoulder.

Four ghostly silhouettes.

Fog.

Black lights.

The crowd's energy was escalating towards maximum velocity.

"Where we're from," Vanian's voice said, "the birds sing a pretty song, and there's always music in the air. This one's called 'Outpatient Therapy'."

The band's music filled the Mozzy, sending shockwaves through the crowd.

Steve gasped.

Having been a long time since Steve heard Bad Apple play live, he was impressed at how much the band had grown. As a young band, their shows were filled with blood-soaked antics and gimmicks. Now, with casual effort, their sound set a gloomy trance over the club. Vanian's words followed, floating with the music like a morning dream. The shyness to his presentation, that vulnerability making him an unwilling member of gatherings was the mystery behind Bad Apple, the band's *it* factor.

Making himself scarce after shows and refusing interviews only bolstered his mystique and the band's allure. Fans ate it up. Bloggers called them a deadly new breath into goth.

The internet made them famous.

Steve knew Bad Apple deserved the attention.

Unlike Danger Shaft, the crowd stood transfixed, snared in Bad Apple's melodic web. Their music pulsated, teetering between noise and angelic hymn. One listener lit a lighter, holding the flame up during Astro's solo. Another joined in with her cell phone's soft blue glow.

Steve saw a woman in the front row singing along, keeping her eyes locked on the singer.

Vanian returned her gaze.

# ♫ TRACK 12 ♫

After their first number, the lighting shifted to purple and green alternating strobe pulses. Vanian looked at Steve to make sure the levels were on point, and the soundman flicked his flashlight confirming they were within range.

The mysterious woman was in her usual spot, watching. Swallowing, he adjusted his capo, securing it on the fourth fret.

"This is called 'Moon Ladder', and it's for all the boys with broken hearts," he said and played the opening lick. The drums and bass entered together during the second measure, and the audience bobbed with the music. Vanian sang:

*The day she left, he built a ladder to the moon*
*Was all alone, but, man, he dug the view*
*Sitting there with little left to do*
*All alone, watch the world so blue*

*Must have found freedom in the Milky Way*
*Seeking out solace in outer space*
*Shooting stars remind him of her face*
*Of her face*

*Sitting in a lunar sea*
*Orbital reality*
*Acting out a fantasy*
*Sleepwalking daydream*
*Where did she*
*Where did she go?*

During the chorus, Vanian saw the redhead swaying, her eyes shut. As she lip-synched along, he wondered what she was thinking. So many nights he'd seen her, hair always in those braids, falling below her neck.

*One day*, thought Vanian, *I'll sneak out in the crowd and talk to her.*

The song hit its second verse:

*She came back, saw that ladder to the sky*
*Wanted up, but, man, she couldn't climb*
*Sitting there, wondering why*
*Nothing left but a few tears cried*

*Must have found freedom in the Milky Way*
*Seeking out solace in outer space*
*Shooting stars remind him of his face*
*Of his face*

*Sitting in a lunar sea*
*Orbital reality*
*Acting out a fantasy*
*Sleepwalking daydream*
*Where did she*
*Where did she go?*

Following "Moon Ladder," Vanian rested his guitar in a stand and took a place behind the keyboards before the band began "Ghost Wood," a song about a hunter finding a murdered woman's ghost roaming the forest where she was killed. Vanian played synths along with Astro's solo, never taking his eyes off the woman. He was singing just for her now, his earlier worries a distant memory, washed away by her presence.

"Thank you so much," he said when the song ended. "We're Bad Apple, and we're glad to be home."

He meant it.

The crowd cheered.

"Carter on drums," he said, motioning behind him. Carter responded with a quick, snappy fill.

"You all know Dar on the bass. He'll be a daddy soon. Show him some love."

More applause.

"I know everyone's taken drinks with Astro," he said. The crowd laughed and cheered as the guitarist tossed out a few picks.

"We also have Kitty Corpse tending the merch table. She's very much a part of the band too. Don't forget, we're accepting canned donations to help those of us who might be going through hard times. It's a daunting world out there. Let's try to keep the candles burning."

Vanian looked back at his band mates. They nodded in agreement, letting him know they were ready.

"Oh, my name's Vanian."

They launched into "Invitation to Love," "Jack's Lantern," "The Great Northern Ghouls," and "Robot Lovers from Mars" without any interruptions before stepping into several instrumental pieces intended for their follow up album. The rolling fog machines and spinning light show gave the concert a surreal atmosphere, trapping the band and audience in psychedelic purgatory.

After a long moment of silence, the purple lights glowed brighter.

"This song is over four hundred years old," Vanian said. "Channeled to me by a Romanian shaman huddled beside a fire as an ancient waxing moon looked on."

They launched into "Gypsy Girl," sending the audience into frenzy.

*Little, beautiful gypsy girl*
*Soft white skin, hair of curls*
*Eyes reflecting silver moon*
*Dance with me this merry tune*

*Fancy delicate gypsy dress*
*Snake green folds, spider webs*
*Filling night with haunted songs*
*Dance with wolf 'till we find dawn*

*Pretty porcelain gypsy hands*
*Chipped black nails, want of man*
*Lips opening upon warm throat*
*Dance with me 'till you must go*

Mainstream tunes pleased audiences, and Vanian learned early on that saving their best material for closing left the audience on a high for the rest of the night. After finishing the third chorus, the stage darkened and Bad Apple slipped offstage, Vanian took one last look at the woman, waving before he vanished.

# ♫ TRACK 13 ♫

S teve brought the house lights up and marveled at the smiling faces. The entire joint reeked of clove cigarettes and stale booze, a pleasant energy hung in the air. Bad Apple had delivered.

One guy wearing a Led Zeppelin t-shirt was proudly showing three punk girls a pick he'd caught, and another group crammed by the backstage entrance hoping to nab autographs. Dar and Carter eventually emerged, signing CD inserts, t-shirts, playbills, and posters. A line extending from Bad Apple's merchandise booth reached the dance floor. Beyond the front door, excited fans lingered and smoked, sharing their favorite moments and after party plans. Two a.m., and Steve knew the diehard partiers would gather at Ms. Newby's for the evening's final drinks.

Mozzy security pushed people out the door.

Bartenders emptied tip jars.

Kitty Corpse, with Carter and Dar's help, packed up unsold CDs and shirts into opaque plastic bins with flip-top lids. Henry emerged from his office carrying a clipboard.

"Bartenders," he called. "When you're finished cleaning your stations, line up outside my office door for the nightly tip outs. Jabberwocky, make sure you've cleaned the fountain nozzles tonight. Steve, help the boys break down onstage."

"Got ya," Steve answered, covering his equipment with a towel to keep dust off the mixing boards.

"Hey," Henry called towards Patricia, sitting at the bar finishing a Mai Thai. "Club's closed. Time for you to beat it."

"Wait," Kitty called. "She's with us."

"She's VIP, Henry," Dar said. "We're hanging out tonight."

"Oh." Henry cleared his throat. "I guess she can stay then." He looked towards the front door and barked, "I want those doors fucking locked and anyone else who isn't working or screwing the band out. Let's get the hell outta here before the goddamn sun rises, folks."

Steve watched Patricia mouth *thank you* to Kitty and Dar. She finished her drink and tossed the clear plastic cup into a garbage can a bouncer was hauling to the back door. Three other overflowing cans waited for dumping in the outside pit. She leaned her elbows on the wooden bar, smiling. Dar and Steve exchanged a sly glance before beginning the breakdown.

# ♫ TRACK 14 ♫

Kitty and Patricia hoisted the last bin into the back of her car while Steve and Bad Apple loaded up the trailer. Most of the parking lot tailgaters thinned, leaving a wreckage of cigarette butts and empty beer bottles. Scattered groups of people still buzzed around the club's front door. As several Mozzy bouncers swept up debris into dustpans, clinking glass echoed in the night.

She watched Patricia shut the car door and hoped introducing her to Vanian was a good idea. Patricia was pretty and talented, but she had been in trouble in the past. She didn't want to set her friend up for heartbreak.

"Oh," Patricia said, "lucky me. A penny on heads."

She bent down to pick up the coin, and Kitty wondered if her own ass would still look good after she had the kid. Temptations waited around every corner in the business, and she didn't want her changing body opening any windows for other women.

Kitty pressed her keyless entry remote until she heard the beep. They walked to the side entrance where a bouncer held the door open. After following the hall and taking a seat next to Patricia at the bar, she yawned and rubbed her eyes.

"Tired?" Patricia asked.

"This has been a long tour, and my body has been all out of whack lately. Thanks for the help with the merch. It sucks not having a hand for that part. After Dallas, I also don't like loading up alone."

"Why, what happened?"

"I was mugged outside a redneck bar." The memory still troubled her.

"My stars." Patricia pulled her braids behind her shoulder.

"It was late, and I hauled all the merch in an alley by myself. I should have waited for Dar or someone, but I was beat and in a hurry for the hotel shower. These two guys cornered me and pulled a damned pistol on me, those fucking hicks."

"That's horrible."

"I wasn't even carrying any money. All they made off with was some lousy t-shirts and posters. When the police came, I told them I was robbed by guys wearing cowboy hats, blue jeans, and boots. They told me that was everyone in Texas."

She didn't tell Patricia how one grabbed her, how close she came to getting raped. Her scream brought out the club's security, and the two assailants scrambled away. Kitty took pride in her ability to handle herself in sticky situations, but those jumpers rattled her.

"Crazy," Patricia said.

"It really shook me up. Outside the New Orleans show, my man helped me load. I kept on looking over my shoulder, even with Dar at my side. I couldn't wait to get back here, where at least I know I'm safe."

"This town's cracked, too," said Patricia. "Back in the day, the arrest log used to take up a quarter of a page in the *News Herald*, but now, it's practically two full pages."

"Shit."

"What's worse is that you always recognize a few names in the damned thing. People we went to high school and Gulf Coast with. Good kids, usually tied up in dope busts or DUIs." Patricia paused before adding, "I was even in trouble."

"Really? What happened?" Kitty leaned forward. She hadn't heard the entire story of Patricia's complications with the law, and if Vanian was interested in her, harmless prying was necessary.

"Got caught with prescription pills. A long story I'd rather not relive."

"Sorry," Kitty said, bummed. The story would have to wait, but if Kitty possessed one trait, it was patience. At least it was drugs and nothing violent. Vanian partied, but he was a pacifist. "I don't wanna pull off old scabs. Want to go backstage?"

Patricia smiled.

"Come on. Let's go," Kitty said, rising from her seat, extending a hand. Patricia took it and stood. Her palm was warm. Kitty led her arm-in-arm to the employee door, pushing it open with her free hand. They followed a tight corridor to the greenroom's door and entered finding Vanian, still in stage makeup, stretched out on a sofa, reading Camus. He looked up from his pages and almost dropped the book.

"U-um, hello," he said, sitting up straight. "I wasn't expecting anyone."

"Vanian," said Kitty, "I'd like you to meet Patricia. She's an old friend of mine and has been following us the past few shows."

"Hi." Patricia raised her hand and wiggled her fingers.

"Yeah," said Vanian as he stood, "I've seen her, er, seen you out there." He held out his hand. Patricia took it. "Pleased to meet you."

"Likewise," Patricia said. "I met you when we were kids. It was a long time ago, and you probably don't remember me. I was at a girlfriend's house, and you were drunk and rolling around her front lawn, tossing leaves into the air and singing to them. I thought it was great."

"I was wild when I was young." He looked at his shoes. Kitty thought his ears reddened.

"That's for sure," Kitty said.

"Most people are crazy," Patricia said. "I'll admit I'm still nuts."

"Crazy's cool," Vanian said.

Kitty loved hearing them talk. Usually Vanian hid within novels, as if what he needed, emotionally, was found on pages instead of the real world. Lost in those lonely songs, reaching out through tormented music. Seeing him not shy away from Patricia was a welcomed change.

"How long are you guys hanging in town?" Patricia asked.

"A few months," Vanian said. "We're recording in the spring then touring during the summer. We played several new tracks tonight, but they...they don't have lyrics yet."

"They sounded wonderful."

"Thanks," said Vanian. "To be honest, this was the first time I was nervous in a while. It felt good."

"I just remembered Henry has our money," Kitty said, winking at Patricia. Ice broken, nature needed to run her course. "I guess I'll let you two get acquainted. I'll be right outside if you need me."

"Thanks," Patricia said.

Kitty looked over her shoulder at Vanian, taking his nervous body language as a good sign. She exited the greenroom, whistling a Flock of Seagulls song.

# ♫ TRACK 15 ♫

Vanian cracked his knuckles, pulling at his sweaty hands. He'd thought he was nervous before the show. This was a whole other chess game.

Patricia looked around the greenroom, her eyes resting on *The Stranger*.

"Good book," she said. "What Camus does with just over a hundred pages is unbelievable. It ties itself up in a neat little knot, and everything, no matter how seemingly arbitrary, makes sense. It's like nothing is there randomly."

"Yeah, it's one of my favorites. Meursault is a lovable misanthrope. He's detached from the world, as if he can't feel. I get in those moods, too, like when I'm writing a song or working on my novel. There are times I wonder if I'm even part of the human race."

"You look pretty human to me," Patricia said stepping closer. Vanian fell into her eyes. Fighting the urge to reach out and run his hand down her cheek, he kept his hands by his side, stuffing them into his pockets.

"I've been writing a collection of absurdist shorts, in the tradition of Daniil Kharms or zaum," Vanian said.

"Zaum, huh? I'm into Dada poetry. Surrealism can clear your head. There's so much nonsense it becomes Zen. In that insanity, a sort of sense shines through. You get struck with the sense that an answer exists in it all, but we're not divine enough to understand it. It's like looking at a complex equation without having the skills to solve it. That gives it the chance to mean something different for each mind."

"Deep." Vanian fought his eyes from tracing her curves. "You're waxing heavy. Finding someone well-versed in books by authors other than Stephen King or Dan Brown usually takes an act of the goddess."

"Did you just say goddess? Are you really pagan?"

Vanian nodded. Normally, he avoided religion talk with people he'd just met, but Patricia was inviting. "I'm a student of all religions, but most of my beliefs are focused around ancient Hellenistic and Roman witchcraft."

"Pretty cool." She tossed a braid over her shoulder. "I'm also pagan, but I practice Gardnerian Wicca. Merry meet."

"Merry meet." They clasped hands again, this time touching each other's wrist with extended index fingers, just above the pulse.

A magical handshake.

Electricity ripped through his arm, her vibrations beautiful.

She withdrew and blushed. "Ah, back to books. I just finished *A Confederacy of Dunces*."

Vanian grinned. "Toole's brushstrokes capture New Orleans flawlessly. The oddball characters leap off the page, and while you're reading those crazy situations, you don't know whether to laugh or cry. Damn, that's a good book. I just read *Exquisite Corpse*."

Patricia licked her lips. "Poppy Z. Brite?"

"No, that's a good book, too, but this one is by Robert Irwin. It's about a surrealist painter in pre-World War II Europe. He spends the novel pining over Caroline, a woman he's not even sure ever existed. Beautiful book. I also read a lot of horror and historical stuff."

"I do, too. To be honest, I devour books."

Another bookworm. Vanian was smitten. "Same. To me books, film, art, and music are divine, proof of a higher power. We just channel them, forge them into reality from the gods and goddesses."

"I'm not much of a musician, but I am a good artist. I draw and paint. Are you into tags?"

"Like graffiti?" Vanian wished his pen and paper prowess equaled his musical ability. He'd painted, but his work missed the mark.

"Yeah. I've been working a lot with spray paint."

"I can dig on some of it. Spray can murals are mind blowing, but a bunch of scribbly lines on a stop sign seems like vandalism."

Patricia's eyes widened. "But it's writing, just in another language. Once you understand it, a whole new world opens. It's magic, if you can decipher the symbols."

"And you write like this?" Turning writing into art, though painfully obvious, had not crossed his mind.

She intrigued him.

"Sometimes, I do. Other times, I throw up art. It depends on my mood. The last time trouble found me, I violated probation by getting busted tagging. I was painting a bad ass picture of Icarus falling from the sky on a power box. I guess you can say I got caught brown handed because I was finishing up his sandals when the cop pinched me."

The words *last time* rattled hard. "Do you usually deface public property?"

"I wouldn't hit a private residence or car, if that's what you're asking. That's lame. I like sneaking out to the tracks at night and tagging trains. Then your art is not stuck on a wall, it's mobile. A lot of people get to see it."

"But they don't know it's your work." Realizing how self-centered the words sounded, Vanian regretted saying them. Patricia didn't seem to mind or notice.

"That doesn't matter. What matters is that your message gets out there. It's guerrilla art, underground, and you can use the subgenre to be playful, to protest, to decorate the world around you. Have you ever heard of wabi-sabi?"

Vanian's brow furrowed. "Can't say I have."

"It's an old Japanese aesthetic associated with tea rituals and Zen Buddhism. They find beauty not only in nature's perfections, its simplicity and simultaneous complexity, but the imperfections also. I see street art as wabi-sabi outside of the organic realm. A blemish on modern, human existence only adding to the mechanical world this species has created."

Vanian was impressed.

Patricia was not only beautiful, she was intelligent.

They looked into each other's eyes—a comfortable silence followed.

The green door opened, and Astro entered. Back in street clothes, his face and hair were wet from scrubbing off his makeup. Astro stopped when he saw Patricia.

"What's this?" Astro said as the door shut behind him. "Vanian, I didn't know you had any friends."

Vanian tightened up inside. The sudden protectiveness over someone he hardly knew surprised him. He wondered if another woman would have pulled the same reaction from him. "This is Patricia, Astro. She's a local fan."

"So, you like the sound," Astro said. "I saw you out in the crowd earlier. Why don't you come to Ms. Newby's with me for last call tonight? I'll buy you a few drinks and tell you about the music we're working on."

How fast the guitarist moved disgusted Vanian. A wave of insecurity surfaced—what if Astro whisked her away before they communicated?

"I was actually talking to Vanian," Patricia said.

Relief washed over Vanian.

"He has excellent tastes in literature and art," she said. "Do you read, Astro?"

"Only smut, toots."

Astro moved closer to her. "I'm more into music. Growing up, I loved smoking a fatty and blasting the Doors on my parents' turntable. Drove the neighbors bananas."

"Books are my friends," Patricia said. "They complimented music."

She glanced at Vanian, and he sensed she was asking him to step in. Vanian hated standing up to Astro—it usually ended in trouble.

Astro slithered to Patricia.

"Let's hit Newby's and tie one on," Astro said. "We can discuss that music you love."

He reached out for Patricia's arm, but she jerked away.

Astro frowned. "What's wrong, baby? I won't stick you with the tab. My treat, honest."

"No, Vanian and I already have plans." She turned to the singer. "Isn't that right?"

"Yeah," Vanian said, amazed. Patricia was special. "We're going to walk on the beach, take in the stars."

"Whatever." Astro's eyes narrowed. "I hope you brought protection because he's pretty dirty, girl. You wouldn't believe the amount of road ass this cat pulled." He grumbled as he walked out, slamming the greenroom door.

"Sorry about that," Vanian said, mortified. "Astro can be…intense."

"That's okay. He creeps me out. Too arrogant for my blood."

"He's talented, but I keep an eye on him. As long as he stays away from hard drugs, we get along."

"He's an addict?" Patricia asked.

"He has moments. Hell, we all do. But he tends to become a monster, powerless to the dope. He keeps his abuse as far as possible from the band. It's better when I don't know what kind of shit he's into."

"Yeah, drugs are bad news. And I am unfortunately well-versed with it." Patricia cleared her throat. "So, are you really taking me to the beach?"

"What?"

"You told Astro we were going to the beach and looking at stars. Did you really mean it?"

She folded her arms across her chest. His eyes followed. She was beautiful.

"S-sure. If you would like, I'll walk you down there."

"Sounds good." Patricia offered her arm to Vanian. He accepted. Locked at the elbows, they exited the greenroom.

# ♫ TRACK 16 ♫

O utside Henry's office, Astro paced.

"What's wrong, man?" Dar asked, lighting a cigarette. He would quit when the baby came, but it was going to kill him. Cigarettes had been a constant companion since he was fourteen. Dependable, he knew exactly what he was getting each time he sparked one. Giving his old friends up would be difficult, but Kitty deserved the best.

"That asshole Vanian cock-blocked me in the mother fucking greenroom. Can you believe that?"

"What are you talking about?" Dar asked. Astro's words sounded alien to Dar's ears.

"I was asking if he was drinking with me, and I caught him hanging with this bitch I'd been scoping all night."

"Nick Cave shirt, red hair?" Dar asked, though he already knew the answer.

"That's the one. Did you have something to do with this?"

Seeing the guitarist so hot over a strange woman amused Dar. "She's a friend of Kitty's. How did he cock-block you?"

"I invited her to a cocktail, but Vanian already laid that poet bullshit on her."

"He must really dig her if he's talking with her, Astro. We both know he'd rather jerk off with *Tropic of Cancer* than mess around with some bubble gummer groupie."

"I saw her first. That was my pussy." Astro drew back and punched the wall. "Fucker."

The outburst surprised Dar. "Dude, calm down. You'll have no problem picking up fresh fish at Ms. Newby's tonight. If Vanian digs her, let him have her."

"Pisses me off," Astro mumbled, rubbing his fist. "Did Kitty get our money yet?"

"I think so. You need money for tonight?"

"Nah, I'm straight. I was just wondering." Astro looked around the empty club. The blaring house lights vamped the magic from the air. "I need a drink. Ms. Newby's?"

"No, thanks. Kitty and I are calling it a night." Snuggling in their own bed sounded wonderful.

"I offered," Astro said. "Didn't realize this band was not only a bunch of wiggle dicks, but getting old, too."

"Where's Carter? Maybe he'll go out with you?" Dar didn't like the look in his friend's eyes.

Astro snorted. "He's outside, fondling the Badmobile."

"That sounds like him. Good playing tonight, Astro."

"You too, man."

"Be safe out there."

Dar left the building, waving without looking back.

*** 

Alone in the club, Astro knocked on the office door three quick times. He knew what was going on behind that door, and he wanted in on the action. A pick-me-up to keep his dick hard all night long.

Henry appeared, beaded sweat glistening on his brow; his nostrils red and swollen. "Hey, Astro, baby, what's shaking?"

"Looks like it's snowing in here," Astro said. "Can I play?"

"Just you?"

"Just me."

"Come on in, boy."

## ♫ TRACK 17 ♫

Patricia and Vanian stood at the end of Beach Access 39's wooden steps, watching dark waves chew the flat shoreline.

"Nobody on the road. Nobody on the beach," he said.

The off season left Panama City a ghost town—another reason its residents became trapped. Spring Break brought money, but after a long winter, most households spent their earnings catching up. By the time fall returned, the cycle repeated itself.

"Smell that salt air," she said. "It heals the lungs, ya know."

Vanian couldn't remember the last time he'd visited the beach at night. In a younger man's skin, he and Dar would jam and drink until sunrise, deliberately spilling merlot for the music gods or fallen comrades. In morning light, red splotches across white sand looked like rose petals or blood drops. After Astro joined the band, the trio would go under the full moon and sing for her, like wolves.

Looking at the beautiful woman beside him, Vanian wished he'd brought an acoustic guitar.

"Just leave your shoes here. No one will mess with them." Patricia kicked off her sneakers and tucked them beside a clump of sea oats dancing to the waves' steady rhythm. Vanian removed his, sliding them into the other side of the shrub. An aglet from one of the laces on his left shoe pointed to the heels of her sneakers.

They walked towards the pier, sand crunching and squeaking under their feet. Other than the crisp autumn breeze and scrambling ghost crabs, they were alone.

"Will your car will be safe at that liquor store?" Vanian asked.

"I've parked there before. No one has ever bothered it."

Vanian watched the wind playfully pull at her braids. He wanted to hold her hand as they meandered past stacked blue beach chairs and boarded up Jet Ski rental huts, but he kept his distance, careful of not overstepping his welcome.

"I forget how nice it is out here," he said. "Trees and rest stops smearing by as we zip from gig to gig have become the norm. I get sick of it."

"I'm happy just being outside," she said.

"Me, too."

"The beach and night are powerful. I feel them rushing through me."

Many pagan religions are filled with a reverence towards the natural world. Paul once told Vanian that magic was a higher understanding of nature, that casting spells and affecting change wasn't as powerful useless you achieved a great oneness with all living things. He was thrilled she was on the same level.

She stopped and pointed to the sky. "Look, a falling star."

Vanian tilted his head, catching a bright white streak slicing the cloudless night. Patricia rested her hand on his arm. For a second, his heart flew with the meteor.

"Did you make a wish?" she asked.

"I did. A shame Mother Moon isn't showing her smile tonight. Usually, I say hello and ask for her protection. I wouldn't mind sharing the prayer with you."

"I'd like that. I'm not really formal. It's been a while since I've opened a circle. I don't call elemental corners when casting spells. Every moment of my life is magic."

"I feel the same way. I have trouble following any one branch of witchcraft. I make my own spells. It gives them a unique power."

"I've made mistakes with magic, misused it when I was younger."

Vanian, surprised by her raw honesty, relaxed at her candid admission. "We all have. What did you do, cast love spells?"

"Love spells always backfire. I've sent negative energy towards people who crossed me, willed bad things to happen to them. I'm still waiting for my threefold."

The Threefold Law states that any energy witch sends out, be it positive or negative, returns amplified three times. Over the years, Vanian, who subscribed to the theory, had met pagans believing the return was as high as twelve.

Patricia looked down, wiggling her toes in the sand. "I also used it for protection during my addict days."

"You're still here, so it looks like it worked," Vanian said.

"I wasn't rushing to get busted, but that happened."

"But if you were casting spells for protection, maybe getting busted was magic's way of keeping you from real harm, like overdosing."

Patricia thought a moment. "I didn't consider that. I thought my self-destruction was evil, so that's why I went to the clink."

"It's beyond good and evil. Your spells probably saved your life. I've learned that there's a balance. A mutual exchange of energy. The universe is on time, for better or worse."

"Whatever you call it," she said, "the course of my life changed. I still drink and occasionally smoke pot, but I'm done with the hard stuff. Art and magic are enough for my happiness."

"Sounds like you've come a long way. Your parents must be proud."

Patricia puffed. "My parents…yeah. I stay away from them. We're on good terms, and all. I have my own life, and they have their world. We just keep it that way. I know I've disappointed them. I feel like shit whenever we hang out. I guess it sounds crazy."

"Not at all. Parents and their children always have issues. Dar and Kitty are expecting, and I wish them the best. There's a lot before them, but they'll be fine. They're survivors."

"What about your parents?" Patricia asked. "They must be proud of their son making his dreams come true."

"Never knew my real dad, he took off when I was little. Mom and I… To be honest, I can't stand being in the same room as her. I watched her transform from a decent human being into a rattlesnake, and it wasn't pretty. In fairness, she doesn't like what I've done with my life."

"What? Become successful?"

"She claims I'm wasting my life because I play music and practice witchcraft. My guitar teacher also turned me on to magic. When she found out, she kicked him to the curb, threatening to call the law and tell them he was molesting me."

"Was he?" Patricia asked.

"Fuck no. He was great to me. When Mom started sucking down quarts, chain smoking cigarettes, and not coming home at night, he looked after me. He was working with her even though she was sleeping around with the late night bar dregs."

"Sounds like he really loved you."

"Yeah. One day I left out a spell book he'd given me, and she went through the fucking roof. Mom thinks religion is brain damage. Really, she hates more things than she likes. I don't know why."

Vanian stopped and looked at Patricia. "I'm so sorry—dumping on you like that. I've kept this bottled up for too long."

"It's okay. I'm actually honored. I did not expect any of this."

"I've seen you at the past few shows. How come you've never introduced yourself?"

"Honestly, I was there for the music. I had free time and extra cash, so I thought it would be cool following you guys along the Gulf Coast. You know, before you get super famous and all."

"Aw, come on." Vanian shook his head. She was a dream. "I find it really easy to talk to you."

"Well then, since we're asking each other serious questions...," she leaned in, her perfume reminded Vanian of burning leaves, "...what is your favorite 80's film?"

Vanian chuckled. The question caught him off guard. "What genre?"

"Um, how about romantic comedy. Do you like romance films?"

"Sure do. I guess *Say Anything*. That scene when he holds up the radio..."

"I wish love was like that outside of movie land," Patricia said. "Things always get tangled."

"Before you date someone, you gotta show them your blood work, your diversified stock portfolio, college diploma...the works. Then after you connect with a person, getting them to stay is a challenge."

"You don't hear a lot of happy stories anymore." Patricia sighed. "That makes me sad. It is so messy out there."

"The world is fine. People are messy. With each life comes the weight of their past—their mistakes, their triumphs, their hopes, their failures. If you find someone patient enough with your clicks and clacks, hang on. It's as fleeting as one of those shooting stars."

"How come no one has scooped you up yet?"

"I keep distant. Scared of getting hurt, I guess. What about you? So smart and hot with two Ts, why are you still single?"

She failed a smile. Vanian wondered if he'd probed too deep.

"I'm a recovering addict," she said. "I had a thing for heroin. Then I got hooked on pills. Tried getting straight, but found myself homeless and rambling around. Failed two piss tests and wound up doing time before going through a rehab program. I was on papers when I got popped painting. That was more time added on. Sucked real bad."

"I bet," said Vanian. He was no stranger to the system. His mom's drinking led to legal troubles, and although Paul bailed her out, Cali refused the straight and narrow. "Looks like you made it out fine."

Yeah," she said. "There are times I still want drugs. It's something I live with, but I'm strong."

The wind howled. Vanian's lips began chapping. Patricia wrapped her arms around herself. "Cold out here."

"Like the cold if we were dead. We might beat the wind by ducking in that kiosk." Vanian pointed to a nearby beach service stand used for renting the blue wooden chairs and matching canvas umbrellas that dot the shore during summertime. "It's the off season, and they aren't going to be renting banana boat rides or Jet Skis till spring break."

She nodded, and they headed over, ducking to enter the structure. They sat across from each other. The waves continued their endless rhythm as wind whistled against posts supporting the rental stand's flimsy wooden roof. It wasn't any warmer inside, but they'd escaped the gusts.

Eyes adjusting to the shadows, he saw Patricia's teeth chattering. "You're still shivering."

"I know. You can sit beside me if you'd like," she said. "I'm not hitting on you, I just think our body heat might keep us both warm."

Vanian thought a moment before joining her on the western end of the kiosk. He sat near, but not so close they touched. "Looks like the winds have changed. Maybe they're telling us something."

"Takes special ears to understand," she said. "I see daytime stars."

"Me, too," he said, "and I don't mean the sun."

"Ever feel like everything's connected?"

"Everyone has a purpose. Most of the time you fulfill your part without even knowing you're playing the game." Vanian licked his dry lips. "We touch lives without realizing it. Sometimes, I wonder what would happen if I wasn't here. If people would be better or worse off without me zigzagging in and out of their lives."

"You've made my world brighter," Patricia said. She reached into her pocket and pulled out a black felt pen. "Check this out."

She began drawing on the kiosk wall. Working with fast, deft strokes, she produced a Bad Apple logo.

"There," she said. "See? I threw a message up, and it's hidden in here. It's like sending secret energy into the universe. Imagine if this was on the side of a train, but bigger. So many people would receive the message."

Vanian now understood how this witch cast spells. "That's pretty cool."

"That's nothing. I'm much better with spray paint."

Vanian took a deep breath and looked at her.

The only light pouring in the tiny shack fell across her face. He leaned forward, brushing his lips against hers before easing into a passionate kiss. Sliding his tongue into her mouth, his groin swelled as his heart pounded out of his ribcage. She rested her hand against his cheek, her fingertips touching a tangle of his black hair. They pushed into each other, and he wrapped an arm around her. He pulled back, looking into her eyes. His soul twitched inside.

"Wow," she said.

They kissed again.

Outside the hut, the wind screamed. Beach sand slamming into the side of the kiosk sounded like metallic raindrops.

"Blessed Samhain, Vanian."

"Blessed Samhain."

Patricia nuzzled Vanian. As he held her close, a strangeness inside arose. He knew the risks with opening his heart.

Behind longing was the fear of losing something cherished.

# ♫ TRACK 18 ♫

Astro's face and throat were numb. Henry's blow was fire, in the running for the best he ever snorted. After sharing a gram and a tumbler of scotch, the club owner excused himself to the closing paperwork.

Exiting the office, Astro found Steve locking the reach-in beer coolers.

"Almost done?" Astro asked.

"Yeah. As soon as I lock this last cooler we can get out of here. Staying at my house right?"

Astro nodded. "We going out tonight?"

"It is Halloween. I heard Nyu and Switch are spinning the outside bar at Newby's tonight." Steve walked around the bar, pulling his keys from his pocket.

"Good. I really want to tie one on."

"Jesus Christ."

"Does that mean you're down?"

"I said I'd put you up. Might as well enjoy the ride. I don't have to work until the weekend anyway."

"Might be the best experience of your life."

"We'll see. I might regret it."

Laughing, Astro threw his arm around Steve and they followed the tight hall. After leaving the building, Steve pulled on the door. Astro glanced over their shoulders, making sure *they* weren't lurking in the corners. He hoped his twist of paranoia was an effect of the powder, that those shadows were just flashbacks haunting him.

In the parking lot, Carter, shirtless and sweaty, was under the Badmobile's hood, loosening the radiator hose with a yellow screwdriver. Astro wondered how the drummer knew what he was doing in the poor light as he slapped him on the back.

"Hey, dick lick. Forget that turd and come to Newby's with us."

Carter didn't look up. "I'm not leaving her and the equipment here overnight."

"Fucking lock that piece of shit up, and let's get faced. No one's messing with that rust bucket."

Astro spit on a bottle broken against the asphalt.

Carter wiped sweat from his brow with his forearm and looked at the engine.

Astro crossed his arms. "Come on, man. Destiny is calling me."

"No thanks." Carter resumed working. "The leak isn't bad. It won't take long getting her running. I have to meet my parents at Thomas Donuts on the West End in the morning. You guys have fun."

Astro shook his head. "See, Steve. This band is losing its edge. Why did my friends have to grow up on me?"

They walked to Steve's black pickup truck and piled in. Astro tried rolling down the passenger side window, but it wouldn't budge.

"Got any metal in here?" he asked.

"Metallica groovy with you?"

"That depends. Which album?"

"*Master of the Puppets*."

"Well played. Your cock just grew three inches. If you said one of their recent records, I would have jumped out and walked."

"Yeah, right. Buying the first round?"

"I ain't scared. The real question is: can you hang?"

Steve shot him a toothy grin and started the truck.

Twenty minutes later they were circling Ms. Newby's crowded parking lot. A gorilla followed a walking banana into the bar, and Astro couldn't wait to see the costumed drunks. Steve finally found a place by the back dumpsters, lighting a cigarette as he stepped out of the truck. Dance music drifted from the outside bar, and Astro and Steve used the back entrance, passing the DJs onstage. Walking to the circular bar, they passed pirates, gangsters, vampires, and zombies.

Everyone drunk, everyone dancing.

Lenard, a tall, slender bartender resembling Anton LaVey, the founder of the Church of Satan, was not in costume. Dropping a few dollars in the tip jar for his last order, Lenard waved at Astro and Steve.

"Here comes a regular—long time no see. How did the show go?" he asked.

"Slayed it," Astro said. "How about a few beers?"

The other bartender, Kim, came from behind the bar and hugged them. "Welcome back, Astro."

"I knew you'd miss me," Astro said, sliding a hand over her ass and wishing he was hard so he could push an erection into her hip. "Are you still seeing that asshole?"

"Yeah, I'm still with Eddie. He's not an asshole, Astro. He treats me damn good."

"No man can satisfy you like me, Kim. You know it."

Steve rolled his eyes as he took the beers from Lenard.

"Hey, let's go inside," he said

"Duty calls," Astro told Kim before pecking her on the cheek.

The men pushed through the cigarette smoke and costumed mob, entering the double doors leading into the crowded bar.

# ♫ TRACK 19 ♫

Patricia and Vanian woke up snuggling in the rental shack. Although the sun was up, it was colder than a normal Panama City Beach fall.

"I can't believe we spent the night in there," she said. "My neck is going to pay for that."

Patricia rolled her head and rubbed her shoulders.

"Think your car's still safe?"

"Yeah, that bar is closed until four in the afternoon this time of year."

Vanian admired Patricia's Bad Apple logo.

"Want to catch a bite?" he asked. "I know a diner near here. We can walk."

"Sure."

They crawled out from the kiosk and headed back to the beach access where their shoes awaited. After knocking off the sand, they walked to Front Beach Road and headed for the diner. Except for a few restless cars, the street was empty. In the diner, they sat beside each other in a booth and poured over a menu as the waitress brought them coffee and water.

"I'm having a ham and cheese omelet," he said, running his hand against the water glass, smearing the condensation. "What about you?"

"Hmm," she said, scratching her scalp, "I'm not sure what I want, something light. Maybe just hash browns or a side of bacon."

"Sounds fun," he said.

She took her eyes off the menu. "Do people ever come up to you and ask for autographs when you're out eating and stuff?"

"It's happened. Usually, I hide out. I'll go to the grocery store and stock up so I don't eat out much. I don't mind talking movies or music with a fan, but sometimes I want to shake the entire scene off my tired wings and not be me for a while. Don't get me wrong, I love what I do. I don't think I can be anything else. It's just once in a while I need a break from…me."

"I understand," she said. "I guess I take it for granted that I can split whenever I want. You're in the public eye, so you can't leave yourself that easy."

"I just kick it on the bus or in the hotel room while Astro parties down and Kitty and Dar do their thing. Carter likes to go out and meet the crowd. He's social like that. Makes for good PR."

"So," she said, "what's the weirdest thing you've seen on the road?"

"Driving or onstage?"

"Driving."

"Well, I saw a UFO when we were stuck in Indiana one night," he told her.

"Really? What happened?"

He took a sip of the coffee, the liquid warmed his belly.

"The Badmobile had been giving us hell. It kept on overheating, no matter what Carter did. We just played a hell of a show at the Metro in Chicago, and we didn't have a lot of time to get to the next gig. We pushed the minivan, and it bit us in the ass. When it finally broke down, there was no one else on the road. It's flat out there, so we decided to camp. We did that a lot when the weather and the terrain were right.

"The sky was bigger than I'd ever seen before. Without light pollution, the stars forming the Milky Way's arm reached across the night. Anyway, Dar and I found ourselves restless, so we were talking by the road, away from the tents so we didn't wake anyone. He saw it first, and when he pointed it out, I couldn't take my eyes off it. It was like a star, but moving erratically. It kept getting closer, until this oval-shaped craft hovered above us. There were flashing red and blue lights, circling a silver disc-shaped core, rising up and down. It stayed in place, dancing in the air for three or four minutes before it zipped away, disappearing around Draco."

"Did you tell the other guys?" Patricia asked, leaning forward.

"No, we didn't. I've never spoken of it before now."

"So, what about onstage?"

He frowned.

"The last time we played Orlando, a woman in the audience slit her wrists while we were playing 'September Tears'. What's worse, other fans egged her on. We've dropped it from the set list."

"I noticed you guys haven't been playing it." She bit her lower lip. "Do you know why she did it?"

"Her parents found a note she left in her bedroom before coming out to the show. Said she was a lonely soul, and that she was unable to connect with anyone."

"Jesus. Everyone faces death alone. That's why you should fill your life with good company and vibes. It only takes a few steps back to see who really cares about you. To see who's going to be there until you make that final solitary voyage into the great divide. I guess there are people who don't find that. Maybe they can't open themselves up enough to allow that in, so they miss out on what life's about. They miss out on all the love out in the world."

"Love's a gamble. People are afraid of the pain that comes along. Beauty's beast."

"The rose's thorn," she agreed. "I've been hurt before. Hurt bad. I was left a wreckage of a person, a shell of what I was. I wanted to curl up and die, take out the pain on myself. It ruined years of my life."

"Everybody hurts…sometimes."

Patricia leaned her head on Vanian's shoulder. He looked at the coffee and the same fiery rivers from his greenroom scrying spell reflected on the beverage's surface. He inhaled the scent of her hair.

"So, do you have a place around here?" he asked.

"When I couldn't live at my parents' place anymore, I moved into a week-to-week efficiency. I was working this taco place, so I was stacking paper. It just wasn't what I wanted to do with my life. When I heard Bad Apple's tour was coming through the Gulf Coast, I took time off. I left on good terms, so I can totally go back if I want to. But I really want to see what else is out there. I don't want to be trapped making burritos the rest of my life. Anyways, I let the efficiency go. I'll probably get another one tonight."

Vanian watched the steam rise from his coffee. "I own a cottage on the other side of the beach. It's not a palace—just a one bedroom, one bath—but it's quiet. It has a pullout couch if you would like to come for a few days."

"Vanian, I—"

"Look, I have enjoyed hanging. I want to get to know you better. I am not suggesting we rush into anything. I just think it would fun to kick it, until you figure out a plan. We can see how we jive together."

"I don't want to be a bother."

"It's no trouble. The company is welcomed. We can watch a few flickers, old horror movies or something. Spin records. I have great vinyl. I would like to see you paint more."

"It does sound idyllic."

He brushed his hands against hers.

"Sure," she said. "But let me pay for breakfast. I'll even throw down on groceries. I'm many things, but I'm not a parasite. I earn my way, and I'm proud of that."

"Fair enough. Hey, you don't mind ghosts do you?"

"Ghosts?"

Vanian tore his napkin into thick strips. "Yeah, my cottage is haunted."

"For real?"

"Yeah, I see her from time to time. I don't know anything about her, but she seems harmless enough."

"Is she like a poltergeist? Does she move shit around and wail in the night?"

"No, nothing like that. I just catch glimpses of her. Scared the fuck out of me the first time I saw her, but as far as I know, she just wanders around. She was the inspiration behind the lyrics to 'Ghost Wood'."

Patricia leaned forward. "Was she murdered?"

"Like I said, I don't know anything about her."

"That's pretty weird."

"So, is that a problem?" he asked.

"No, ghosts I can handle."

# ♫ TRACK 20 ♫

Astro woke up after two p.m., tangled in the blankets of the woman he'd picked up from Ms. Newby's. Fragments of the previous night returned to him. Henry's blow was good. Real good. Steve wanted to leave after one beer, but Astro was charged up from the cocaine.

He'd met her by the vodka rack...

She was dressed as a vampire's concubine, and Astro was drawn to her healthy cleavage and short velvet dress. When he looked at her tits, he wanted blood. She recognized him from the show, buying him Hunch Punch at last call to wash down a few last minute peppermint schnapps shots.

They were pushed from the bar to the patio with the rest of the drunks, given five minutes to finish their cocktails.

"I like it hard," she said. "And rough."

"Can you keep up, little girl?"

She grabbed his crotch. "Can you keep *it* up?"

"Watch your tongue," he said, kissing her.

They hopped a taxi, and Astro groped her under her top as she instructed the driver to take them to her North Lagoon flat. Her nipples hardened between his thumb and index fingers. He pinched them hard, and she slapped him, giggling. Astro bit her neck, working his hand past her thigh and rubbing her panties through fishnet stockings. When the cabbie dropped them off, she paid for the ride.

Inside, she tore into the guitarist, dragging him straight to her bedroom. Astro ripped off her costume, pleased she was shaved under her panties. He wasn't wearing anything under his jeans. She started opening a condom, but he was inside her before she freed the prophylactic from its package. He wrapped her hair around his fist, jerking her head back as he thrust harder and harder between her legs.

She came first, her body shivering underneath his unyielding pounding. Not wanting to look at her face anymore, he turned her over and took her from behind. She started insisting he put on the rubber, but he wasn't interested in her pleasure. She began drying up, and when she complained, he fucked her harder.

When he finally found release, they collapsed panting. He heard her breathing slow, and he sat up, lighting a candle on the nightstand.

"Don't tell me you're finished," he said.

"You can't be serious," she said. "We just went at it for, like, an hour."

Astro took the candle, pouring melted wax across her tits. She yelped and sat up.

"Fucker, that hurt."

Astro laughed. From his crumpled jeans, he pulled out his pocket knife.

"How rough do you like it?"

"Get that thing away from me," she said.

"Happy Halloween, baby."

She started to scream, but he covered her mouth as he slid the blade across her breasts…

The green satin covers stuck to Astro's chest and thighs as he rubbed the sunlight from his tired eyes. Unsure if she was unconscious from alcohol, sex, or abuse, he shook her gently. When she didn't respond, he assumed it was abuse and relaxed.

He didn't know the woman's name.

He slid out of bed, gathering his clothes and knife from the carpet.

After dressing, he glanced at the sleeping woman, unable to decide why he'd found the wench attractive enough to bang in the first place. Without liquor goggles, she was so common, so unlike his usual type. He wondered how he achieved and maintained an erection with that ogre in his arms as he shut her bedroom door, placing an imaginary wall between himself and the slumbering object.

Outside her bedroom, a Persian cat *meowed* and followed him to the kitchen where he guzzled three light beers from her refrigerator and helped himself to a piece of steak from a Styrofoam to go box, leaving behind a pile of soggy French fries and a hardened dinner roll. He didn't want anything in the pantries, so after rooting through her purse for what was left of her menthol cigarettes and a few loose dollars, he lit up and prepared himself for an afternoon walk.

In the living room, he grabbed a DVD copy of *A Clockwork Orange* resting beside her TV, tucking it under his arm. He was scoping out her CDs when shadowy movements caught the corner of his eye. He glanced, but there was nothing there. Figuring it was traces of the LSD he'd eaten when he was younger, he shrugged it off and started for the door.

The Persian *meowed* louder, tripping him as he walked, so he grabbed the cat, snapped its neck, and tucked it under his arm. He left her home unlocked, tossing the corpse in a neighbor's trashcan and walking down Allison Avenue towards Steve's house where he would try to hole up until his head stopped throbbing.

# DISC II

# KNOT WORK

ANTHONY S. BUONI

# ♫ TRACK 1 ♫

Patricia parked her car underneath the Dead End sign. The sun was sinking fast, and long-leaf pine trees gently waved in the breeze.

"I can't believe I'm doing this," Vanian said.

"Relax. You're gonna love it. You said you wanted to watch me paint. Well, this is part of it."

She reached in the back seat and pulled up two plastic bags filled with spray paint cans.

"There's a trail that will take us to a fence. It's easy to get over, but once we do, we have to be quick. We'll have to cross a clearing to one of the open cars, and it's in eyeshot of the guardhouse. We don't want any attention from the bulls watching over the trains. As soon as we get inside, we'll be fine. As long as we keep our voices down."

"I feel like a juvenile delinquent."

"Shaking up your soul, rock star?" She winked before getting out the car.

Vanian took a deep breath and followed. He wished he knew a spell for avoiding cops.

The trail zigzagged through the trees. They passed a dingy mattress in a clearing that was part of a hobo camp. A circle of mismatched red bricks and broken cinder blocks encased charred logs and half-burnt magazines. Empty cans and beer bottles were piled by an overturned school desk. A few more twists and turns, and they came to a chain link fence. The tracks were visible, not far ahead.

Vanian sighed. "I was worried it was going to have barbed wires along the top."

"I'm crazy, not stupid. I know this part sucks, but it is easier to come along the backside than cutting across the road from the mall. You're exposed. This way it's just a dash before we're in there."

She leaned forward, kissing him slow, warm against the cool, crisp dusk. Vanian pushed himself into her. When they separated, she scrambled up the fence, her agility amazing. In no time, she was on the other side, smiling. Vanian grabbed the cold fence, unable to remember how long it had been since he'd climbed one. It wobbled under his weight, but after building up momentum, he was able to clear it.

When his feet touched the ground, it was as if he crossed over into another world.

His heart pounded. Patricia mouthed the words *be quiet* and pointed to her left. Vanian spotted the guard hut, but it was too far to see if anyone was in there.

"That one there is our girl," she whispered, motioning towards a rust-colored boxcar, the side door wide open, inviting. "Ready?"

He nodded. She counted down with her fingers—*three, two, one*—and they raced to the car. Reaching the railroad car, Vanian was surprised how tall the sliding door was. Patricia was inside with a fast leap, holding out her hand to hoist him up. With her help, he pulled himself in the boxcar's belly. Patricia pulled him to the corner of the car where they squatted down, listening.

"Were there any bulls in the shack?" he asked.

"I couldn't tell. If they come up on us, run to the mall. We don't want to lead them to the car. We can backtrack for it later."

"Sounds good."

"Just be careful when getting over the couplings that hold the trains together. I once got my shoe stuck in one and thought I wasn't going to make it."

Vanian looked around inside the empty car. "Any idea what you're going to paint?"

"Yeah. How about you?"

"Me?"

"Yeah. I'll take this wall over here, and you can start on the other side. We can meet in the middle."

"Patricia, I'm not really good at drawing things. I've never used spray paint before. I wouldn't even know where to begin."

"Don't worry about that. Have fun with it. Life is a series of experiences. This is one way to grab it by the balls and squeeze."

She reached into a plastic bag and pulled out a can of brown paint and shook it, a rattling sound echoed in the car.

"What's making that noise?" he asked.

"It's a metal ball bearing inside the can. It helps agitate the paint inside the can, mixing it with the propellant so the paint comes out in a smooth coat instead of clumping."

"Oh."

"The nozzles were different. They were easier to paint details with. I've learned to adapt. What color do you want?"

"Um, silver."

"Good choice."

She handed him a can. He shook it as she stood up and approached the back wall. Studying her canvas a moment, she glanced over her shoulder before attacking the wall with the spray. Vanian watched as her wide, bubbly lines slowly formed an outline of a giant owl. It was not long before she began adding the feathers, beak, and eyes.

"That's pretty good," he said.

"Get to work, Vanian."

He looked at his side of the wall, clueless where to start. He tested the nozzle, a burst of silver streaked across the metal. It pleased him. He released reservations, letting the paint fly. They worked in silence, the sound and smell of aerosol filled the boxcar. Vanian was lost in the moment. Before he knew it, he'd painted a silver skull adjacent to a pentagram, coloring the uneven arms and legs green, yellow, red, blue, and the top point a combination of the four. Vanian found the process cathartic. He looked over at Patricia's piece, impressed with the owl's details.

"That's awesome," he said.

"It's interesting that you painted a skull. I chose an owl because they have complex magical meanings. In ancient Greece, they were seen as fortuitous, wise. In Rome, they were bad luck, often preceding death or disaster. There's folklore that counts the number of hoots to divine luck. Then you put up a pentagram, also a magic symbol for protection, and sandwiched it with a skull, which can mean death or wisdom, too. It's balance. Vanian, I believe we just cast our first spell together."

"I was thinking that when I stepped back and observed our work," he said. "It's in a secret spot. Unlike the outside of the train, no one will see this."

The images shimmered, the colors coming to life with a muted radiance, enough to illuminate the interior.

"Can you feel the energy?" she asked.

"This isn't vandalism. It's art...it's magic."

She kissed him. "It might not alert the bulls, but let's gather our tools and scram. We made our mark."

A cool windless night waited outside the boxcar. They collected the paint cans and darted back to the fence, climbing over and following the trail back to the car. As they headed back to the beach, Energy coursed through his veins, inspiring lyrics.

# ♫ TRACK 2 ♫

Astro crumpled a beer can and tossed it on Steve's coffee table, knocking over the aluminum pyramid they'd built while playing video games. He'd been living with Steve, taking up residence in his spare bedroom. The arrangement was working out. Steve kept a quasi-normal schedule, and Astro was up from dusk till dawn, so they managed to stay out of each other's way. The rent was cheap, and Astro had cash from the tour.

"Want to get out?" he asked.

Steve shotgun blasted another zombie in the head before pausing the game. "I don't know, man. I'm already getting drunk."

"You pussy. We're out of beer, and we still haven't gone to the liquor store. Come on, let's go out. I'll throw down on this bender."

"Fuck, man."

"I don't want to hear your bitching. We're going out, and we're getting hammered. I'll try sharing the women I pick up with you, but no promises. At the very least, you can have sloppy seconds."

"Gee, since you put it like that, I can't wait."

"So, we're going?"

"Nah, man. You go ahead and have fun. You have the key. When you get back, blast the music if you want. Fuck the neighbors, I can sleep through anything."

"All right, wimp. What am I going to do if I wind up with more tail than I can handle?"

"You know where my bedroom is. Point them to the door."

Astro pulled on his shoes and started to leave.

"Hey, Astro."

"Yo?"

"Bring back beer and a bottle of rum. Maybe a couple of nice cigars. Tomorrow, I'll throw down with you."

"Sounds good. See you then."

"See ya."

The night welcomed Astro. Crisp but not so cold that it was uncomfortable. Astro lit a cigarette and headed towards the bar, the beer buzz nipping at his eyeballs. He was still pissed about Vanian and the redhead, vowing to give him seven levels of hell when they jammed again.

His thoughts drifted to the ugly women he picked up, wondering if he'd pulled out before ejaculating. Her face's terror when he began cutting forced his orgasm too fast, especially when he cupped her mouth and fileted a silver dollar-sized hole in her arm. When her body slumped, he pounded her, diving into his usual fantasy that he was fucking a corpse. He still tasted her blood.

He was nearing Joan Avenue when he saw them, this time full on instead of dancing in the corner of his eyes.

Three shadowy forms, looming beyond a streetlight's illumination. Drawing near, they did not move, hovering at the edge of the light. The streetlight winked out, engulfing them in darkness.

He shrugged it off, assuming Henry's shit was cut with hallucinogens. Rubbing his nose, Astro pushed on to the bar, quickening his pace.

## ♫ TRACK 3 ♫

While Dar was watching an MMA fight, his cell phone rang. He touched the screen and placed the receiver to his ear. "Hello?"

"Is it just me, or do you also have the itch?" Vanian's voice asked.

Dar laughed. "What's up?"

"We should jam tonight."

"I thought we were taking time off. Less than a week since the last show isn't what I'd call down time."

Dar was relearning normal life. He was spending serious time with Kitty, falling in love with her again. Without the pressures of touring, he was able to concentrate on bringing another life into the wicked world. Kitty washed away his worries. She gave him strength. One look vanquished all doubts and fears. Dar knew he was a lucky man.

"Let's just say I've been inspired," said Vanian.

"Did you hit it off with that Patricia chick?"

"She's pretty cool, man. Got stuck on her. She's been crashing at my cottage."

"You're not moving too fast are you?"

"No. We're not sleeping together, if that's what you mean."

"You're not?"

"There's definite interest. We're sparking like crazy, but taking our time. She's staying over here, but she's been sleeping on the couch."

"That's fucking weird. But I'd expect nothing less from you. So where are we practicing?"

"Over at Carter's. We've already been talking today. He has his kit ready at his parent's beach house," Vanian said. "I can't wait for you to hear these new riffs I've been tinkering with."

"Sounds good. I know Astro has been crashing at Steve's place. I'll give him a ring and see you in an hour or so."

"Ciao," said Vanian.

Dar hung up the phone, pleased his friend found happiness.

"Details, details," Kitty said. "Are they an item?"

"Looks like that's how they're landing. He says they're taking things slow."

Kitty clapped her hands and bounced in her seat.

"Why are you so happy?"

"It's about time Vanian let someone in. He seemed so lonely when we were on the road."

Dar shook his head. "We're going to get a jam in over at Carter's."

"That's great. I might go by my parent's. Work on damage control."

"Cool. Maybe we can take them to lunch soon."

"I'll throw that out there. This will blow over soon."

Dar nodded. He hoped so.

# ♫ TRACK 4 ♫

Astro snorted a line of coke the size of his pinky off a mirror. Blurring time with Henry—drinking screw-top scotch and ripping rails—was now a daily affair. Today, Henry wore shorts and a Hawaiian shirt as he paced.

"Let's make lots of money, baby," he said, taking the mirror from Astro. "Once my man gets the shit from Miami, we move it nice and easy. Maybe only touch a few heads so word doesn't get out."

"I know the right people to sing to," Astro said.

"You wouldn't tell the band would you?" Henry asked, dumping more powder on the mirror.

"Fuck no. Carter would beat me over the head with the fucking Bible, probably make me go to rehab. Vanian would sit me down and want to discuss feelings and shit. Bastard hypocrite. He parties, but he would see me dabbling with it as a move against the band. Dar wouldn't give a shit, but Kitty has his balls clenched in her talons. She'd make him give a damn."

Henry chopped up the drug, turning the heap into two huge lines.

"I just want the business to be down low, ya dig me?"

"I dig it. You need start up cash?"

"No, baby. That's covered. I just don't want my face on the game. I have a respectable business to attend to."

"Right."

"We'll both make a mint. My guy isn't in it for the cash, he just likes fucking with the world."

A slow smile crossed Astro's lips. "What are you in it for?"

Henry passed him the mirror. "Lots of reasons."

Astro picked up the rolled up hundred dollar bill but before snorting the cocaine, his cell phone rang. "Fuck."

He set the mirror down on the table and looked at his phone. "It's Dar."

"Answer it."

"Don't really want to."

Henry scrunched his brow and rubbed his nose. Astro sighed and answered.

"Yo. What's up? Practice tonight…aren't we on break? Christ. I guess I'll be there."

He hung up and tossed the phone on the table, finishing the coke. "Man, I gotta run. We'll talk about this later."

"Consider my offer, baby. We get this done, and that's more money. More money means I'll be a happy Henry."

# ♫ TRACK 5 ♫

Astro flipped the switch on his amp. It came to life with a deep hum, like the buzz surrounding slot machines in a casino. The ash dangling from Astro's cigarette fell, exploding on his shoelaces.

"Where's Vanian?" Astro asked. Carter, tightening the nuts on his symbols, shrugged. Astro groaned. "Man, this is supposed to be down time."

"Maybe he wants to strike while the iron is hot." Carter tapped his snare. "'Gypsy Girl' is getting downloaded like crazy. With Meow handling another pressing of the single, it's smart to have a follow up. Keep the market saturated."

"Fuck that," Astro said. "I want a break."

"Relax, dude," said Carter. "We're keeping our skills sharp and our communication flowing. Plus, it's fun. That's why we're doing this, right?"

"Whatever." Astro sighed. "Your parents stock any booze in this joint?"

"They practice temperance."

"What the fuck am I supposed to drink?"

Carter hit the snare. "Try water. We have it in bottles if you don't like tap."

"Water? Yuck. Don't you know the government puts mind-controlling agents in that stuff so they can force you to do their bidding?"

"Have a soda then."

"Gross. That high fructose corn syrup makes you fat and keeps your dick soft." He adjusted the strap on his shoulder. "Have you ever wanted to fuck a cartoon character?"

Carter looked over at him. "What?"

"I'm not talking about those Japanese ones where the floppy titty school girls jump up and down. I'm talking about the animals."

"Like that cat lady on *ThunderCats*?"

"That's closer."

Carter shook his head. "No, man. Never."

"There's something not right with you. You know about the groupie hierarchy, right?"

"Can't say that I do."

"It works like this: the bassist and drummer can have equally hot groupies. The keyboardist doesn't get a groupie unless there are enough for the singer and guitarist to have two each. Bassists are sterile. It's the constant low vibration of the bass guitar near their junk that makes their sperm swim into walls. The bassist's groupie is allowed to be as hot as the rhythm guitarist's groupie, but not as hot as the lead guitarist's groupie."

"If the bassist is sterile, how come Kitty is pregnant?" asked Carter as Dar entered, wearing a t-shirt that looked a beer label except it said *Bukowski* in red letters.

"What the fuck are you talking about," Dar said. He rested the bass next to his amp and cracked his knuckles.

"I was about to tell Carter he can't fuck anyone better looking than me. It's the law."

Carter laughed. "Given the fact that you usually give the time to ugly bitches, I guess that means I'm better off playing with myself for the rest of my life."

"Looks like you're getting a good start."

Dar cleared his throat. "Been forever since we simply practiced. You guys been taking care of yourselves?"

Astro snorted. "That depends on what you mean by that."

"How's the little lady?" Carter asked.

"She's doing well. We've been decorating our apartment, you know, getting ready for the baby and all."

"It's hard to picture you as somebody's papa, Dar," Carter said. "How long does she have left?"

"Seven months."

"Hear that, Astro? Lucky number seven."

Astro didn't look up. His guitar strings caught the light. Vanian entered, guitar case at his side and wearing a long-sleeved black turtleneck hanging over worn blue jeans. Black painted fingernails unhooked the guitar case's latch, and he pulled out his axe, strapping her on.

"Evening, guys," he said, attaching the chord leading to his amp. "Glad to see you."

"You look good, Van," Dar said, adding with a shrewd smile. "Practically healthy."

"Thanks."

"So," said Carter, "what do you have brewing in that noggin of yours?"

"You may be surprised," Vanian said, strumming an open G chord. "Ready?" Dar nodded, and Vanian began to play. He started in G, finger picking a melodic pattern. He moved to A minor, then to D major, finishing the riff with open C. The music sounded like Victorian-era chamber music. By the time Carter homed in on a proper drumbeat, Astro stopped picking.

"What the fuck is this?" Astro asked, stopping Vanian in mid-riff.

"I think 'Emptiness by Candlelight' is a pretty cool name," answered Vanian. "The lyrics are about a lover searching for his spouse after fighting a long, gruesome battle. He's war weary and longing to hold his woman, and—"

"Like I said," Astro said, "what the fuck is this?"

"It's an idea," Vanian said. "I've been thinking about a concept album. Maybe set it in Greek mythology, or perhaps an epic not yet heard. Something romantic and dark; bittersweet nectar drenched with soul and passion."

"You're turning us into a fag band," Astro said. "I'm not feeling it."

"It's hot with two Ts," Carter said. "I like the idea of a concept album—doesn't happen much anymore. My heart's runnin' round like a chicken with its head cut off."

"Let's give it a try, Astro," Dar said, tapping out a bass line based on Vanian's chord progression. "What else you got, Van?"

"I have a heaver riff, Astro," he said, depressing the fuzz box's foot pedal, changing the guitar's voice from classical twang to ferocious growl. "Nice and simple, with a twist of distortion. I'm calling it 'Dowsing Rod' because writing the melody was like using sticks to find water."

The music was slow and heavily influenced by old Delta Blues. The chords were simple, A minor and F major, and Vanian's steady down stroke strumming gave the notes a choppy edge. Carter entered in with a tribal beat. Dar picked added a hypnotic bass line. Astro plucked out harmonics, adding heavy atmosphere to the mood.

Vanian sang:

*Hunting under dark moon*
*Searching for a glimpse of you*
*Dowsing rod show the way*
*To your arms within this maze*

"Stop, stop, stop" Astro said. "Man, you have this groovy vibe and these terrible words. Is this another album about love?"

"In a way, yes," Vanian answered.

"Fuck that," Astro said. "Why don't we concentrate on darker themes?"

"Like what?" asked Carter.

"Like abortion or grave robbing. We're a goth band. Let's poke around the twisted shit," Astro said. "Why don't we write a song about a father raping and killing his little slut daughter in a brothel after they gobble armloads of meth cut with bath salts? Call it 'Cherry Popper' and make it a secret track."

"Man," Carter said, "my grandmother listens to our sounds. I don't want her hearing depraved rape messages on something with my name attached. Explaining that to my church would be embarrassing."

Astro laughed. "Well, what about a song about riding in a car with Lucifer? You know, Satan rides with the top down so his hair can blow."

"We're not a satanic group," Dar said, crossing his arms. "I thought the only allegiance we pledged was to music."

"Vanian's always singing about the moon and the stars," said Astro. "Serious pagan undertones, man. If that's not kneeling before something other than music, I don't what is."

"There's a way to be subtle about things," Carter said. "Like, poetic, right? I love classic horror movies because they only hinted at the gore, working the imagination. We should be the same way with the sound. The more left unsaid, the better. I like the idea of having love as a backdrop, too. The Dark Wave movement has always been romantic and sad. Look at the Cure or the Crüxshadows. Beautiful vibes but sad and about unfulfilled love. Man, that's what it's about. That's what *we* should be about."

"Wait, now," said Dar. "I like darker. We are supposed to be brooding, and discontented relationships are only a fragment of goth. What about including songs about monsters and Lovecraft and death. Fuck, how about a man eating plant like the tat on my leg? Pretty to look at but hungry for human flesh."

"We should embrace the nefarious," maintained Astro. "The fucking dark side is where it's at. Do it better than the Black Metal outfits, more theatrical than those goofy splatter rock groups."

"How about this?" said Vanian. "A double-disc. One light, focused on love and healing, the other the blackest album ever conceived? I'm a Libra, and balance is key. With one side romantic with a tint of sorrow, and the other side embracing the monstrous corners of human nature, we can create unprejudiced scales. I haven't seen it done before."

"We can make it a total gimmick," suggested Dar. "One CD with a black label, the other white."

Carter rubbed his chin. "Make the entire tone of the cover art contrasting colors. Red and blue, or green. Black and white. Clashes that both excite and aggravate the eye."

"I like it," said Vanian. "What do you think, Astro?" The guitarist said nothing, his palm muting the guitar strings above the pickups. "You can write the twisted shit, and both you and Dar can throw in a lot of lead vocals, giving me a chance to maybe show off my guitar panache."

"I'm not playing anymore tonight," Astro said, unplugging from his amp. The black chord coiled at his feet like a moccasin as he pulled off the guitar. "Go on ahead without me."

"Aw, man," Carter said, "that's not cool. You're part of the sound and decision-making. We can't have a good jam without your input."

"I'm—I'm just not digging it. Maybe it was all the fucking touring or the drinking, but I need a break." The other members exchanged looks. "We can do this shit another day."

He set the guitar down and left the practice room.

*\*\**

"What the fuck was that?" Dar asked.
"Do we go on?" Carter asked.

"I'll go talk to him," Vanian said, pulling off his guitar and setting it back into his case. "We'll call it, boys."

"Fuck, I didn't get my groove on." Dar thumped out a scale on his bass. "What a prick tease. Hello, is there anybody out there? I wanna play."

"Another night." Vanian sighed.

"You don't think he's leaving us, do you?" whispered Carter.

"Every little thing's gonna be all right," assured Vanian. This wasn't the first time he had to calm his friend. He pushed open the door and followed the hall until he reached Carter's living room. Astro was spread out on the couch, drinking bottled water. "Are you cool, Astro?"

"Fuck off."

"We're compromising here. Let's do more than compromise, let's collaborate. I respect your ideas. Lay them down. If it's time you need, then we'll chill a few weeks. We've been through a lot and—"

"I said 'fuck off', Vanian. You think you're special 'cause you can string bullshit lines of poetry together and carry a tune while strumming elementary chords. A brain dead giraffe could pull off your grade school guitar work."

"Astro, don't—"

"Hey, look, ball buster," Astro voice was louder now. "No one made you den mother, and you keep on pulling rank like you're the master of ceremonies. You ain't running shit, Van."

The rest of the band emerged from the practice room. They kept their distance, huddled together in the living room's egress.

"Did I do something to piss you off?" Vanian asked. Astro leapt up, shoving a finger in his face. Dar positioned himself to break up the men if punches flew.

"You walk around like you know every goddamned thing, but you're just a needy little bitch, Van. You're too clingy to have a woman, that's why none of the twats you've dated have stuck around. You're looking for something that doesn't exist. Some bullshit fairy tale you'll never find. This is the real world, pal, so quit fucking whining about love and grow the fuck up."

Vanian stood there in shock a minute before saying, "I've been seeing Patricia, and it's been good for me."

"That little cunt from the last show? The townie? That bitch is a fucking whore, and the whole beach knows it. She was pulling me into the men's room for a handy before we played, but I told that slut I wasn't interested. I can't believe you fell for that shit."

"The way I remember it," Vanian said, "you tried to get her to go to Ms. Newby's with you before she shot you down and went out with me. If you're ticked off at me over a woman, we need to squash it ASAP. This is stupid shit, man. I want to slap skin before it goes any further." Vanian wasn't aggressive, but bringing Patricia into the mix flipped a switch inside of him, something dark and protective. "You need to stop playing like you're so damned hard and get your head out of your asshole."

Astro swung, knocking Vanian in the jaw. Vanian fell to the floor. Astro jumped on him, slapping and clawing at the singer. As they fell, Dar wrapped his arms around Astro, squeezing tight while lifting him away from Vanian.

"Chill out, Astro. This isn't cool. I'll fuck you up, man."

Astro howled like an injured animal, swinging and cussing as Dar, much larger than the guitarist, pulled him towards the front door. Carter rushed to Vanian's side, making sure he wasn't injured.

"Fucking monkeys," Astro screamed. "You pretend you're something, but I'm outta here. I'm through playin' with you jerk offs. Don't you forget about me. I'll be bigger than Metallica or Slayer, assholes. You're finished. Bad Apple's finished. As for you, Vanian, your heart will betray you. If I catch you out and about, I'm fucking you up. There's going to be people you don't even know looking for your ass. I'll fucking kill you, asshole."

Dar fumbled for the front door's handle and tossed him out. After slamming and locking it behind the screaming mess on the porch, he leaned against the door and caught his breath. Astro had scraped his face, drawing blood across his left cheek.

"Did he just quit the band?" Carter asked.

"That's what it sounded like," said Dar. "He was a madman. It's all the drugs. I've never seen such a crazy look in his eyes."

Vanian was panting. The negative energy tore at his emotions and made his lower lip tremble. "I'll...I can talk to him tomorrow. I didn't mean for that to go as crazy as it did. I'm so fucking sorry, you guys."

"That's fucking bullshit," Dar said, looking at the rest of the band. "We don't need a loose cannon in this outfit. I say we throw that fucker out. Give him a fucking wake up call."

"No, no," Vanian said. "We need to let shit cool off and talk about it later. I don't want to lose him. Not like this."

"I'd say this sucks," Carter said, "but that's obvious."

"Tell me about it." Dar groaned. He looked at his hands and shuddered. "I can't believe how close I came to beating him to pieces. What's happening to us?"

# ♫ TRACK 6 ♫

Vanian entered his cottage, resting his keys on the bar separating the living room from the kitchen. Patricia sprawled out on a pullout mattress in front of a flat screen TV, watching a silent movie and drawing in her sketchbook. She looked up and smiled when he entered, but her joy dropped at his worried expression. She closed the sketchbook and tossed it on the floor.

"What's wrong?"

"Practice was shit. Astro got angry and quit the band."

"What? This ever happen before?"

"No. He went nuts." Vanian sat on the bed beside her, pulling off his black sneakers. After a moment, he rubbed her shoulder blades, working his way down her spine. "He's held onto a lot of anger, and he took that shit out on me. Kind of messed my head up."

"You cool?"

"Yeah," he said. "Just sending out positive energy for a swift resolution."

"How about a cleansing ritual?"

"I usually practice alone, and I haven't opened a circle in a while, but I'd be honored to let your energy join mine."

She kissed him on the nose before turning off the television and folding in the sofa bed. Patricia tucked her sketchbook under a cushion.

Vanian moved to the kitchen, opening a cabinet and pulling out a black velvet box, a gift from Paul that contained magical tools: four anointed candles—green, yellow, red, blue—and an athame, or ceremonial dagger. Given to him by a Salam witch he had the privilege of sharing a glass of ritual wine with during a great winter solstice feast, the athame pulsed with power in his hands. He treated each item with respect, careful not to taint the tools with negative thoughts. After filling a ceramic bowl with Gulf water they had gathered in a glass decanter during a walk along the beach, Vanian set it on the coffee table.

He positioned the candles around the room, one for each compass point—North, South, East, West—and extended a hand, inviting Patricia into the center of the circle they formed.

"I invite you to cast this circle with me, to cleanse any and all negative energy attaching itself to us," Vanian said, looking in her eyes. Her energy flowed into his, raising the hair on his neck and arms. Beautiful and powerful—a rare combination.

"I accept your invitation with an open heart."

He struck a match, moving clockwise to light each candle. After, he dipped the athame's tip in the ceramic bowl and rubbed the Gulf water along the blade, visualizing a white, purifying charge. Vanian raised the point to the air, starting at the green candle to repeat the same clockwise motion, chanting, "By the power of three times three, I cast this circle around thee and me."

Patricia joined in the chant. When the circle was cast, Vanian rested the athame on the table. They kneeled facing each, fingers touching over the bowl and the blade.

"I want you visualizing the negativity in you, see it spiraling," Patricia said. "That bad energy is twisting clockwise. See it tightening into a jagged knot. Now use the power of this circle to send the spiral widdershins, breaking down that negative knot until it is as loose as a piece of yarn, blowing in the breeze. Let go. Let go. Let go."

The weight lifted from his soul, sweet relief.

"Send that negative energy you released into the water of the Gulf, where it can be neutralized."

Vanian sent the energy into the water.

"We'll meditate for a few moments. Let the calm of today and tomorrow pass through our souls."

They sat in silence, savoring the moment.

"Is there any magic you would like to address in this sacred circle?" Vanian asked.

She pulled him close, kissing him and spinning his head. His muscles relaxed as they explored each other. Their mouths created the perfect balance—a harmonious blending of longing flesh.

He could kiss her for eternity.

Chests pressed together, their hearts beat in time, breaths synching. As he'd never experienced before, all his worry dissolved. Nothing existed outside of the combusting universe they created.

She slid a hand along his ribs. He'd never wanted anything or anyone so badly. Pulling away before he crossed any boundaries, he fell into her eyes. Not only did he look in her soul, she peered into his. After brushing her cheek, she smiled and bit her lower lip.

"Patricia, I—"

She interrupted him with a kiss.

How could anyone be so perfect?

This wasn't a drunken one-night stand or a friendly romp to pass time and blow off steam. She effortlessly led him to wondrous new lands, places he'd been too afraid to expose his heart of glass.

Awe and fear tingled through his pores.

He pressed his hips into hers, lifting her Cheshire Cat t-shirt to expose her pierced nipples. Her body was kinetic divinity, and she offered him passage with an eager nibble on his neck. She moaned when Vanian ran his thumb against her nipple ring, tugging gently as his teeth caught her earlobe. The noises she made was the sweetest of songs.

Remembering the importance of balance within the circle, he returned the invitation to explore. Taking her palm and slipping it between his thighs, she grabbed his rigid penis and pulled her skirt off with her free hand.

He couldn't remember the last woman he'd been with. Worse, he could not remember the last time he'd had sex this close to sobriety. The circle's heightened magic added to his vulnerability. She removed his pants, tossing them with her skirt.

Vanian surrendered.

By slow route of her knee and thigh, his fingers tentatively found their way to massage her velvet until she grew moist. He took his time, her pleasure his only concern as she writhed under his caresses. Patricia tensed, and Vanian's heart skipped.

Had he moved too fast in spite of his caution?

Switching from submissive to dominant, she pushed him supine, spreading a leg over his hips and easing herself onto his hungry cock.

Both gasped.

She rocked over him.

Skull cradled beneath her red locks, he tilted her head back and exposed her neck to more kisses.

Two entwined as one.

The universe paused.

Everything was right.

He flipped her over, pushing deeper inside. She raised her leg on his shoulder, tightening herself around him. Sweat ran down his back. He hooked his thumb in her mouth, and she chewed on it. Her teeth were sharp, but her gnashing produced pleasure that echoed through him.

How long did he have?

Would he please her before losing control?

"I," he, said, "Patric—"

"Me, too."

Exploding, the release felt as rare and wonderful as a firework in a November sky.

They crumpled in each other's arms with a mutual groan.

Clinging together, their breathing returned to normal, and they basked in the warm, candlelit afterglow.

She lit a joint and blew out slow smoke rings that wobbled in the air above them before dissipating into the darkness. He toked as she made circles on his sternum with her ring finger.

"So is this a romance?" she asked.

He rolled over and looked her in the eyes. "It would be vulgar if you continued sleeping on the couch."

Smiling, she took the joint from him. "I wish I could bottle this moment up and drink it forever."

"Would have to be a pretty big bottle." He brushed her hair from her eyes. She took another hit, and they kissed as she held in the smoke. "Maybe more than one."

The candles flickered, casting their nudity in shadows.

# ♫ TRACK 7 ♫

Astro leaned forward, taking a cocaine-lined mirror from Henry. "Fuck those guys," he said, holding a rolled-up two dollar bill between his thumb and forefinger.

"With all due respect," Henry said, "Bad Apple is your ticket out of this shit hole. Most bands around here would sell their souls to have half the shot you cats do at the big time."

"Vanian's a one hit wonder, and he knows it. He thinks he's so fucking clever 'cause he's read a few books about witchcraft and constellations, but really, he's a fucking hack. He doesn't have it together enough emotionally to run with the bulls."

"You're speaking out of anger. You guys go way back."

"Since we were fourteen."

"Right. There's no need for this animosity. You guys are on the verge of being household names. To piss it away over creative differences...that's garbage, Astro."

Astro rolled his eyes before sucking up one of the lines into his left nostril. He passed the mirror and bill to Henry, pinching his nose. The drug always made his sinuses run, and he didn't want to waste any of the expensive substance. "You know, I want to do something different. Musically, I mean."

"Like what?"

"I really dug those Danger Shaft kids. Their approach to noise was fresh. Brutal, even. Like they were raping sound in the asshole without lube. There's promise in them, and I was wondering if they want to get things going."

Henry snorted his rail, rubbing the mirror with his index finger and massaging the leftover grains on his gums. His habit ran deep, and there would be no end to his hunger tonight now that he had a trusted dust buddy.

"Look, Astro, you each play an integral part to the Bad Apple sound. It happens when the four of you come together with your different personalities and jam. It's like four pieces of a puzzle. If you subtract any of it, you lose the magic. All the great bands had members with different musical tastes. The best of the best were able to fight like teenage girls and then kiss and make up."

"Save it, Henry. I don't want to go back. I want to move on."

"Haven't you been sleeping at Steve's? What are you going to do for work?"

"Fuck it, I'll crash on the beach. I have cash saved and enough talent in my little finger to blow this scene wide open. With our little game, I'll be sitting pretty. Fuck Bad Apple, I'm out." He looked at his feet a moment, and an emptiness opened inside of him. It had dwelled there a long time, but finally found reason to emerge. "Pass me another rail, will ya?"

"No problem, amigo. Plenty more where that came from." He rubbed his nose and passed the mirror. "So, have you thought about my offer?"

"Yeah, I'm down. Just let me know when."

"I'll let you know when my guy gets his shipment in. Keep this info under your balls, man. Don't go yammering about this all over town."

"I hear ya." Astro snorted a line. "Hey, what are you cutting this shit with?"

"What do you mean? I don't step on my powder."

"I swear this shit is cut with hallucinogens or something. I've been seeing weird shit lately."

"Flashbacks from the LSD you kids did in high school. You're lucky that hippie shit didn't make your dick fall off."

"Fuck you."

"No, really. What kind of weird shit have you been seeing?"

"These people, man. But they're not really there. Like smoky shadows, three of them…I guess."

"I'll say it again, lucky your cock didn't fall off putting all those chemicals in your brain. No, my shit is straight. Top of the food chain here. I don't sell it, so there's no need to cut it."

Astro snorted another line. "Guess I'm stressed. Nothing another drink won't cure."

# ♫ TRACK 8 ♫

C arter pressed the phone's receiver close to his ear.

"It's late, Carter," Anabelle said. "What do you want?"

"Whatcha been up to?" he asked.

"I just got back from the club. ScottEG and JKaos were spinning tonight. I drank too much."

"Well, make sure you drink a glass of water before you crash. It will keep your head from pounding when you wake up."

"You're not my father, Carter."

"Excuse me?"

"We need to talk," she said. Carter could almost smell the vodka on her breath.

"That doesn't sound good. Wouldn't you like to hear how we're not taking time off? How Vanian has been cranking new songs at an amazing speed, and the concept album about things lurking in all of our souls we're creating?"

Annabelle snorted. "No, Carter. I don't. We need to talk about me and you."

"Go ahead, shoot." Carter dreaded where this was going.

"I'm lonely, Carter," she said. "While the rest of the world moves on, I'm stuck living a lie because this talented musician I know is too chicken shit to own up to his real self."

"That hurts."

"I don't care if it hurts; it's true. We're playing this stupid game so you can save face, and I'm fucking sick of it. I love you, Carter, but I need a man who can be there for me. I want to go out to dinner and a movie from time to time. I want to have a laundry buddy. I want to be held at night and wake up next to someone, for Christ's sake."

"Please don't take the Lord's name in vain."

"At least Jesus had Mary Magdalene to snuggle up with during those cold biblical nights."

"That hurts," Carter said. "Look, I don't want to fight right now. I just wanted to tell you I was thinking about you and that I love you for what you're doing for me before I called it a night."

"Is that all?"

"Other than thank you? Yeah, I guess it is."

"Damn it, Carter. I didn't want to do this like this, but…I've been seeing this guy, a local here."

Carter rubbed his eyes. He could feel a headache coming on. "Oh yeah?"

"He has his own business, and he treats me really good. He doesn't understand our relationship, and he wants me to clean up my baggage so we can have a life. Together. That means no pseudo-boyfriend who can't face the truth."

"You want me to tell you it's okay to start seeing this guy or what?"

"The funny thing is that I don't want or need your blessing, Carter. I'm seeing him whether you like it or not. It's actually been going on a while. I didn't want to hurt your feelings or put you on the spot."

Carter balled his fist and hit his leg. Betrayal from someone who knew all your dirty little secrets sucked. "Yeah, thanks for that."

"I have needs, and what we've been doing isn't healthy. Not for me and not for you. You can't change what you are, Carter. As soon as you face facts and accept it, your life will be so much better."

He heard a guy's voice in the background but couldn't make out what he was saying. He swallowed hard, but the lump wouldn't go away.

"I need to get going, Carter. Don't call me for a while. Maybe until you can be honest with yourself and the rest of the world. Take care."

She hung up the phone, leaving Carter sitting at the kitchen table, alone and sad.

## ♫ TRACK 9 ♫

Dar and Kitty sat in front of the television, watching *Little Shop of Horrors* and sharing a bowl of microwave popcorn. He rubbed his hand across her arms, soothing her upset stomach as the singing plant wooed the nerdy florist.

"How's the new music coming along?" she asked.

"Some days it's easier than others. It's weird not having Astro around, like we're missing a limb. The rest of us have to pull harder to get the sound we want, but it's not bad."

"I told you he was becoming erratic. He's been changing for a long time now."

"I guess we're all changing."

"That better not be a fat joke," she said.

Dar leaned in, kissing her on the lips. She ran her hands down the side of his face, tracing his stubble under her fingers.

"Are you ready for this?" She rubbed her tummy.

"Is anyone really? I know I'm ready to spend the rest of my life with you two, and that makes me happy."

"I have a favor to ask of you, Dar. You might not like it."

"Fuck," he groaned, leaning back into the couch. "Let's hear it."

"I want you to lay off the booze for a few weeks," she said. "Dry up so we can spend adult time together."

Dar was silent a few moments. Some nights partying went too far, but he made sure it didn't interfere with his relationship.

"Can I have a beer or two before bed at night? You know how I toss and turn."

"A beer here and there is fine, but we should start acting like adults since we're about to spawn and all."

Dar sighed. "Cool, I'll lay off. You're just going to have to do something for me."

"Oh, yeah, like what?"

An evil grin crossed his face as he moved in for the kill.

# ♫ TRACK 10 ♫

Astro poked his head in the shed where Danger Shaft rehearsed. The band was sitting around, drinking quarts of malt liquor and smoking cigarettes over a game of poker. Nostalgia flooded him. A few years ago, Bad Apple rented a shed, practicing most days after work late into the night. Another lifetime now.

"Gentlemen," Astro said.

The guy he recognized as the singer looked up from a porno mag. "Hey, you're the guitarist from Bad Apple, right?"

"Yeah. The name's Astro."

"I'm Eamon. Mike here plays guitar, and that's Orlando on the drums." The other guys indifferently waved before returning to their quarts and cards.

"Nice to meet you guys. I have to say, I love your shit. You guys are brutal."

"Thanks. We fucking hate trendy music, so we try making as much noise as we possibly can. Guess it's our mission statement."

"I can dig it," Astro said. "How long have you been playing?"

"Over two years. Henry lets us play the Mozzy once a month, but that was the biggest audience we've ever performed for."

"How'd that shit feel?"

"Like I was alive, but the soundman was not on his game."

"What do you mean?" Astro asked.

"He wouldn't let us get loud enough. He kept on adding too much reverb, too. I mean, that shit works for Bad Apple, but we like it raw."

"Yeah" Mike said, "We're destroying eardrums, not wooing women. No offense, but Bad Apple is fucking music, not fighting music."

Astro loved their passion. They were pissed at the world and taking it out with rock and roll. "None taken. I actually wanted to see if Danger Shaft would be interested in my services."

"Are you asking to manage us?" Orlando asked.

"No, you guys don't use guitars, and I wanted to throw in my skills as a fretsman."

Eamon smirked. "You want to join Danger Shaft?"

"Yeah. Charles Manson used rock and roll to incite his followers to kill, and we could be the next chosen ones. I bet my noise jives with yours, make those fucking ears bleed while we take their hard earned dough. Maybe we can take Danger Shaft to the next level."

"We don't want the next level," Eamon said. "We're not playing music to make it or sell out. Hell, we're not even playing music."

Astro didn't follow. "What do you mean?"

Orlando took a long pull from his quart. "Danger Shaft isn't about a record deal or selling t-shirts. We're about fucking shit up."

"Yeah," Eamon said. "It's cool as fuck you're into us, but we just don't get down like you, man."

"I see," Astro said, feeling like falling hail inside.

"You should come out to the Mozzy next week," Orlando said. "We're playing a show with Pig Chicken Suicide."

"I'll be there. Bet it." Astro had no intention of being there. "Well, I won't waste any more of your time. I'll catch you guys at the next gig."

Offended, Astro left. Those kids had no idea what they passed up. He wasn't into working with amateurs. He was once a member of a famous band, way out of league for a bunch of kids. As Astro headed towards the closest bar, dark clouds swelled in the sky.

# ♫ TRACK 11 ♫

Patricia poured over the Gyro Café's menu, deciding between the classic gyro with tzatziki sauce, onions, and tomatoes or the supreme with grilled mushrooms and feta cheese. Vanian sat across from her, his folded hands resting on the table. They were the only late afternoon diners in the restaurant, and Vanian soaked up the pleasant atmosphere.

"Hummus today?" he asked. "It's excellent here."

"Um, sure. I can't decide if I want the extra stuff on my gyro or not."

"Go for it."

The waitress returned, resting two beers in front of them. "Here you go. Are we ready to order?"

Vanian looked over to her. "You ready?"

"Yes," she said, drawing out the *s*. "I would like the super gyro today. Did you say you wanted hummus, Van?"

"Yeah," he said. "An order of the hummus, and I'll also have the super."

"Would you like fries?" the waitress asked.

"Nah," he said. "Do you?"

"No, not today."

"Sounds good, guys," the waitress said. "I'll put in your order. The hummus will be up in just a few moments."

"Thanks," Patricia said before the waitress disappeared behind the bar.

"You ever see that Molly Ringwald flick, *Pretty in Pink*?" Vanian asked after sipping his beer.

"Yeah, why do you ask?"

"It's the saddest movie I've ever seen."

"And why is that?"

"Because of Duckie," he said.

"Duckie?"

"Yeah. He's obviously the right choice for Molly Ringwald's character, Andie, but she's too self-absorbed with that rich guy to notice. Duckie proclaims his undying love for her throughout the movie, and she doesn't even care. Instead, she hooks up with the rich guy before he heads to college. He's going to break her heart in a few months, but she's happy for the moment, and I'm supposed to be copasetic with this."

Patricia laughs, bringing the beer to her lips. "The rich guy's name is Blane, by the way."

"Oh, good form." Vanian winked at her. "Worse, although we see this unknown woman giving Duckie the fuck-eye before the credits roll, we know he's not going to be happy without Andie. I'm saying they ended the movie too soon."

"Really?"

"Really. Flash forward a few months to when Andie is broken-hearted because that same rich asshole she's in love with is fucking three university women with one of his sleazy frat brothers. Fortunately for Andie and audiences all over the world, Duckie is there to take her hand and show her what real love is."

Patricia's eyes sparkled. "And what is real love, Vanian?"

The waitress rested a plate between them; a soufflé cup overflowing with hummus and surrounded by fried pita triangles.

"You need anything else?" she asked.

"No thanks," Patricia said. After the waitress left, Patricia locked eyes with Vanian. "So, what is real love, Vanian? You're not getting out of this that easily."

"Well…real love is patience, understanding for someone else's clicks and clacks, working together through the hard times, and being there whenever you are needed. Sharing that internal contentment with someone special."

"Will you stand before me?" she asked.

Bells hanging from the door announced another patron's entrance. A busty blonde in a yellow sundress with matching expensive handbag sauntered towards the bar.

"So," Patricia said, "You really believe Duckie was better for Andie than Blane?"

"Absolutely."

"Well, as a witness beyond the fourth wall, you know Duckie is better suited for Andie, as well as the people surrounding Andie. But what matters is what Andie wants. The rich kid may break her heart down the road, but at that moment, she wants him. That's what's important. I see Andie down the road becoming her father, a single parent struggling. As for Duckie, he'll die lonely and bitter."

"Like I said, the saddest movie ever. I don't know if I can go on with that in my head." Vanian looked at the window at the cars in the parking lot. Cumulonimbus clouds swelled over the magnolia trees lining 23rd Street, and Vanion's knuckles ached with the promise of rain. "I really feel bad for the Duck-man. I don't know if I could wait and wait for the woman I love to reciprocate the emotion. I would go crazy outside of that absolution."

"What if I needed time? What if I put us on hold to figure shit out, forcing you to wait for me? Would you just give up?"

Vanian raised his hands. "Touché, gorgeous. I would not give up. I would wait as long as it took. I wouldn't like it, and I'd like seeing you with another cat even less. I'd wait for you, but I'm not an idiot."

"What's that supposed to mean?"

"I'm just saying—"

Before Vanian finished the thought, the blonde stood next to him.

"Hi, um, I saw you sitting over here, and I was wondering if I could meet you?" she said, twirling her hair in her fingers.

Vanian locked eyes with Patricia.

"Have a seat," she said.

The blonde sat between them, leaning towards Vanian. "You're the singer for Bad Apple, aren't you? I've seen your pictures in the *News Herald*."

"Guilty party," Vanian said. "This is Patricia, my girlfriend."

The blonde ignored the last part, closing the already narrow gap between her and Vanian.

"How long are you in town for?" she asked.

"We're in no hurry to tour again," he said. "We recently lost a long-time member, and it's changed our sound considerably."

She giggled. "I bet you guys still kick ass."

"What did you say your name was?" Patricia was unable to hide the aggravation in her voice.

"My name is Julia." She rested her fingertips on Vanian's arm.

"Are you from around here, Julia?" Patricia asked.

"I'm local," Julia said. "I moved here about three years ago for my job on the Navy base. Anyway, Vanian, some friends of mine are having a party tonight. If you'd like to come over and have a few drinks, you're more than welcome to join us."

"I appreciate your offer, but Patricia and I have plans."

Julia leaned over, whispering in Vanian's ear loud enough so Patricia heard, "Oh, leave her home. The invitation was for you."

Patricia stood up.

"Look, bitch," she said. "Go back to the bar and eat your food. Let us have our peace."

"Pity," she said before returning to her seat at the bar, passing the waitress holding the couple's gyros on a serving tray.

"I'm—I'm sorry," Patricia said after the waitress left. "I'm such a freak."

"She was overstepping her bounds. You did nothing wrong."

"I know what you do puts you way out in the public eye," she said. "I also know there are people in love with the image of you. The tortured rock star poet. I am lucky enough to know the real you. When we started hanging, I was worried that you wouldn't like me because I'm a fan. But I'm no groupie. You know that."

"I do." Vanian reached out and grasped her hand, rubbing her fingers with his thumb.

"I don't want you or anyone saying I am a groupie," she said.

"I saw you in the crowd before we met in the greenroom. To be honest, I told Dar I wanted to meet you. He just facilitated the moment."

"Well, then, I guess I have to thank him."

"Yeah, me, too."

"Stand...stand by me," she said.

"You make me happy. I haven't felt that way in a long time."

She smiled, covering her blushing cheeks with her hands.

They looked at each other.

"Here's a thought," she said. "What if Andie really belongs with Blane?"

"What?"

"What if they stay together? Life is funny, and it is a possibility."

"Things don't wind up that fairytale," he said.

"What would you call this?"

"Wonderful," Vanian said, leaning forward for a kiss.

## ♫ TRACK 12 ♫

D ar's hands shook. While Kitty was visiting her parents, the alone time found him craving beer. There were three unopened bottles of merlot in the refrigerator, but his promise to Kitty prevented him from dipping into the red wine. He opened the pantry and stared at food he didn't want to eat. The cereal, sardines, and cookies did not strike his mood. He reached into his pocket and pulled out his cell, dialing Vanian's number.

"Bacon bits," Vanian said. He usually strayed away from answering the phone with 'hello' because he believed it was another way people were trapped in habits and routine.

"Hello, Van, I need to get out, man. Kitty's at her mom's, and I'm going stir crazy."

"Patricia at a friend's house," Vanian said, "so I have the night free. How does Newby's sound?"

"I'm supposed to be staying off the booze. I'm drying up."

"We don't have to drink. We could go to a restaurant. How does that sound?"

"I'm not hungry?"

"Well," said Vanian, "any suggestions."

"Newby's is fine. I can have one or two and be fine."

"Cool. I'll see you there in twenty."

"Thanks, Van. There is a lot banging around in my head."

Dar closed his phone and grabbed his keys off the kitchen counter.

\*\*\*

By the time Vanian made it to Ms. Newby's and ordered red wine mixed with diet soda from Lenard, Dar was three beers deep and punching in punk rock songs on the internet jukebox.

"Taking it easy tonight?" Vanian asked. If Dar was seriously drinking, keeping up with him would be impossible. Once his alcohol train got rolling, there was no stopping it.

Dar shook his head. "Man, my head's goin' nuts. I don't know if I'm ready to be a father."

"I don't think anyone is. You just have to make your own way and run with it. Cheers." They clinked beverages and took a long pull from their drinks. Vanian looked around at the people, drinking away their problems and money. Was he any better than these lost souls? "What are you worried about, man?"

"What if I fuck him up? The sins of the father, right?"

"You said 'him' again. If you are worried about the way you're living, change. Sometimes you have to grow up. If the band's going to hurt you guys, maybe we should call it quits."

Van hated the words as soon as they left his tongue, but reality was reality. He could never tear his musical brother away from his family, no matter what it meant to Bad Apple.

"Fuck that," Dar said. "I know I can't go on forever, but for now this is what I need."

"It's a job. If I thought it was interfering with Patricia and me, I'd drop it in a heartbeat."

"You really dig this bird?"

"Yes. I…I'm in love with her."

"Have you told her that you loved her yet?"

Vanian's face burned. "No."

"She's the one, huh?" Dar asked.

"Not a doubt in my mind."

"Is she working anywhere yet?"

"No. Off season here sucks balls. There's simply no work to be had. Makes me wonder how anyone gets by after summer."

"Kitty and I were talking, and she had a good idea. She knows Patricia is bad ass with paint, so she was wondering if we, Bad Apple that is, should hire her. She can help with designing the new CD's art and help sell t-shirts at shows. There's constantly new orders on the website, and she can help Kitty fill them and get them to the post office."

"That's not a bad idea."

"We're getting bigger, and with Kitty pregnant, she could use the help. I know our next tour is going to be different with the baby and all. An extra set of hands will make things a lot easier."

"I like it." Vanian scratched his head. "Sounds like we're crossing over from band status and forming a tribe."

Kim, the other bartender on duty, slid up, hugging both men. "Hey, guys. I'm sorry, but I threw out Astro earlier."

"Fuck," said Dar, "what did he do?"

"He tried to punch a regular for playing country music on the jukebox. I'd seen Astro drunk a million times, but he was so angry tonight. There was something in his eyes, something I didn't like at all."

"Yeah, he's been moody as hell lately," Vanian said. "Is that guy still around? Can we buy him a shot to apologize?"

"No, he split right after Astro. About fifteen minutes ago."

Vanian frowned. "Damn."

"We'll do a shot then," Dar said. "Whiskey?"

"It's going to be one of those nights, is it?"

"Hey, if I'm messing up, I'm messing up large."

"Have it your way, but we're taking a cab home."

"You're buying, Van."

Vanian nodded, and they bellied up to the wood.

## ♫ TRACK 13 ♫

"Fucking Danger Shaft," Astro grumbled to himself. "Fucking Bad Apple."

Too many Long Islands at Newby's were making his head spin. Even the crisp fall night did not clear the hangover already creeping into his brain. He started a fight with a guy at the jukebox, so Kim asked him to leave. She was no different than the other women Astro knew. She longed to swallow his semen before he fucked the dog shit out of her. The desire came off as aggravation, but Astro knew how the game was played. She'd get her chance; he was only waiting for the right moment to rip her panties off and fulfill her wishes.

They would all get their turn, it was up to him to decide when.

One day they would realize his greatness and regret the bullshit they put him through. Bad Apple, Danger Shaft, his parents—they would beg forgiveness. By that time, the real paychecks would be rolling in, and Astro wouldn't need them or their approval. He would have real friends, high rollers. He knew it was only a matter of time before he climbed out of the gutter and took his proper place, strolling alongside gods.

Stopping to sneeze into his arm, he looked up and saw a person's silhouette standing in the middle of the sidewalk. Far away from the nearest streetlamp, its features were hidden in shadow, but Astro saw they were taller and thinner than he was.

"Got a cigarette?" he asked. The form did not reply. It stood there, unmoving. "Hey, just being friendly, asshole."

He started walking towards it, but stopped. Another shadowy figure appeared on his right, standing in the street. The hair on his arms stood up. Realizing he was looking at the things that had been following him, he turned to go the other way another one waited behind him. The sexless form billowed, moving like smoke. With no eyes, no human features, it existed as a shifting curtain of atmosphere.

"Back the fuck off, man. I don't want any trouble."

There was nowhere to run. To his left was a wooden fence too tall to scale. The creatures approached, misty arms extending outwards. Astro curled up against the fence and tried to scream, but their icy touch blinded his eyes with white hot cold, filling his nose and mouth with thick smoke reeking of damp earth and rot.

# ♫ TRACK 14 ♫

Clearing the bong's smoke-filled chamber, Patricia's eyes watered. The hit of Lucio's hydroponic marijuana felt like a wrestling match in her lungs. She held in the smoke. Good pot was difficult to come by during the off season. It would be tragic to waste such high-grade shit. Sinking back into Lucio's expensive leather couch, the techno music and marijuana swallowed her up.

Sitting across from her, Lucio held a bright green bud with tweezers while using a pair of scissors to snip the fluffy flowers from the pale green stem, taking time to stack the red and blue hairs in a separate pile. An aficionado, Lucio always scored the best shit, medical grade smoke he refused to touch with his bare hands as not to destroy the bud's delicate THC crystals. He also wouldn't snort cocaine outside of anything other than a rolled up hundred dollar bill. Lucio's arrogant eccentricities didn't bother Patricia. She'd learned to go along with his moods years ago.

"Not a goddamned seed in any of it," he said. "It makes for great smoke, but I can't grow my own batch."

He popped the stems in his mouth and began chewing, destroying evidence of contraband.

"You're letting me take a bud to Vanian, right?"

"Are you really serious about this...musician?"

"Yeah. When we hooked up, it was like a missing piece of my life fell into place. I couldn't be happier."

Lucio cracked his knuckles before loading the bong's bowl with another clump of weed. "I've known you a long time, Patty."

"Don't call me that."

"Sorry, Patty. Anyways, I've known you a long time, and after Hunter fucked you over, you were an absolute pain in the ass."

Patricia looked at her fingers. Her nail polish needed touching up. "I know."

"The dope was one thing, but I didn't know if you were going to off yourself or fuck every guy in town or what. That shit didn't look good on you."

"Junkie doesn't look good on anyone," she said. "Looks like you've been losing weight yourself, Lu."

He shook his head. "This isn't about me. I can handle my shit. You, on the other hand, were a fucking mess last time your heart got broken, and I won't see that happen again. I'll have to shoot that motherfucker. So help me God, you know I'll do it, too."

Patricia gave him a nervous smile. Lucio was dangerous, but she trusted him. Years of friendship showed her that he was harmless until provoked. He was one of the only people on the planet who'd seen her shoot up. During her active addiction, her habit was a shameful, solitary one. She would score, taking the smack or pills or whatever and locking herself away to face her demons alone.

There was even a romantic connection between them when she returned from Portland, but they didn't gel as a couple. When the romance fizzled, they managed to maintain a close friendship.

"I know, I know." She handed Lucio the lighter. "You don't need to worry about Vanian. He has a heart of gold."

Lucio ignited the lighter and sucked hard. The bubbling bong filled with smoke. He pulled out the slide and cleared the chamber with one mighty breath.

"Are you really off the smack?" he asked, his voice strained from holding in the hit.

"Yeah. I just drink and smoke pot now. It's all I need. The other shit was fucking killing me. Now, I am trying to have a life, ya know? So far it's working out."

Lucio replaced the slide and refilled the bowl, handing it back to her.

"How much can you kick down?" she asked.

He reached into a cigar box and tossed her a rolled up baggie. "Here's a half ounce. It's what I can spare. For a friend."

"I really appreciate it." She tucked the weed in her pocket, smelling her fingers before resuming her work with the bong. If only they made perfume that smelled so sweet.

"I bet you do." He watched her as she filled and cleared the chamber. When she rested the bong on the table, he reached back into his cigar box and extracted an eight ball of brown powder.

Her eyes widened. "Fuck, man. What's that?"

"Your favorite. Some skag I shipped in from our neighbors down south."

"Put that shit away, Lu," she said, standing. "I don't want to even be in the same room as someone using."

Lucio stood up, stepping over the coffee table and standing in front of her. He was too close for comfort, and she stepped to the side.

"Come on," he said. "We could fly together. I'll show you a good time. It's been a long time since we were together."

"I told you. I'm with someone now."

"Yeah, but he ain't me. I have two Viagra. I can keep it up all night."

"Thanks for the buzz, but I have to go." Patricia grabbed her keys off the table and started for the door.

"When he fucks you over, don't come crying to me, Patty. When your heart's broken, that's on you."

"Fine," she said. "I'll call you in a few days. Till then, jerk off. I'm not your whore, got it?"

Lucio yawned. "Yeah, you're his."

Patricia frowned and left, slamming the door and vowing to never see or speak to him for as long as she lived.

## ♫ TRACK 15 ♫

"**W**hat the fuck are you doing, man?" Steve asked as Astro pushed his couch against the front door.

"We gotta barricade ourselves, Steve. It's the only way."

"The only way for what?" Steve crossed his arms as the guitarist grabbed chairs from the kitchen.

"The fucking shadow people. They're out there. They're coming to get me."

"I get it. You've done too many drugs. You want me to call a doctor?"

"No! No doctors. They won't be able to help me."

Steve shook his head as Astro stacked up the chairs, reinforcing the couch. "Did you burn your dealer? Are drug lords after you?"

"These things aren't human. They're of the night, 'cept they can come out during the day. These things are out to get me, Steve. These things—"

"Aren't real, dude. You're fucking spun. You haven't eaten solid food or showered in days. You drink every drop of booze we bring in the house, and, frankly, you look like fucking shit."

Astro looked up and Steve saw the madness in his eyes. "You're with them, aren't you?"

"What are you jabbering about?"

"You know goddamned well what I mean. The shadow people. You're working for them, aren't you?"

"Don't be ridiculous. Come on, help me get this shit out of the way and get some fucking sleep. The sandman will do you right."

"You think I'm going to sleep?" Astro screamed. "I go to sleep, and they'll get me. You'd like that, wouldn't you?"

"That's enough. You got ahold of some bad shit or something. I'm calling for help." Steve turned on his cell phone, but Astro jumped him, tearing it out of his hands and smashing it against the wall. The phone shattered into pieces, scattering across the living room.

"Fuck you, man. Fuck you. They're not getting me."

"Get out," Steve said. "Get your ass out of my house. You've gone crazy, man. I was lending a hand, looking out for an old friend, but something's wrong with you. Come by tomorrow, your shit will be on the porch. I want you out of my sight."

Astro stood in his face. Steve flinched, looking for a shield or weapon to defend himself.

"You want me out of your goddamned house. Fine," he said, his demeanor normal as if nothing happened.

Astro's sudden calm chilled Steve.

"Yeah, man. It's a good idea. Tomorrow you should check yourself into rehab. You need help, dude."

"Yeah," he said softly. "Help. I'm out of here."

He removed the furniture blockade he'd constructed. Steve watched as he pushed the chairs and sofa aside.

"If you don't see me again, you know who did it," Astro said before leaving.

Steve sat down on the floor and stared at the mess in his living room. He didn't have much, but he'd worked hard for his things. Replacing the damaged furniture would cost a fortune. Astro, born with a silver spoon stuck up his ass, didn't give a fuck about anything outside of his cock and dope anymore; his repulsive insanity and drug-fueled devolution was now metamorphosing into something dangerous and scary. Steve rarely burned bridges, but he couldn't ignore the signs.

Time to pull the plug.

He stood and picked up the landline—a phone attached to the kitchen wall—dialing the number to the Mozzy.

"Mozzy," Henry's voice said.

"Hey, it's Steve. Some fucked shit just went down here."

"What happened?"

"It's Astro. He flipped his fucking lid, like he took some bad dope."

"Was he fucked up?"

"You could eat breakfast off his pupils."

"I'm sure I'll see him sooner or later, Steve. I'll see what the fuck is going on with him."

"He needs help, man." The pleading worry in his own voice startled Steve. Always the club's go-to guy, the genie who fixed all the problems on and off stage, Steve realized he didn't have a solution.

"I'll talk to him. Don't worry about it." Henry paused a moment and added, "You're okay?"

"Just rattled. I have a mess to clean here, but, yeah. I'm fine."

"Good. I'll let you know when I talk to him."

"Thanks, boss."

Steve hung up and grabbed an overturned chair.

# ♫ TRACK 16 ♫

The taxi stopped in front of the cottage with a metallic squeak. Vanian, still drinking wine, was having trouble giving directions to his home, telling the cabbie to turn down the street before his. When the driver finally found it, Vanian hugged Dar and handed the cabbie several wadded-up five dollar bills.

"Does that cover it?" he asked.

"And then some," she said, smiling at the generous tip.

"Make sure he gets home in one piece," Vanian said. Dar was spread-legged and slumped in the back seat.

"No problem."

Vanian opened the door and stumbled out. As the cab pulled off, the headlights cut through the darkness, illuminating magnolia overlooking the twin pine trees at the end of his driveway. Vanian dropped his keys. Swearing, he fumbled around the pine straw and sand until he found them, shaking off the dirt. The cab's taillights were already shrinking in the distance, delivering Dar to a catfight. Vanian walked up the steps and tried inserting the key into the lock. Before figuring it out, Patricia opened up and stood, arms crossed, in the doorway.

"Late night?"

"Hey, pretty lady," Vanian slurred. "How are you?"

"I've been waiting for you, Van. I thought we were going to watch a movie and eat ice cream when I finished at Lucio's."

"Dar called and he was going through hell, so I caught a few drinks with him at Newby's."

"A few drinks?"

"Well, maybe more than a few. I messed up, didn't I?"

"No, it's no big deal. I was worried about you, that's all. We'll talk tomorrow," she said. "Let's call it a night."

Vanian lowered his head and started for the hall. Patricia reached out and grabbed his sleeve. When he stopped, she mussed his hair. "Get rest. You need to sleep it off, and I need to go job hunting in the morning."

She sighed and mussed his hair before wrapping her arms around him and leading him down the hall, helping him into bed before turning out the light.

*** 

Vanian opened his eyes, unsure how long he'd been sleeping. In the dark bedroom, Patricia's soft snores rose beside him. He rolled over and took a drink from a water cup he kept on the nightstand. Reclining, the ghost, dressed in her usual white blouse and black jeans, floated out of the bedroom. Instinctively, he started to rise, but Patricia stirred. Seeing the dead was nothing new to Vanian, but he'd never communicated with the phantom dwelling in his cottage. He scooted close and wrapped his arm around Patricia. As his eyes closed, their breathing fell in time.

# ♫ TRACK 17 ♫

Kitty flipped through the channels, dissatisfied. MTV's garbage reality shows and humdrum format had infected the other music stations, and nothing interesting was on the premium stations. She wasn't sure if it was the pregnancy or Dar being out late making her irritable but suspected a combination of both.

When she was little, she wanted to be a famous artist after her father took her to a downtown gallery. The artist community was odd, but their beautiful work made her beg her parents for an easel and brushes, imagining herself hanging beside her favorite Louvre masters. Although still hanging onto those dreams, she was more than content to be a part of Dar and Bad Apple with Dar.

She stopped on the History Channel, flashing images of the Greek underworld. Taking a sip of chai from her favorite brown coffee mug, her mind floated to Dar and his taste for intoxicants. She really didn't mind the drinking, but there was the baby to consider. Dar treated her well. Most men didn't give a damn about their mate's feelings, but he was different. A rare breed. He was always concerned about what went on in her head, careful to give her space when she needed it, even when they were on the road with three other personalities.

She glanced towards her cell phone. Would he answer if she called? A stone bust of Hades flashed across the screen, and she wasn't sure about life after death.

A cab, engine grumbling and suspension squeaking, pulled up their driveway, and Patricia grabbed a copy of *Good Omens*, pretending to be lost in its warm pages. The book was an old friend, and Dar would never suspect the turmoil in her head. Dar entered, and she looked up from the dog-eared pages.

"You smell like a brewery."

"I feel like one," he mumbled.

"Is this going to continue when the baby comes?"

"What do you mean?" he asked.

"Are you going to party away your life?"

"I wasn't planning on it."

"I know that you're a musician and all, but an example is going to have to be set for our daughter. I just want to make sure it's the right one."

Dar sighed. "Do we have to do this now?"

"I think so."

# ♫ TRACK 18 ♫

Vanian, carrying an envelope, walked up the path to his mother's trailer, the yard in its usual disarray. Empty beer bottles and sun bleached cans poked out from the brown patches of overgrown weeds and sandspurs. Cali had been threatened by neighbors about the lawn before. Vanian normally made excuses to clean the property, but lately, it felt like a waste of time.

He knocked on the dented door. Stale liquor and cigarette smoke burned his nostrils as Cali answered. Dark brown speckled her tattered pajama bottoms and white t-shirt, and Vanian wondered if they originated from whiskey-spiked coffee or vomit.

"Oh, it's you," Cali said. Her over-pronounced Southern drawl became worse with each passing year. Because her voice pulled Vanian's attention to how she spoke rather than what she was saying, the phony honkytonk grated against his ears.

"Yeah, it's me. How are you, mom?"

"You bring me cigarettes, boy?" she asked.

"No," he said, "I did not. May I come in?"

"Be my guest. The place is a mess, but you already know that."

Inside, Vanian frowned. No matter how much work he put into Cali's home, she kept it trashed, as if she enjoyed living in squalor. The smell of garbage and cat piss nauseated Vanian, but he found a place on her tattered sofa beside a stack of old newspapers.

"What about beer?" Cali asked. "Bring your mama something delicious to swill on?"

"I'm not helping you harm yourself. You're special to me. I want you around a few more years."

"Listen to that," she snarled. "My rock star son wants his mommy. I thought I pulled you off the tit decades ago. It don't matter. What I really need is a cigarette. You know how much them bastards are nowadays? I swear, all that money for a dumb plant in a box. I'd be better off growing my own tobacco."

"I want you to quit drinking, mom," he said. "If you keep this up, it'll kill you. Then what will I have?"

"What will you have?" she mocked. "A bunch of money, for starters. Fans that call out your name wherever you go. They don't know the weird shit you put me through growing up. All those goddamn monster movies and satanic albums."

"Look, here's a list of the AA and NA meetings in town." He handed her the envelope. "Go check it out. Maybe you can find peace in those rooms. Maybe you can't. All I'm asking is that you try. After you hit a few, call me. There's a lot we need to talk about."

She held the envelope, a puzzled look across her face. "You can't be serious."

"I am. I also came by to tell you I've been seeing a woman."

"Well, it's about time. I figured you were queer. The way you and Paul always got along, I thought he popped your cherry."

"That's bullshit, and you know it. Paul is a good man, and you fucked it up. I can't believe he gave you this house to wreck. It's a waste. You're a waste."

"Is that any way to talk to your mother?"

"Probably not, but when you start acting like my mother, I'll talk to you better. I'm not staying long. I just wanted to make sure you were doing well."

"Just come and go, don't even bring me a cigarette. I guess I have to get one from next door."

"I'll see you later, mom."

Vanian rose and left. Visits with Cali always proved emotionally draining, but today the negative energy seemed to glue itself to his soul. He tried pushing away the dark vibe, but the more he pushed, the more it swallowed him like black tar. As he walked down the street, he couldn't wash off the dirt from her house.

# ♫ TRACK 19 ♫

Patricia and Vanian left Panama City Beach and headed north on Highway 77. Before connecting with Interstate 10, the couple turned right, following State Park Road to the green and brown tollbooth at Falling Waters State Park's entrance. They paid admission at the guard hut and drove in, following the winding, down sloping road to a large, empty parking lot.

Exiting Patricia's car beside the campground bathrooms, picnic area, and water fountain, they walked hand-in-hand to a butterfly garden. The plants used for attracting the insects were brown, withholding their vibrant displays until spring returned. In the center of the octagonal garden, Vanian and Patricia relaxed on a curved concrete bench suspended by Dorian pillars. She rested her head on his lap, breathing in the fresh air.

"It's so peaceful out here, Van. This is how we were meant to live, isn't it?"

"Probably. It's nice to sneak away from reality and get in tune with nature."

"I bet this garden is beautiful in the spring. I wish we had enough space to plant things. We could grow herbs for cooking. Orange trees, so we can squeeze our own juice in the mornings. And tomatoes. Nothing tastes better than fresh tomatoes."

"I'd love a real piece of property. We could raise a magical garden to rival Babylon's. Maybe lure butterflies of our own."

"Shame they aren't buzzing around today."

"We can bring them here."

"What?" Patricia asked. "It's too cold. Most of the butterflies migrated elsewhere or died."

"I can sense there are a few more out there."

"How do you call them?"

"Here." Vanian sat her up, standing behind her while wrapping his arms around her waist. Security washed over her. "Close your eyes. Feel the world around us. With your heart."

She complied. After her mind cleared, she became aware of the surrounding forest's pulse.

"There's enough warmth within you to call those butterflies out from wherever it is they're hiding. You don't even have to say a word. Just concentrate on bringing them near. Try the spell I taught you. Use your inner beacon and draw them out with your soul."

Her breathing steadied, finding a similar rhythm as when she mediated in that sweet spot between sleep and consciousness—not quite awake, but not totally consumed with dreams. Visualizing, her heartbeat turned into a torch, burning brighter and hotter with each breath. The inner light intensified until the fire gently spread outward, filling the garden with her energy.

"Look," Vanian whispered.

She opened her eyes. The woods had come alive. Fluttering Monarch butterflies floated around them. One landed on her hand, peacocking its orange and black wings. Vanian pointed to the woods and she gasped. The butterflies weren't the only creatures she'd lured out. A family of deer watched at the tree line. Dozens of singing birds circled overhead. Crawling out from under the bathrooms, an armadillo wobbled its way to the garden. A green anole crawled onto her lap and bobbed its head.

"Did I do that?" Patricia asked.

"Yes."

"Now what do I do?"

"Thank them with your soul."

She closed her eyes again, thanking and blessing the woodland creatures for hearing her call. Before reopening her eyes, she turned to face Vanian, kissing him deep and slow. After parting their lips, they locked gazes.

"I'm in love with you."

"I'm in love with you, too."

Neither wanting to break eye contact, they sat in comfortable silence.

"I didn't want you thinking I was rushing you or compromising the way you do things," she said. "I know this sounds crazy, but it's right.

My mom once told me that you just know about these things, that you feel it deep inside. I know what she meant now, Vanian. I love you."

"I feel the same. You've brought so much to my life. I'm thankful to know you."

"I'm glad to know you, too." She squeezed him. "I want to treat you right, Van. I've had a twisted past. There are things people will tell you about me that aren't true. I'm the first to admit that I've done wrong, but I want to live better. I want to have a better life...with you."

"I don't care about then. Life's about moving forward. I'd like to move forward with you."

"I just worry that—"

Vanian placed his finger to her lips. She bit her lower lip, understanding.

"Words can only do harm," he said.

"I'll always be there when you rain," she said. "No matter what, I'll be there."

They kissed again before heading down a trail leading to the park's namesake. Centuries ago, the local limestone gave way to sinkholes appearing throughout the area. One such natural pit opened across a creek's flow, causing the stream to plummet a hundred feet into the deep crater. Vanian led her through the winding path, weaving in and out of other sinkholes before a wooden stairway escorted them down to a platform overlooking the chasm. The previous night's hard rain fueled the waterfall as it cascaded into the ravine. The site throbbed with power, and the lovers clung to each other enthralled with its beauty.

She gasped. "I had no idea this was here."

"It's a magnificent world. You have to look for the exquisite among the hideous, but even ugly is attractive in its right. I believe you called it wabi-sabi, the imperfection making things beautiful."

"I've never met anyone like you," she said. "You see things your own amazing way. You find beauty in the smallest, most trivial things, and you have a knack for making people rejoice in life."

"Can I tell you something?" he asked. "Something about myself I haven't told anyone."

"Vanian, tell me anything."

He sighed. "I use magic in my music. Always have. As I became serious about blending music with spells I was writing, more people took notice. I didn't mean any harm, I was just creating atmosphere. I told you Paul was my music and magic mentor, right?"

She nodded.

"He's a witch. The strongest I've ever met. People would be scared if they knew how much power he possesses. The funny thing is that he never uses it. He found balance in music, hanging out with other people interested in rattling their ear drums, letting music guide their souls. He loves enlightening people about bands, and he is one hell of a music coach.

"I don't know where he draws his strength, but he was passing that power to me. Mom sensed the change in me was more than puberty. She knew he was teaching me magic. Finding that old spell book was the ammo she needed to end their already strained relationship. The things she said...to both of us. People don't deserve to be treated like that. Especially if they're any kind of decent. She'd been slipping so long, and he encouraged me to not give up on her, that she needed patience and love. Love is all you need. But when she told him to leave and threatened to call the cops on him for sexually abusing me, I knew that whatever love she had left was gone, dried up. I was looking at a soulless woman, not my mother. I have not seen Mom since."

Patricia reached out and touched his shoulder. His pain broke her heart. If only her words and kisses could stitch the pieces back together.

"Worse, I blame myself for her loss of humanity. If I hadn't left that book out, Paul and I would have continued our lessons. Maybe she would have found her way again, and we could have been a family. I destroyed both of their lives."

She embraced him, wishing her arms could wash away every bad thing that had ever happened to the man. "Vanian, you can't blame yourself. The universe is on time, remember? Everything is in its place, running like clockwork. Life can suck, but it is a string of experiences, building us up to a more complete whole. Your mom isn't really gone. She's lost, but there's always hope. In the end, all we can ever have is hope."

"I try, Patricia. I really do."

"You don't talk much about your mother," she said. "Who was she before she slipped away?"

Vanian looked at the water cascading into the abyss.

"She's complex. Her parents disowned her for getting pregnant with me so young. She dealt the only way she knew how, always using the bottle filling up that piece in her heart she couldn't. I know it was hard with the bullshit jobs and needy child, so I don't blame her for anything. She just ran from her problems."

"Where is she?"

"She holes up drunk in town. Look, I don't want to come off like she neglected me when I was growing up. That wasn't the case at all. She wasn't always drunk. It started as an occasional thing for her to blow off steam. As I grew older and more independent, she took to the sauce because she saw me leaving. Her parents, my father—no one would stand by her. The people in her life left her behind, and it broke her."

"That's so sad. I'm sorry, Vanian."

"I've come to terms with my life. I'm happy." He looked into her eyes; the gaze stroked her soul. "I've never been happier."

"You two will reconnect one day. You strike me as one who doesn't leave many loose ends. Something as meaningful as this you'll see to. I'm sure of it."

"Maybe."

"I want to meet her," she said, tugging at his hand.

He frowned. "I'm not so sure that's a good idea."

"Come on," she said. "You're becoming successful. A hot song and new material in the works. You two need a lot of catch-up time. Plus, you can introduce us."

"I don't know."

"Here's an idea. Thanksgiving is coming up. We can drop by her place tomorrow and offer to cook turkey dinner."

"You are incredible. Tomorrow, we'll drop on by there. If she gets weird, we'll split."

"Sounds great." She hugged him. "It'll be wonderful, Van."

Putting her arm around him, they watched water tumble down the hole.

"I have a spell I can show you," she said after a few moments.

"Yeah?"

"Come on, let's find someplace open."

They walked along a trail, passing a lake with a roped off swimming area. A sign depicting an alligator warned bathers that the reptiles were known to reside in the water. Entrance in the lake was at their own risk. The path coiled through rows of slash pines before opening into a flat, grassy field. Patricia grasped his hand and took him several paces from the path.

She made him face east and spread his legs at a forty-five degree angle.

"Plant your feet flat on the ground," she said. "Now lift your arms up over your head and point your open palms to the sky. Make sure your fingers are spread so the wind can pass through them."

Vanian cracked his knuckles before lifting his hands.

"Now close your eyes. Focus your negative energy in the center of your chest. Clear out your soul's dusty corners. Anything that's bothering you—your mother, Astro, worries about recording—tighten them up into a ball. Once you've gathered your apprehensions together, divide it, and push it up your arms. Let it work its way up like an electrical arc on a Jacob's ladder. When it reaches your fingertips, let the breeze lift it away. The air will shuttle it to the sky. As the energy elevates, imagine the clouds circling overhead. They will attract the energy, soaking it up like a sponge. When the clouds capture it, the sun and sky's power will neutralize the energy. When it rains, the water will be charged with positive vibrations, giving this land a drink for the plants and animals."

She looked up. Cirrus clouds aligned themselves into a wide-reaching spiral. His knotted, complicated energy lifted up, getting pulled into the twisting sky.

"Vanian, look."

Opening his eyes, the clouds absorbed the expelled negative energy. Transforming from thin, wispy brushstrokes into fluffy cumulus clouds, their color shifted from white to dark gray. Lightning flashed, and the sky opened up, drenching them with hard rain.

"Damn," she said. "You've been holding a lot inside."

The downpour was hard and fast. Within a few moments, the blue sky returned. A rainbow arched across the sky.

She kissed him, and they walked back for the waterfall.

## ♫ TRACK 20 ♫

Carter and Dar sat in the corner of a fast food restaurant's lobby, eating double cheeseburgers and watching cars outside the tall glass windows overlooking Thomas Drive. Dar took a loud slurp from his soda, washing down French fries dipped in mayonnaise.

Carter chewed slowly. Annabelle's departure hadn't sent him on a self-destructive rampage, but his mood had flattened, soured. Though he loved burgers, his sandwich tasted like cardboard, and the sweet soda hurt his teeth.

"I wish I ordered extra pickles on this sandwich." He swallowed, wiping ketchup from the corner of his mouth. "Vanian is getting serious with Patricia. What do you make of it?"

"Fuck, it's his life. He's happy." Dar picked up his burger. A piece of onion poked out the side of the sandwich, so he shoved it back under the crown of the bun. "He needs someone who'll stick by him. She's a nice woman. Kitty adores her. They're not out trying to change each other. They're existing together. I guess time will tell."

Carter was happy for the singer, but with Astro acting so erratic, he wondered if the band could take another external complication.

"Lately, days just don't seem the same. Are we really recording without Astro?"

"It looks like it. We've covered a lot of ground over the past week. I tried talking to him, ya know."

"Who, Astro?"

Dar nodded. "He left Steve's and has been staying in a roach hotel downtown. I went over there to try and smooth things out, but it was like pissin' up a rope. He said I should quit the band before Vanian has me sucking him off between songs."

146

"Astro has a way with words, doesn't he?"

"He told me he had a different idea about where his sound should be going, and we weren't it anymore. He wants to play like that Danger Shaft outfit that opened for us."

"Danger Shaft? That bunch of hacks?" Carter cocked an eyebrow. Those kids were beneath the guitarist. "You've got to be kidding me."

"I don't know if he really meant it, or if he was trying to wood tick his way under my skin. Either way, it appears the break's final."

"Fuck, man. Goo goo g'joob."

Dar slurped his soda. "Pouring like an avalanche and coming down the mountain."

Carter blinked. Maybe it was the drugs or the drink, but Dar seemed a little spaced out. "What is?"

"Everything. I can feel it."

"You're just nervous about being a daddy."

"Maybe. Or maybe I'm worried about growing up."

"You look pretty grown to me."

"Thanks, Carter."

"Are Kitty's parents warming up to the idea?"

Dar rubbed his eyes. "Yeah. Getting better there."

Carter rubbed his chin. "Are you guys going to have it baptized?"

Dar smirked. "Are you serious?"

Carter looked at the ketchup and mustard mess left behind on the burger wrapper. "Annabelle broke it off with me."

"That was a weird relationship."

"Gee, thanks."

"All right. What happened?"

Carter picked at the top of his ear and fidgeted in the seat. "She found a homegrown cat."

"Carter, you know we don't judge, man."

"What do you mean?" This was ground Carter did not want to approach. His inner circle was already wobbling. No need to send everything crashing down.

"I mean, you can love who you want, and it doesn't really matter."

Carter tensed.

"Look," Dar said, "we don't mean to hurt you when we pick on God or call you a fag. You're the best drummer I've ever heard, and playing with you is amazing. That's all that matters."

Carter stopped eating and looked at food as if it were a dead pet.

"I swear," Dar said, "this month. There's definitely something in the air. A lot of shit has been going down."

"Maybe it's the end of the world," Carter said softly. He gnawed on the thought, wondering if anyone would notice if the world really did end.

# ♫ TRACK 21 ♫

Allowed to serve booze until four a.m. by Bay County law, Ms. Newby's was packed at three in the morning. A favorite last call spot, the true alcoholics started their evening cocktails there before pub crawling up and down Thomas Drive and returning to finish their evening.

Lenard mixed Astro another Long Island, careful to make it light. Although Astro was a good tipper, he was quick with his fists, and Lenard didn't need that madness in his establishment. He placed the drink in front of the guitarist, taking his money. At the register, Kim watched the rocker take a large gulp.

"We knew all the answers, and we shouted them like anthems," Astro screamed, raising his Long Island ice tea above his head. He uneven footing caused liquid to splash down his arm and chest. "Did you guys see that? I just spilled that all over my pussy."

Lenard heard Astro using his Bad Apple status to hunt free drinks and a warm place. After being turned down by several women, he bellied up on a barstool.

"You know, Lenard, Panama City's lesbian population has exploded as a result of the local asshole hillbillies. No one here knows how to treat a woman."

"Is that so?"

"It is, my good man. I'll show them. Tonight, I'm fucking a late night diva so hard her mother will cum. That's how real men do it. Deep dick those dykes until they're straight."

Kim shot Lenard a look.

"The lunatic is on the grass," she said.

"Shit, he's probably on a lot more than that," Lenard said as he stuffed the change in the tip jar. "He'll be dead before they cut another record. All we'll have of that great talent is a few witty memories and several bastard children."

Kim snickered.

"Nothing to laugh about, Kim. I've been in this biz a long time, and I'm watching a friend throw his life away."

"Look at the drunks in here," she said. "Who isn't guilty of that?"

Lenard sighed, nodding. The bar scene was a wreckage of lost souls. The world needed love, nurturing, and understanding.

"Lenard," Astro said and pointed to the rum rack. "Let's talk to those dripping slits over there. They look lonely."

"You cool back here alone for a few minutes?" Lenard asked Kim.

"Yeah," she said, uncorking a bottle of merlot. "Keep him out of trouble"

Lenard followed Astro as he wandered to a pair of girls wearing cowboy hats, jamming his thumbs in his pockets. The tall blonde looked up from under her hat and smiled, tossing her spiral curls.

"Howdy, stranger," she said with a thick accent. "You look like a fella that might want to buy little old me a whiskey shot."

"Show me the way to go home," he said. "I'm tired, and I wanna go to bed."

"Slow down, Buck Rogers," she said. "First thing's first. You have the wrong impression."

"Funny how secrets travel," Astro grinned. "I can tell you've never been this far before. I'd like to be the guy to show the bone."

She rolled her eyes, looking back at her girlfriend and turning her back to the men, resuming their private conversation. Astro furrowed his brow.

"Come on, man. Let's go outside. I need fresh air."

"Whatever you say, man." Lenard glanced at the bar where Kim appeared to have things under control.

Astro took another long pull from the drink, stumbling through the door leading to the outside bar where a cover band cranked out Southern rock standards to an intoxicated horde. Most of the folding tables and chairs were pushed against the back wall, so patrons could dance to the live music. Astro and Lenard found seats at the horseshoe bar near the darkened jukebox.

Whistling, he pounded his fist on the wood. "Yo, barkeep. Lenard and I demand more Long Islands."

"Easy. I work here, remember," Lenard said. Astro's behavior was wearing on his nerves.

As the bartender made the cocktails, Astro realized Vanian and Patricia were sitting at the other end. Waving her hands in the air, she was talking to a man in a striped golf shirt while Vanian scrawled in a composition notebook with a ballpoint pen.

Astro squinted, resting a twenty on the bar.

"Look what the cat dragged in," he mumbled, rising. "Hey, you." Vanian looked up, breaking away from his writing. Astro staggered towards them, Lenard close behind. A few rogue splashes jumped from Astro's cup, landing on the concrete as he weaved towards the couple. "I want to tell you something."

"Hey, Astro," Vanian said. "You doing all right, man?"

"Piss off," he slurred.

Vanian leaned back as he rested his pen on the half-filled page.

Astro crossed his arms. "Say something. Anything. Your silence is deafening."

"What do want me to say, Astro? Distant conflicts unresolved. I love you. There's no need for you to be a pariah from the band. You belong with us, in Bad Apple. It's not the same without you."

Astro slurred. "You're a monster. I'm gonna make sure the world sees it. You may have fooled them, but I know. I know the real ghoul that you are. Sending those...those things after me."

"What are you talking about?" Vanian asked.

"You know goddamned well what I'm talking about." Astro shifted his bloodshot eyes to Patricia. "Both of ya."

"No ghouls, no witches here to scream and scare them," Patricia said. She looked him up and down. "I see angles trapped within the ice."

"There are no angels here. No fucking angles here, missy. Leave them kids alone."

Astro finished his drink with one mighty gulp. He drew back his arm, throwing the ice-filled cup at Vanian. The cubes burst free of the cup, raining over Vanian's notebook, smearing his fresh words. Astro pounced, fists balled.

Lenard reacted. In an instant, his arms were around the guitarist. Astro unleashed a string of obscenities as Lenard and another bouncer dragged him outside. The commotion was so intense the band ceased their cover of "Bad Moon Rising" and watched the fray unfold. As Astro was tossed into the street, he waved his fist at the bar.

"You've got a hell of a lot to learn about rock and roll. I'll get you, Vanian. You'll be sorry. You'll regret ever meeting me."

Back inside, Lenard rested his arm on Vanian's shoulder.

"Are you okay?"

"Yeah," said Vanian. "I'm all shook up."

Patricia straightened her hair. Her hands trembled. Vanian turned to her. "How about you? Are you okay?" She nodded, reaching out to him.

"What are we going to do, Van? He said he was going to get you. Doesn't that make you worry?"

"He's just drunk. I bet he'll regret it in the morning. If he even remembers saying anything."

"Shit," Lenard said, "That's a hangover in the making that I wouldn't want any part of."

"Let's rest." Patricia tugged on his sleeve. "We have a big day tomorrow."

"Sure," Vanian said.

She rested her head on his shoulder.

Lenard smiled. They made a cute couple. He looked through the plastic covering the open air barroom and saw Astro strolling down Thomas Drive, shaking his head and talking to himself as he became smaller and smaller until he was nothing, nothing at all.

# ♫ TRACK 22 ♫

As Vanian escorted Patricia up the overgrown path leading his mother's trailer, her palms sweated. He'd warned her Cali's trailer was raggedy, but she wasn't prepared for its squalor. The feral lawn, overrun with dollar weeds and sandspurs, reached out for the couple. Beside the front door, thorny climbing vines consumed a rusted dryer missing its lid. Tin foil plastered the windows, even covering the yellowed, cracked transom. Across the bent door, uneven black letters in grade school penmanship read *we don't dial 911*.

Vanian's silence concerned her, but she knew she would have to be strong.

The three wooden steps creaked as they ascended. Would support both of their weights? Fidgeting, Vanian rubbed his wrists where a silver bracelet dangled. Sweat beaded his forehead. They'd spent a lot of time together, but she'd never seen him so uncomfortable.

"You ready?" she asked, scratching his back. He looked down and inhaled deeply.

"As much as I'll ever be. I have to warn you, Mom can be—"

Patricia brushed her finger across his lips, cupping his stubbly cheek with her hand. He managed a weak smile, nodding twice.

Vanian took one last long look at her. He knocked three times. His mom opened the door carrying a bottle of rotgut vodka, a slender menthol cigarette dangling from her lips. Dressed in a tie-dye t-shirt and ratty frog pajama bottoms, she looked Patricia up and down, sneering.

"Hello, Mother," he said. "Patricia, this is Cali, my mom. And, Mom, this is Patricia. My girl."

"Pleased to meet you," Patricia said. She extended her hand, but it remained untaken. Cali's unforgiving stare screamed silent judgements. Patricia had seen the same look when she was strung out. She'd come so far, healed and grown so much, but Cali's disapproving glare ripped the scab away. Awkwardly lowering her hand, Patricia bit her lip.

"Did ya bring me cigarettes?" Cali asked.

"No, Mom. You know I don't support cancer."

"What about beer? Did you bring some beer? You know how thirsty I get."

"Sorry, no beer either."

"Then why is the big time rock star coming round here? Don't you have a bunch of fans that need you right now? Or has success finally pulled the rug out from under you?"

"Mom, I wanted to visit. Can we come in?"

"Whatever," she said, disappearing into the darkness. Patricia and Vanian exchanged a glance before following.

Inside, the acrid smell of cat urine burned Patricia's nose. She wanted to open a window but was too afraid to touch anything. The trailer looked as if it hadn't been cleaned in a decade. Piles of outdated News Herald back issues were stacked to the ceiling in the kitchen, and the living room wall was covered with clippings.

"Have a seat on the couch," Vanian's mother said, motioning with her arm. "Damn cats have been tearing up the upholstery. Little bastards."

"I don't see any cats," Patricia said, sitting next to Vanian on the couch. She hated to imagine what those dark splotches were on the armrest. "How many do you have?"

"Thirteen. They're mostly outside cats though." Her hands trembled as she unscrewed the vodka's cap and took a large gulp. "The way they keep having kittens, I need to get you to buy me stock in cat food. Not that they actually eat here or anything."

"So what's new, mom? Have you been taking care of yourself, getting exercise?"

"Fuck," she coughed, lighting another cigarette with a clear blue lighter. "I don't need exercise. Cutting out articles is all the damned exercise I need. Keeps my brain sharp."

"Mom loves Sudoku and articles about local and national government conspiracies," Vanian said. "She cuts out the puzzles, comics, and strange news."

"What else are you into, Cali?" Patricia asked. There had to be something beneath this woman's prickly shell, and world be damned, Patricia was going to break through. "Do you like art or books?"

"I don't remember anyone talking to you, doll face," Cali said. "Now, Vanian, honey, are you sure you didn't bring me anything to sip on?"

"No, Mom. I actually wanted to tell you the good news," he said. "One of my band's songs is doing really well. We're making money finally. We've been gearing up to record a new album."

"Is that so?" Cali asked.

"Yeah. Patricia and I have been dating a few weeks, and I also wanted you to meet her. We're planning on cooking a bird for Thanksgiving, and we were wondering if you would be interested in coming out to the cottage for dinner?"

Cali snorted. "That's so fucking cute. Young love. It always starts with cuddles and lofty promises, but when it comes down to it, no one can exist with anyone but themselves. There's no such thing as love. One of these days, you children will figure that out."

"Well, Mom, I believe in love. That's why I'm here now. Because no matter what, I love you."

"Then get me beer," Cali said. "I'm sick of potato juice. Beer would settle my ulcers. They've been acting up lately. It's the damned noodles I've been buying. The grocery store has been out of the good kind, so I've been stuck with those crappy ones. Crappy noodles and chicken with poison interlaced with the meat."

"No one's poisoned your chicken."

"All the food's poisoned. The government is killing us with the very thing we need to survive." She took a drag from the cigarette. "Having you was a trap, you know that, Vanian. I wanted to do things, see the world. You came along and fucked up my life."

Patricia cleared her throat. She'd never heard anything so mean before.

"I heard you are good at the crosswords," Patricia said, anxious for better conversation. "Did you see today's? I'm stuck on a four letter word for a mine entrance."

"Don't try and think about it, poppet," Cali said. "You'll only pop a fuse in that cute, little brain of yours."

"I guess we're hitting the road." Vanian stood, pulling Patricia up by the arm. "It was good seeing you, and I guess I'll come by later."

"Wait," Cali said. "What about my beer? Are you going to buy me a case or what?"

Vanian pulled out folded cash and tossed it on her cluttered coffee table. They left, not saying another word until they were in Patricia's car. Before she turned the ignition, Vanian leaned over and kissed her.

"What was that for?" she asked, grateful they were out of the smelly trailer and back in their private bubble.

"I don't care how lonely I get, or how fucked up my life gets, I'll never treat myself that bad." He looked forward, jaw clenched.

Patricia nodded, turning the key and putting the car into gear. "How does she afford what she has?"

"Paul gave her the trailer. She gets disability. Food stamps too, I suppose." He sat in silence a moment. "I hope this doesn't change your opinion of me."

Her heart melted. How could one man be so tender, so wonderful? "Of course it doesn't."

"It kills me. It really does."

Patricia drove as Vanian fumbled with the radio. After pausing on a few stations, he turned it off.

"I'm such a dumbass."

She looked at him. "Why do you say that?"

"Because I am enabling her. I give her cash. Cigarettes and booze too. I know I should cut her off completely, but I just can't. She's my mother, and if I don't take care of her, she will waste away."

"I understand why you help her," Patricia said. "It's very noble. You, Vanian, are a fine man."

She reached over and rested her palm on his thigh.

"I'm sorry I have baggage," he said.

"Who doesn't?"

"Fuck, do you think I'm crazy?"

"No, I think you're wonderful. Can I take you out for Chinese food? Let's gorge ourselves on crab rangoons and egg rolls."

"Sounds perfect."

She rubbed his leg, steering the car to her favorite Chinese buffet.

# ♫ TRACK 23 ♫

The hotel room was trashed. The stench of stale booze hung over the whiskey bottle and beer can graveyard. Isolated, Astro's only companions were drugs and alcohol. He'd consumed a smorgasbord of intoxicants from painkillers to hallucinogens, attempting to keep the shadow people at bay, but the further he fell down the rabbit hole, the closer they were.

He squeezed the entire contents of an eye drop bottle filled with liquid LSD into a coffee mug, mixing the drug with sweetened water and absinthe. Each time an acidhead drops, a piece of their mind remains in the great beyond, and Astro knew he was not coming back from this trip. He'd never taken so many doses at once, but he did not fear. He knocked back the coffee mug, emptying its contents with one gulp. He tossed the mug over his left shoulder, hearing it thud somewhere in the room.

"Look up—the sky is falling," he said. "Is this the real life? Is this just fantasy?"

He stumbled over his boots and kicked them under the bed. There was no use for shoes anymore. That ever-present voice inside reminded him the sun might not come up again.

Live for today, it hummed.

But when you live a certain way, the Devil demands payment. Old Scratch whistled a melancholy ballad at the crossroads, and there would hell to pay when he punched Astro's wicked card. That is the way it goes.

A palmetto bug inched across the wall. He scooped it up, letting it crawl in and out of his fingers.

"Really I'm not actually your friend, but I am," he told it before crushing the life from the insect. The cracked exoskeleton poked into his hand, pinching. Its center was sticky and tasted salty.

Astro's hatred burned white hot for Vanian and Patricia. The singer constantly steered Bad Apple down a shit path, dulling their edge and turning the sound into a wheelbarrow filled with weeping pussies. He ruined whatever he touched. Just like his fucking mother.

Patricia was even worse. She was *his* conquest that night. Vanian broke one of the sacred man rules by hooking up with her. Now they were playing house, acting as if she wasn't planning on jumping on another cock as soon as she had the chance. Astro knew it wouldn't take much for him to penetrate her.

Even better if it happened on Vanian's bed.

The first wave of LSD slithered its way down his lumbar vertebrae. Already the walls were breathing, and his surroundings were more dynamic. Plugged into the moment, he heard sounds he didn't know existed. Stomach flipped-flopping, his tongue became a worm burrowing in his dry mouth.

Something caught his ear. In the bathroom, a winged beast covered in gray and purple scales dripping with thick slime had replaced his reflection in the mirror. His gifted fingers were now long talons, and clawed feet protruded from frayed black jeans. The shadow people surrounded him, patting him on the back and whispering in his pointed ears as they fed him more smoke from their swirling bodies.

He rushed to the bathroom, punching the mirror. His vision blurred with the smashing glass, the shards smeared with red. He pulled back and cradled his wounded hand. Blood oozed from between his fingers, splattering beside his feet on the brown carpet.

The blotches transformed into pomegranates before rotting into crawling maggots.

Feeling dirty and old as the drug took full effect, he reached for a razor...

# ♫ TRACK 24 ♫

Bad Apple began the slow process of recording their second album. More people were involved with the disc, and Vanian did not like the new extra hands during the process. Astro's departure worried him. His guitar was an essential voice, and its silence during sessions unnerved the lead singer. Their producer, George Bearden, pushed for a slower sound.

Vanian found the constant retakes laborious, preferring the music to unfurl naturally, but playbacks sounded promising. While George mixed tracks, Rumi poems and horror comic books distracted the singer, often providing snippets of inspiration for the songwriting.

The band worked late in the night, finding the proper mood somewhere between the witching hour and dawn. Once every forty minutes or so, they'd break from their work and shoot bourbon, chasing it with room temperature imported beer.

Dar played more keyboards, using sustained notes that hung in the air like a storm cloud. Vanian strummed power chords and simple, catchy fills accenting the riffs. Carter's slow beats drove in the final coffin nail with a skeletal hammer, tribal and primitive.

In the mixing room, George and his sound tech, Benny, ran a strict 'no outsiders' policy. Friends, wives, and girlfriends were distractions to working artists, and time was money. Kitty and Patricia did not mind, pooling their creative minds to design the album's look while the band recorded. The record costs were skyrocketing because Vanian insisted making sure each nuance was acceptable. At first George protested the perfectionism would lead to unfulfilled tracks, but they were persistent, seeing most tracks through at least a rough draft.

It was about checks and balances, something Vanian understood well.

"Good job, boys," George's voice flowed into the soundproof room from a set of black speakers affixed to the ceiling. "That last one needs room to breathe. Let's try something else. Have any other ideas?"

"I have one I wrote last night," Vanian said, pulling out several crumpled diner napkins and smoothing them out on a music stand. Written the night before, his atrocious handwriting dripped of Irish whisky and exhaustion. "It's called 'Missing You'...it's about Astro."

George frowned. "Is a tribute to the newly estranged guitarist a good idea?"

"I don't know," said Vanian, "but it has to be said."

Silence hung in the air for a moment. Maybe his timing was wrong.

"Let's hear it," Dar motioned. Relieved, Van loved that he could always count on his friend.

"Ready?" George asked. "We're rolling."

Vanian put his fingers in C major and sang:

*Vanished this midwinter's eve*
*Someplace wild, scary, and free*
*Searching hard to believe*
*Not really sure what you need*

The rest of the band joined in. Vanian was surprised at how fast it all clicked, as if the tune had been in the air, waiting since the beginning of time to come alive. The song was moody and slow, snaking through the mixing booth while George and Benny adjusted levels.

The door opened behind them, and a shadowy figure entered.

Vanian moved into the chorus.

*Life's a stream*
*A flowing dream*
*Thoughts of glee*
*On nameless streets*
*You'll find a way*
*A better place*
*Or lose your face*
*And go insane*

160

Vanian looked through the glass separating the recording room from the mixing room. Behind George and Benny, Astro stepped from the darkness and into the recording booth's dim, red light. He'd shaved the hair on his head and eyebrows bald, his face and scalp now covered with nicks and gashes from the razor. He watched them play, chewing on a yellow toothbrush.

Though the sight of the guitarist broke his heart, Vanian didn't lose a beat. He kept crooning to his lost friend.

By the end of the song, George and Benny, glued to their headphones and the mixing board, still hadn't noticed Astro's presence. When the music ended, Vanian waved.

"Hi, Astro," he said. "Want to jam?"

Astro frowned. "Here's a fucking song lyric for you: anytime before cooking donkeys, everyone forgot giraffes. How igloos justify knowing lovely mannequins near octopi parts quintessentially reject subsequent technology under various watermarks. Xylophone...yes, zebras."

The microphones in the mix down booth picked up his voice, allowing Vanian and the rest of Bad Apple to hear him.

"What are you talking about?" asked George. "You look like shit, Astro. What happened, man?"

"I ran," Astro said, "so far away. I couldn't get away."

"Ran from what?" asked Vanian. "Is someone following you?"

"I'd give it to you if I could, but I borrowed it."

"Look, Astro," George said, "We're making a record here. If you want to go in and lay down riffs, by all means go ahead. But if you're interrupting this session with your fucking whack job nonsense, then I'm going to have to ask you to leave."

"Astro, man," Vanian said.

"You guys didn't deserve me. I've got blisters on my fingers anyway," Astro said in a soft voice before turning and leaving the mixing room.

"What the fuck was that?" Benny asked. "Was he okay?"

"I should go after him," Vanian said, pulling off his guitar. In that moment, he knew his old friend was gone. What stood in his place, however, was a mystery.

"Wait, cat," George said. "Let him go. We have work to do. I liked the last number, but I'm not sure if it's right for the album. Why don't we try that 'High Priestess' song again? I have an idea about the bridge."

"I want to keep that one," Vanian said. "It stays."

"Look," said George, "I just—"

"It stays," Vanian said again.

George and Benny exchanged a glance.

"Sure, baby," George said. "Anything you want, you got it."

"One more time," Vanian said. "Now I want to do something different on the chorus. I want to add another measure because there's something else I want to say."

# ♫ TRACK 25 ♫

Vanian led Patricia down Beach Avenue by the hand.

"Um, where are we going, Van? What's with the secrecy?"

"Gotta keep you on your toes," he said. "You know, I have my ways."

"Never a dull moment," she said. He took a right on Mystic towards Thomas Drive. They stopped at an abandoned building where Vanian proudly stood. "What is this, Vanian?"

"This place was a pizza joint. Fuck, I can still smell the melted cheese. I was friends with the owner's son, and he was a guitar genius. He was crazy about punk rock and David Bowie, so when I wasn't learning from Paul I learned a bunch of Vandals tunes and spent hours with 'Let's Dance'. It's hard to believe how far I've come since those days."

Patricia loved his sensitivity and nostalgia, it warmed her heart.

He leaned against the brick wall. "I just found out it's getting torn down so they can sell the land."

"Well, Vanian. You keep on stressing how you don't want to lose control over the sound, so why don't you buy this place, turn it into a studio of your own? Maybe you can snag it cheap."

Vanian reached into his pocket and pulled out a white gold, ruby engagement ring, getting down on one knee.

"Patricia Morrison, will you marry me? I love you, and I want to spend my life as your partner. You've given me something I haven't had in a long time…hope. I want to share the bourdons and joys, my entire life with you. I don't want to ever lose you."

Her eyes watered. The ring was beautiful. Vanian adored simplicity in his music, writing, and life, but the ring he was offering was so elaborate. She saw age behind it. In the afternoon sun, the rock sparkled like a miniature galaxy. For a second, she was light-headed.

"I—" she said. "I'd be honored to be your wife, Vanian." Sliding the ring on her finger, Vanian held her hand and kissed her. He sang:

*You are the night*
*Swimming through my soul*
*Ending all my pain*
*A secret never told*

*You are the star*
*Deep darkness I roam*
*Showing the right path*
*A candle lighting home*

They looked into each other's eyes, knowing the universe wasn't such a bad place when you were truly loved.

# ♫ TRACK 26 ♫

"You can't escape the fly," Vanian said to Dar and Carter as they shared a joint between sessions behind the studio.

"What?" said Dar. "Are you sick?"

"That's what we should call the new record." Vanian passed the joint to Dar. The new effort was coming along. Intense trust between the band and their producer made three of the eight tracks they'd finished really pop. "Gypsy Girl" was still selling strong on the internet, and their video was getting constant new hits.

Things were going well.

"And why should we call it that?" Dar asked.

"Well, do you remember Cronenberg's remake of *The Fly* with Jeff Goldblum and Geena Davis?" Vanian had caught a late night viewing of the film and something he'd never noticed in the movie spoke to him.

"Yeah," Dar said. "That fuckin' movie. Man, when he's falling apart and keeping his pieces in jars in the medicine cabinet—he had his cock in one of those things. Christ, that shit still looks gruesome."

Vanian didn't lose a beat. He'd given the idea a lot of thought, and the guys needed to hear this. "I remember reading this book called *Hardcore Zen*, and it mentioned the movie in passing. This one paragraph talked about how we're connected to the collective consciousness like he was to the fly, but I found deeper meaning in it."

"Here we go," Carter said.

"At first, he transports himself through this teleporting device without knowing he's been joined at a molecular level with the insect. He's rejuvenated, as if he can do anything. He becomes a better lover, able to fuck like a teenager. He's strong. So strong, he breaks a man's ulna and radius like a matchstick while arm wrestling in that crowded shit kicker bar. He is so confident about this sudden transformation he wants to pull Geena Davis into the machine so she can experience the glory of his invention to the fullest. It is not until later that he realizes a contaminant tainted the machine."

Vanian licked his lips. The words leaving his tongue tasted wonderful.

"The fly," Dar said.

"Right. Those scaly back hairs keep on growing no matter how much he shaves them, foreshadowing the terror that's lurking ahead. He runs tests and discovers a second passenger in the telepod, and it becomes clear their DNA is conjoined. So, he panics. He experiments, attempting to separate himself from the bug, but it's useless. They are one. Inescapably connected."

"Like me and Kitty now," Dar said.

Vanian imagined their kid misshapen and murderous before getting his mind back on track.

"Sort of, except you guys aren't having a horribly deformed creature, you're bringing a child into a loving family."

"Good point."

"Anyway, he eventually accepts the fact that he's becoming a monster. He begins making children's videos about how flies vomit on food before consuming it."

"That shit's so fucking gross," Dar laughed. "I love it."

"What I'm driving at is that the fly is in us all. You can't escape it. You have to accept that you have already bonded with your choices. You are the product of whatever you've done in the past. No choice is good or evil, it's beyond that, but there are consequences to your actions. Like Frankenstein, the things you create come back to haunt you."

"You can't escape the fly," Dar said.

"You can't escape the fly," Carter said, nodding. "Why that title?"

"There are two major themes on this disc," said Vanian. "There is a lot of love and healing, but there is also a lot of loss. Astro's absence resounds on the tracks. I'd be bullshitting if I said his touch wouldn't bring this record to perfection. There is something missing from each number, and that missing variable is Astro. We're stronger with him than without him."

Dar took a swill of a ginger ale.

"But," Vanian continued, "that ugly thing inside of him is coming out. It's always been there, lurking behind the alcoholism and the drugs and the music. It's what made him so passionate in the first place. He can't avoid it any longer. He can't escape the fly."

Carter scratched his eyebrow. "That's heavy shit, man. An entire album to Astro?"

"For me, it's a love letter to Patricia and a lament to Astro. The balance of light and dark. I didn't set out for it to be that way. It just sort of happened. I loved the idea when we pitched it to Astro, and it evolved."

Dar laughed. "Magic, right?"

"Magic," Vanian said, his whole body tingling. "I believe it's magic."

"Will George go for it?" asked Carter.

"I can only offer the title as a suggestion, but it's our band. We do what we want."

Dar finished the ginger ale, crumpling the can in his fist and burping. "It's hot, Van. Two fucking Ts, man. Two fucking Ts."

## ♫ TRACK 27 ♫

"What do you think about this one?" Patricia asked, holding up a sketch she'd completed for the band's new album cover. Charcoal smudged her fingers and palm.

"I love it," Kitty said. "I think I've figured out the problem we were having with the liner notes."

"Van's story?"

"Yeah, I got the text wrapping to work. It—"

Her hand went to her belly.

"Are you all right?" Patricia asked.

"Yeah, my baby girl is just a little restless today. The pictures of the instruments look good. I also want to go with a different paper stock than we did for the first record. Something thicker and glossier that feels better in the hand."

"Sounds legit."

"Patricia, I need to ask you something."

"Shoot."

"I'm not trying to piss you off, or anything," Kitty said.

Looking back at the album cover, Patricia traced her thumb over the band's logo. No conversation starting this way was ever good.

"You can ask me anything," she said.

"I really don't want to piss you off, but it's been bugging me." Kitty swallowed hard. "Look, I remember when you went to jail. Before you got busted, Janessa was going around telling everyone that she and you were working for Hunter. And I don't mean running dope."

This wasn't the first time that the rumors surfaced. She crossed her arms, deciding that playing dumb was the best move. "What do you mean?"

"I heard you were turning tricks to support your dope habit."

Patricia chuckled. "Do you think that sounds like me?"

"That's why I'm asking," Kitty said. "I guess I'm straight up like that."

"I was shooting dope. Mostly smack, but pills sometimes. I was always safe. I never shared needles."

"Ever been tested for anything?"

"Yeah, all the time. I'm clean." Patricia made an X over her heart with the pointer and middle fingers on her right hand.

"How did you pay for the shit?"

"I slung a little to keep myself in the game. I'm not proud of that. But, Kitty, swear to the stars, I would never, never sell my body."

Kitty thought for a moment. "I believe you. I trust you. It's just been eating at me. I wanted to clear the air."

"I know people talk about me. It's how people in this town are. So damned bored with their own lives, they have to stir shit up to feel better. I guess in all fairness, I deserve some of it."

"No. No one does."

# ♫ TRACK 28 ♫

The Bad Apple show was the Mozzy's best night in three years. Henry needed a few more like it to line his pockets, especially with the business deal he was plotting with Astro. Bad Apple's next album was going to propel the act into superstardom, and Henry wanted to launch the record at his club before they played larger venues. After that, it would be a few years before they grew desperate enough to play his shit hole again. He wasn't worried about them turning their backs on him. Vanian was a classy guy, and the years his band spent maturing on the Mozzy's stage would be reason enough to have them launch their newest recording where it all began.

His bag of cocaine was running low, and he knew his dealer had some fire powder just in from Miami. Life was good.

Henry pulled out his cell phone, dialing Kitty's number.

"Hello?" she answered.

"Kitty, baby. It's Henry."

"How are you, doll?" Her voice was friendly, like a paper bag full of sunshine. Henry wondered what it would be like to climb her, and a twang of jealousy towards Dar stirred within his heart.

"I know the boys are almost done another album. How's that coming along?"

"It's called *You Can't Escape the Fly*. From the finished tracks I've heard, it cooks. Patricia and I have been designing the album's look."

"Ah, so you two have been working together?"

"Yeah, we make an efficient team. She actually designed the album's cover and came up with the idea of having no band picture, just photos of their instruments with their names underneath it."

"That's creative," Henry said. "She and Vanian are getting along as well, I take it."

"Like the moon and poetry. Yeah. Vanian has a short horror story on the back two pages of the record's insert, and the centerfold is the last sonogram the doctor gave Dar and I."

"How have you been?"

"I'm not sick in the mornings anymore. I've also wrangled in Dar and slowed down his boozing."

Henry laughed. "I bet he's a bear to live with."

"No more than usual. He's been really great." She burped. "How's the club?"

"That's actually why I've called. I wanted to lock the band down for the record release. The last show was good for business, making me a happy Henry. I wanted to have them back and really throw down, maybe get the cops called on us for noise ordinance."

"It's a great idea. I'm sure the guys will, too. When we get closer to release, we'll book the party with you."

"Thank you, Kitty. Dar is a lucky man."

"Goddamned right, he is. We'll be in touch, Henry."

"Perfect. Ciao, baby."

He hung up the phone and sharpened a pencil. He railed up another line and dialed his dealer's number. "Lucio, baby. How ya doing?"

# ♫ TRACK 29 ♫

Astro walked to Lucio's Colony Club home.  Many of the neighborhood's houses sported luxury cars and pleasure boats. After business, he planned on taking a cab back to Henry's to bask in their drugs.  It would be a hairy couple of days following the deal, and Astro hoped the shadow people would leave him alone long enough to enjoy himself.

He remembered their first real conversation.

After seeing the gargoyle in the bathroom, they explained they had unveiled his true form, what he looked like without the deception of human existence.  They told him Vanian was holding him back, how Astro would have gone so much further if he'd just stepped from behind the singer and made music for himself.  His obedience marched him to the unemployment lines, begging for scraps.

By the time the trip leveled out, Astro realized he was surrounded by three of the Otherworld's lost souls.

Neither solid nor defined, the featureless forms whispered into each other's ears and pointed at Astro as he huddled, clenching his pillows. They enjoyed the pathetic wreckage Astro had made of his life.  They danced at his bedside, mocking his failures.

Astro tried pushing them away, but after shoving the nearest tormentor, his hands were covered with sticky black goo.  He rubbed them on the sheets, but the coagulated glop wouldn't wipe away.  The slime attached itself, burrowing under his skin and marking his soul so the shadow people could find him wherever he hid.

Ants marched through his veins.  Astro wasn't sure what they wanted, but they always lurked nearby, whispering and judging.  They loomed even in well-lit places, and he knew they would not rest.

The next day he'd seen Bad Apple in the studio, and he wished the shadow people would have tormented Vanian and the boys instead of following him.

No one said life was fair.

After admiring the stained glass sidelights, he knocked on the oak door, putting on his best smile. Lucio answered wearing black slacks and a white silk dress shirt.

"Jesus, you look like fucking shit," he said. "Lose a bet or something?"

"I had head lice," Astro said. "Didn't want to waste my time with those bullshit shampoos."

"I got crabs from a Paris hooker when I was backpacking Europe," Lucio said. "Try taking care of that in another country when you don't speak the language."

He let Astro in, and the two men followed a wide hall towards a spacious living room.

"Sorry about the little lady," Astro said. Lucio shot him a look. "I heard through the whispers."

"Shit happens." Lucio cracked his knuckles. "She was getting into weird stuff. It was only a matter of time before she OD'd. No secret there."

"She was balling one of your buddies behind your back, wasn't she?" Astro asked. Lucio nodded slowly. "Fuckin' A. With friends like that, right?"

"It was tragic," he said. "Care for a glass of absinthe?"

"Sure."

Lucio walked over to his bar and removed a fifth of Moulin Vert he'd acquired the last time he passed through France. He pulled down a special glass goblet from the overhead rack and set it beside the green bottle. Next, he opened a drawer, producing a flat absinthe spoon and several sugar cubes.

"I hear you're out of Bad Apple," Lucio said as he uncorked the green fairy. "I kind of dug the sound."

"We had...artistic differences," Astro said. "They're a bunch of goons, too."

"Pity," Lucio said.

He poured the green alcohol in the cup, adding two sugar cubes. As they soaked up the booze, he produced a bottled water from a reach-in refrigerator. He fished out the sugar cubes with his fingers, placing them over several wavy holes in the spoon's center. The spoon's pointed tip rested on the glass's rim. He struck a match, setting the saturated cubes ablaze. Astro watched the blue and red flame dance over the sizzling sugar with childlike fascination.

The shadow people were watching, too. Whispering, judging.

When the flame burned out, Lucio turned the spoon over, dropping the cubes into the liquid and stirring it up. He used the pointed part to chop the sugar.

"And now the magic." Lucio poured the spring water into the concoction, turning the green liquor opaque. "Ah, the tipple that tipped Van Gogh."

He passed the glass to Astro. The licorice aroma teased his nostrils. A long pull filled Astro's mouth with the milky swill, burning his esophagus all the way to his stomach. The hair on the back of his neck stood up. Astro passed the glass to Lucio who wolfed the drink down.

"A fine drink between businessmen," he said, setting the glass down. "You bring the cash?"

Astro pulled out a wad of bills from his coat and handed it over. Lucio didn't bother counting, screwing him was not wise. He stuffed the cash in his pocket and pulled out a briefcase from behind the bar.

"You can see yourself out," he said. "Tell Henry I'll be in touch."

Astro nodded and left his host pouring another glass of absinthe. Already the green fairy's wings ran through Astro's hair. He heard the shadow people's whispering in the palm trees as he opened the door and stepped into the darkness outside.

Judging. Whispering.

They wanted blood; they wanted pain.

Catching a cab at the nearest gas station, the trip to the Mozzy felt like three lifetimes. The club's side door was unlocked, and Astro rushed to the office, locking the door behind him.

Astro watched over Henry's shoulder as he opened the briefcase on his desk. The case was filled with two plastic bags, two-thirds filled with white, one-third brown.

"What the fuck is this?" Henry said, pulling up the brown bag. "This doesn't look like blow."

"Did he make a mistake?"

"No, Lucio doesn't slip like that."

"My guess is the brown stuff is heroin," Astro said. "I'd have to taste it to make sure."

Henry shook his head. "Man, that's a train I'm scared to board. Can you flip it?"

"I can flip it, cat," Astro said. "But I need time."

"Yeah, I don't know anyone that plays this game," Henry said, scratching his head. "That's a fast one."

"I know someone who parties like that." Astro licked his lips. This was too perfect. "I just have to wait a few days before I can step to her."

"How long are you going to need?"

"Month, tops. Maybe more, maybe less."

"Excellent," Henry said. "You wanna get high?"

"Goddamn right I do. Line 'em up."

Henry pulled out the white bag, leaving the heroin in the case. He pulled out a pocket knife and cut open the bag, breaking off a solid chunk.

"Fucking Christmas," he said before rolling up a two dollar bill. "Have you been naughty or nice?"

Astro wasn't sure how to answer, but he figured the shadow people would have something to say about it.

# ♫ TRACK 30 ♫

"I have great news, guys," Kitty said. "Gather around."

Bad Apple huddled around her in the studio.

"I got a call from Sally, my New York connection. She's booked Bad Apple on *The Late Show*. The mainstream has picked up on 'Gypsy Girl' and is wondering what you guys are about."

"Holy fuck," Dar said.

"No shit, right?" Kitty looked at the band. "They're flying Bad Apple out of Pensacola and putting you up for a few nights so you can do the taping. It's a quick trip, so you three are on your own, but you're in good hands with Sally."

"When do we leave?" Carter asked.

"Two weeks."

Dar scooped her up in his arms and spun her around, kissing her.

"I need to call my parents," Carter said.

"I'm calling Patricia," Vanian said, pulling out his cell from his pocket. Before he dialed, it rang. "How's that? She's calling me now. Talk about synchronicity."

"What's up?" he said, answering. "I have great news."

"Van, you need to come home." Her voice was stressed. Fear gripped him.

"What?"

"Paul's here."

"He is?" He was surprised. Paul had never visited his apartment.

"Yeah. I'm sorry, but your mother's dead."

# DISC III

# TRAGEDIES

# ♫ TRACK 1 ♫

Cali's funeral was on a Wednesday. Vanian, Patricia, Dar, Kitty, Carter, and Paul were the only attending souls. Standing in the cold drizzle, black umbrellas shielded them from the weather. Vanian paid for the plot in Panama City's Greenwood Cemetery. Knowing Cali would not have wanted a priest, Vanian and Paul opted to say words a few words around her gravesite.

"Mom wasn't perfect," Vanian said. "I would like to remember the good times, before she lost her way. That is all you can do for anybody. Remember the good times."

He took his place beside Patricia, mad at himself for lacking anything more to say about the woman who brought him into the world. He couldn't stand before the people that knew him and lie about what a great person she was or how much he loved her.

Could ever forgive her?

Paul stood beside her casket and cleared his throat. "Cali was a unique woman. We met over cocktails at the No Name Lounge, and she stole my heart. I had the privilege of sharing many years with her, and they were the happiest of my life. It was the only time I ever had a family. It was sad when that chapter of my life closed. I have not spoken to her in a long time. Who knows how she spent her last days, but I hope, wherever she is now, she finds the peace that eluded her during this lifetime."

Tears welled in his eyes as the group disbanded.

Vanian and Patricia followed Paul to his house on the beach for quiet drinks. Vanian had not seen his old mentor's home, having been years since the two men spent any real time together.

Inside they settled in the living room. Paul uncorked a bottle of cognac and filled three tumblers with the amber liquid.

"To your mother, Cali." He raised his glass. Patricia and Vanian raised theirs. "You've grown into quite a talented musician, Vanian. I'm proud of you."

"Thanks, Paul. I had a great teacher."

"Your fiancé is beautiful," Paul said. "You've done good, boy."

"She means the world to me," Vanian said. "I realize how lucky I am."

"You both are embarrassing me," she said. "I'm lucky, too."

"Just be loving and kind towards each other," Paul said. "It's funny how easy it can be to lose the way. Eros is a tricky cherub."

"Eros?" Patricia asked.

"The god of love. He makes it possible. Attraction, lust, true love. He aims his arrow into the hearts of mankind and watches their worlds tumble. Although he grants us a great gift, he can be a scam artist. He'll lie to you in a second, but he can't help it. He's an eternal child. I hold no grudge against him. His arrows changed my life when I fell for Cali. It was an adventure."

"I always thought it would be her liver that quit working," Vanian said. "Would not have guessed it would be her heart."

"Before things turned bad between us, she was so warm. There was so much love in her, so much possibility with you both. I'm sorry I've put so much distance between us, Vanian. The nature of our separation was complex, and I hated that you were dragged in the middle. I just wanted the best for you two. I wanted to hand you both the moon."

"Last time I saw Mom, she told me I was a trap. That she wanted to see the world, and then, I came along and ruined her life."

Paul set his glass down. "Oh, Vanian. I cannot claim to know why she would ever say such a horrible thing to you. That's not right, no matter how you look at it. I know she was afraid of losing the people she loved. Abandonment was a huge deal to her. Sometimes, I wish I could pinpoint where her life veered so far off course. May she'll find her course on the other side."

Paul drained his glass and poured another.

"Forgive me, but I'm confused," Patricia said. "That's twice you've mentioned her in an afterlife. I know Cali shunned religion, so what do you mean?"

Paul looked at her.

"The universe's great secret is that it's all true. Whatever you believe in, you have the power to make real. There are many different dimensions, all touching and sharing this plane of existence. Where I believe in magic, a balance between many goddesses and gods, others put their faith in one all-knowing God, and we're both right. Everyone brings unique pieces to the world. That is what makes it such a dynamic place to live. That same dynamism extends beyond life, and, regardless of what most people might perceive, death is not the end. Some souls go to heaven, others are reincarnated, and others may find a dark place filled with sorrow. Although she did not subscribe to any organized religion, I worry even death did not offer peace, that her troubles spilled into the next realm, trapping her between the here and the there."

"Like purgatory?" Patricia asked.

"In a sense. Who knows for sure? I have yet to cross over to the Otherworld, though the temptation has presented itself to me. From time to time."

"Suicide?" Vanian asked.

"No, not like that. In my studies, I found an old spell that makes the boundaries between life and death very thin. It summons Charon, the ferryman who escorts the dead across the Acheron, the River of Pain. He escorts those who can afford it to the Otherworld, hence the tradition of placing coins of the eyes of the deceased. It is Charon's fare, and those lacking it are doomed to wander the shores for eternity, or until someone pays their passage."

"You have a spell to summon death?" Patricia asked.

"Not Death, child. No man wishing to greet old age would dare beckon him. Death wears a flashy suit, and picking up his tab is expensive. This spell just summons a vessel to the Otherworld, into the land of the dead."

"You're not considering using this spell to go after Mom are you?" Vanian asked.

"No, but I would be lying if I said the thought didn't cross my mind. But so much hurt has passed between us. I don't know if I am strong enough to survive the journey into the Otherworld, let alone find her. Then what? Do you think Hades, god of the dead, will let me just waltz out of his domain with her? Even if I could convince him to let me have her, what would life be like once we got back here? I am still in love with Cali, this is true, but the sad thing is that our paths are different. Her sojourn and mine are no longer the same, and they haven't been for a while."

Paul filled their glasses again.

Outside the frogs sang to the night in harmony with crickets.

## ♫ TRACK 2 ♫

Dar packed a duffel bag, dreading the flight out of Pensacola. Not much frightened him, but airplanes topped that short list. Whenever he boarded one, turbulence and lightning always plagued the ride. Kitty bought a box of nausea pills for his trip, and tucked them into his carry-on.

"If you start getting woozy, take these."

"I've tripped balls on those things," he said. "Before I knew what real acid was all about."

"It's a wonder you're still walking around," she said.

"I should have been in jail a thousand times," he said. "Or dead at least three times."

"Well, I believe we have a purpose. We co-create our own fate."

"Everything's connected," he agreed. Pajamas were cozy against his skin. The fan circulated the air in the bedroom, raising gooseflesh on his bare shoulders.

"I'm going to miss you, Dar. This will be the longest we've been apart in months."

"I'll miss you, too. I go crazy when I'm without you, but at least it's only for two days. We'll play the show, hit a bar or two, and be back before my side of the bed is cold."

"What if a city minx turns her peepers your way?" she teased, adjusting the cleavage on her blue nightgown. "I know there's going to be all sorts of artsy trollops eye-fucking you."

"Well, I'll glare and tell any bitch that tries reeling me in that I'm a happily spoken for man. Vanian won't allow any cheap hussy worm her way in. You know how he cock blocks."

Kitty smacked him in the shoulder. Hard.

"What do you want to name the baby?" she asked. "Have you given it anymore thought?"

"It depends on if it's a girl or boy. We could find out right now if you'd just ask the doc."

"Don't you want it to be a surprise?"

"Whatever you want, Kitty. With the drinking and drugging I've done, I'd be happy just to know it has ten fingers and ten toes."

She punched him again. "I love you, fucker."

He kissed her, tugging at her nightgown.

## ♫ TRACK 3 ♫

The plane's scheduled departure time was a quarter after nine. Patricia and Kitty drove the trio to the Escambia County Airport in the Badmobile, where they said their goodbyes in the lobby.

Dar promised Kitty he'd bring her an old book from a dusty shop. Vanian straightened Patricia's engagement ring before kissing her earlobe. Carter hugged Kitty and told her to take care of the Badmobile four times. She agreed, even pinky swearing with the drummer. The group exchanged hugs. Cater boarded first, waving once before disappearing down the hall leading to the plane. Kitty kissed Dar, grabbing his ass.

"Come back in one piece," she told him. "There's a little one that needs her daddy around."

"When I get back," he said, "there's gonna be a little one that's fed up with his daddy poking him in the head."

"Him?"

"Just a figure of speech."

"Uh huh." Kitty kissed Dar one last time before sending him down the hall.

Vanian and Patricia held each other tight. He'd grown accustomed to having his body pressed against hers—they fit together. Lying alone in bed would be the hardest thing. Each night her breathing was a lullaby, each morning her energy buzzed. Drowning in her pheromones, he wished she could travel along, too.

"Come and go with me," she said. "It's going to be a lifetime till I see you again."

"It's only forever. Not long at all." He failed a smile. "Don't stop believing."

"When are we going to get married? I want to set the date."

"Let's swim out tonight, love," he whispered in her ear, giggling. "When I get back. We'll ease the neon nice and low, go down to the courthouse, and get hitched. In the spring, we'll have a real ceremony, proper and classy."

They kissed as an announcer boomed over the loud speakers—final boarding.

Patricia looked to the sky outside towering glass windows. "Bring my baby back to me."

"It can't come quickly enough," he said, kissing her one final time before racing down the hall to the plane.

In the air, Vanian opened a copy of Camus' *The Plague* that Patricia bought for him the day before. Carter played video games, listening to the sound through earphones. Dar sat next to a window, watching the wing.

The captain warned turbulence lurked ahead.

## ♫ TRACK 4 ♫

O n the way home, the women hit the outlets and ate supper at McGuire's Irish Pub. They split an order of supreme nachos, chasing the enormous pile with a dark beer. Afterwards, they hit a shoe store before returning to Panama City just after dusk. Kitty dropped Patricia off at her home, hugging her friend.

"Call me, Patricia. We can do lunch before the guys get home."

"Sounds great," Patricia said, carrying several shopping bags. "This is so exciting. When we have the ceremony, will you be my bridesmaid?"

"I'd be honored. Actually, Dar and I want to ask you and Vanian to be our baby's godparents."

"For real?"

"For real. You two are so fucking awesome, it's only natural," she said. "Man, it's going to be weird without my man around. I'm spoiling myself. I'm getting a manicure and a pedicure. Hell, I'm eating out both nights."

"Let me know when you're pampering yourself. I'll join you. Maybe we can throw down on deep tissue massages."

"Mm, sounds nice," Kitty said. "I'll call you."

They hugged again.

"Please do," Patricia said. "Take care."

Patricia waved goodbye, and the Badmobile pulled out and drove away. She realized how empty the house was going to be and wondered if she would finally see the ghost.

She walked to the door and unlocked it, entering and fumbling for the lights. After flipping the switch, she gasped, dropping her bags on the floor. Astro was sitting on the couch, his hands behind his shaved head. He looked pure evil.

"Hello, kewpie doll."

"Jesus Christ, Astro," she said. "You scared the fuck out of me."

"Lilly Munster ain't got nothing on you," he said. "I know why he's so crazy over you."

"Shit, Astro," she said. "Are you all right?"

"A creature made of sunshine; her eyes were like the sky."

"Look, if you want to talk to Van, he's outta town for a few days. If you leave a number, I can have him call you when he gets back."

"You want to get high?" he asked. "I know you like points."

"Look, I'm not into that shit anymore. I went through hell and back to kick, and I'm not about to start again."

"One little taste will pick you up."

The shadow people hissed from the corners of the room.

"What the fuck was that?" she asked. They materialized, twisting and curling around each other like a den of snakes.

"Don't worry about my friends. Here, I have a hit ready for you."

"Fuck you, Astro. You've been fucking losing it, man. You know what that shit does? It ruins lives. It cost me friendships, relationship, sanity, freedom—I can't do it again. I won't lose what I've worked for."

***

Astro was finished with chitchat. He reached under his legs and pulled out the claw hammer that smashed the back window, a crude but effective break-in. Patricia backed up, wide-eyed and speechless. She started to turn, but with a great swing, he smacked her across the head. Patricia fell to the ground, bleeding.

"Die, die, die, my darling." He leaned over and whispered in her ear. "Die."

She was still breathing, shaking from the sudden impact. Astro unfolded a black cloth containing thirteen loaded syringes on the coffee table. The shadow people huddled over his shoulder, supervising his work.

"You have to meet my beautiful serpents. They bite, but it will be a kiss you won't forget."

Her breathing was shallow, labored, and Astro kneeled over her, tying off her arm using his belt as a tourniquet. When her veins popped up, he slid the first point under her skin, injecting the drug into her bloodstream. Her facial expression contorted. Astro's dick swelled against his leg. He shifted his erection out of the way before moving to the next needle. And the next. And the next. Involved with his work, it was unclear when she stopped breathing.

After injecting the final hit into her arm, Astro pulled her pants off and ran his fingertips along her pale leg, from her knee to her pubic line. She needed a shave. He pulled her legs open. Resting his palm on her right hip, he licked her thigh before spitting on her vagina. Sliding his pants over his ass, he positioned himself for insertion. Her pussy didn't respond like a living lover's. He forced himself inside, planting unreciprocated kisses over her lips and breasts. His machine-like thrusting violated her until his loins rubbed raw. As her body heat faded, he fucked her harder and harder, unable to achieve release. He pulled out and tried masturbating over her corpse, but still climax eluded him. When his penis rubbed raw and he could take no more, he collapsed beside her, his eyes drawing shut.

The shadow people gathered. Patricia was now the ferryman's property. Her final voyage was beginning as Astro slumbered peacefully beside her, dreaming of playing guitar for a winged reptile.

# ♫ TRACK 5 ♫

Bad Apple landed in New York after a rough flight. Dar swore aloud they were going to die every time the flight hit turbulence. Vanian read most of *The Plague* and couldn't wait to buy Patricia a copy of Kafka's *The Metamorphosis*. Carter loved the bumpy moments on the flight, even getting a pair of wings from the captain and pinning them to his coat.

They took a cab to the hotel the network arranged, checking in behind a man who looked like Hunter S. Thompson. In his room, Vanian tried calling Patricia. When the answering machine picked up, he assumed she was shopping or hanging out with Kitty, so he showered and watched the Weather Channel to see what the radar maps looked like.

The band ate at Japanese restaurant with *The Late Show* producer and Sally, enjoying an ostentatious hibachi show and fresh sushi. They toasted warm sake before walking up and down the strip, hitting the more exotic spots. Carter bought a plumed trilby from a haberdashery. Dar found an antique store and bought Kitty Depression-era jewelry. Vanian bought Patricia several occult books. They found a goth bar where they were recognized by a young Wiccan couple and finished the night drinking Vampire's Kisses—a cocktail consisting of raspberry vodka, peach schnapps, champagne, and splashes of cranberry and grenadine—in a darkened corner while discussing music, horror movies, and love.

Back at the hotel, Vanian tried calling home again, but gave up, not wanting to wake his love. The shots helped him fall asleep, and he passed the night in dreamless slumber.

# ♫ TRACK 6 ♫

Astro trashed the cottage, breaking LPs and tearing pages from books. He ignored the incoming phone calls—too much work at hand. He covered Patricia's body with cushions, flipping the couch over into a makeshift coffin. He poured out the liquid in the fridge, smearing peanut butter over the kitchen walls. He snapped the DVDs in Vanian's collection and crushed his guitars, scattering the pieces in the bedroom before pissing on them. The photos documenting Vanian's life were wadded up and boiled in a large pot. Astro poured the soggy mess into the sink.

Once he was sure he had ruined Vanian's life, Astro curled up in fetal position in the corner of the trashed living room. The shadow people horseshoed around him.

"I did what you asked," he sobbed in his knees. "I gave her to you."

"You took her life," the center one hissed. "She is worthless now."

"Well, that's not my fucking problem." His gaze met the sexless, floating forms. "Now, release me. Like you promised."

"You know what to do." The creature extended an arm, filling Astro's mouth with icy smoke. Images of razor blades cutting into his arm flooded his mind, his vision blurred with dripping blood. "Down the road, not across the street."

He nodded, rising.

Astro filled up the bathtub and entered, fully-clothed. At the same time Bad Apple was filming their *Late Show* segment, Astro slit his wrists long ways down his arm and soaked in the bloody water, closing his eyes and letting the world's weight finally dissolve. The shadow people gathered one last time around the vessel that was Astro's broken life and wept.

# ♫ TRACK 7 ♫

Vanian was worried. In spite of numerous efforts, he couldn't contact Patricia. He refused showing the guys his concern during the trip, but when Kitty picked them up in Pensacola, he broke silence.

"Have you heard from Patricia?" he asked her as they shoved their bags into the van.

"No," she answered. "We were talking about pampering ourselves, but when I called, I didn't get an answer. I wound up getting busy at my parents, and time ran out."

"I see trouble on the way," Vanian said.

"Oh, don't be melodramatic," she said. "Don't worry 'bout a thing."

Vanian said nothing as he finished loading his bags. The normal two hour drive back to Bay County took over three with traffic. The world wasn't quite right, and when they finally pulled into his driveway he rushed to the front door. The house was unlocked, and with a flick of the light switch his world crashed down.

The cottage was in shambles, his possessions destroyed and strewn about the living room. An arm poked out from the overturned couch, and he rushed to flip it over. Underneath, Patricia's lifeless body stared open-eyed, her expressionless gaze locked on the wall behind him.

Vanian wailed. Tears streamed down his face. Dar rushed and froze in the doorway.

"What the fuck?" Dar asked.

"Call the cops," Vanian said.

"Fuck me," Dar said. He searched his pockets. "Where's my fucking phone?"

Vanian whispered to Patricia's body. Kitty screamed at the front door. Dar dialed 911.

When the cops came, an officer found Astro's body in the bathtub clinging to a wet and tattered copy of J. D. Salinger's *The Catcher in the Rye*, the only book not demolished. It took three policemen to pry Vanian from Patricia. He didn't fight them, but he wouldn't let go of her. Finally, Vanian succumbed to Dar's arms. Several uniforms strung out yellow tape across the cottage door. The flashing lights made the street look like Christmas. Neighbors peered from their windows, gawking at the sideshow.

"You're staying with me and Kitty," Dar said. "We have extra space and a pull out."

"It wasn't her time, man," Vanian said. "This shit's not fair."

"Dude, we'll jive later. Let's get outta here. It's been hell, but it'll be all right."

"No," Vanian said. Dar frowned. "It'll never be all right again."

Three shapes huddled in the shadows.

Vanian looked up at the shadow people standing in the hall.

# ♫ TRACK 8 ♫

Thunder grumbled, rain and tears indistinguishable during Patricia's funeral. The attendees surrounded her closed casket carrying black umbrellas and heavy souls. Vanian stood by her mother as the preacher read the 23rd psalm.

"This is your fault," her mother told him in a hushed voice during the service. "Acting out a rock and roll fantasy while my baby girl gets murdered."

Inside, Vanian was broken glass, his heart torn from his chest and stomped into waterlogged gravel.

After the service, Vanian rested a purple tulip on her coffin, blessing her life with a quiet prayer. He returned to the hearse, leaning against the hood for balance. Vanian listened to his labored breathing, how it blended harmoniously with gravesite lamentation. Weeping in chorus with falling rain and the wind's whispered dirge.

Everything was music.

Dar stood beside him while Carter held a few feet back.

"Van, I...I don't know...," Dar said.

"There's nothing to say, Dar. She was too young. We were just...we were just beginning." Vanian wiped tears from his eyes. The rain matted his hair against his face. "She was robbed from me. Astro stole her. Her beauty, her laughter. It's fucking gone. And for what?"

"He's in hell now," Carter said. "I know we don't share religious beliefs, but trust me, there's a special torment for those who commit such heinous deeds."

"Astro's not even having a proper burial," Dar said. "They're cremating his body next week and shipping the ashes to the islands."

Dar squeezed Vanian.

Vanian knocked his arm off.

"It isn't fair," he said. "This wasn't supposed to happen. We were going to get married and grow old together."

"You can't know what is going to happen," Carter said. "No one can. Sucks, but we have to deal with it. She's in a better place, man."

"There is no better place." Anger coursed through Vanian's veins.

Thunder echoed across the sky. The rain came down harder, muddy runoff soaking their dress shoes.

"Let's go home," Dar said. "I'm soaked. I can use a drink. We all can."

"Home," Vanian said. "I have no home. Not anymore. I'm going to get her back."

"That's crazy talk," Carter said. "It's not like you can hop a boat, man. She's dead."

"Death is not the end," Vanian shouted, water pouring down his face. He sobbed. "I'm getting her back."

## ♫ TRACK 9 ♫

Sitting in flickering candlelight, Paul was reading a magical herb book by Scott Cunningham when the knock came. He put down the text and answered, finding Vanian standing in the downpour.

"My stars, son, come in. It's a hazy shade of winter out there."

Vanian entered, shivering from the cold.

"I have towels and dry clothes you can use. I figured you would come here soon, I just... I'm sorry I wasn't there today. One funeral a month is plenty. I have altar candles burning for Patricia. Let's get you dried up before we talk."

Paul fetched Vanian a towel, sweat pants, and a plain gray t-shirt.

"Seems like this town is going crazy. Did you hear about that woman who was strangled a few weeks back? In her own home, too. Can you believe it?"

While the musician changed in the bathroom, Paul opened a bottle of cognac and filled two tumblers. Vanian slumped on his couch, cradling the liquor. In the living room's northern corner, candles glimmered on Paul's altar. Burning frankincense filled the air

Paul sat beside his student, rubbing the tumbler's rim with his pointer finger.

"I saw the performance on TV. You sounded good. I know your next gig at the Mozzy is postponed. When you decide to play out again, I'll come out and show support."

"I want the spell to summon Charon. I want to travel to the Otherworld to find her." Vanian didn't take his eyes off the altar. What secrets did it hold?

"I was worried you were going to ask for that."

"It isn't fair, Paul. She was taken from me."

"Life isn't fair, Vanian. Sometimes it's a mouthful of sugar, and other times it cuts you up. But there is an order to the universe we are obliged to follow."

"Fuck order." Vanian gulped the cognac. He barely tasted the burn.

"Crossing over is just the first step. What do you intend to do about Cerberus, the three-headed hell hound? How about Hades, what do you intend on saying to him? There's no telling what a living man will face once he goes beyond death. Many souls from the Otherworld despise being dead, and they will stop at nothing for a chance to live again. That makes you a target. It's too dangerous."

Vanian's eyes locked with Paul's, filled with love and pain. His mentor had aged since they were close. Though his face now showed crow's feet and brow creases, Paul's eyes still sparkled with mischievous wonder.

"I'm going, with or without your help. The way I see it, I can go about it three ways. I can spend every penny and moment I have pouring over books and talking to mystics, hoping to stumble upon the spell. It's a needle in a haystack, but if you figured it out, I have a chance. I can kill myself, but that limits future options."

"Or I help you," Paul whispered.

"I'll take the risk of crossing over, confront whatever is out there. In my heart of hearts, I know I can find her and bring her back."

Paul sighed. "Death has many dimensions. Within it are different realms. Go to the Otherworld, you might find heaven...or hell for that matter. There's not a doubt in my mind you possess the will to find what you're seeking, to successfully navigate your way to Patricia. I don't know if I could forgive myself if you didn't come back."

"You wouldn't have to," Vanian said. "It would be on me. I'm not asking to put any weight on your shoulders. I'm asking because you have always been my mentor. I understand the danger involved, but, you see, I have no choice. Patricia was taken from me, and I know evil forces were at hand. I've seen them."

"Them?" Paul asked.

"Shadow people. Three of them have been following me. They never get too close, but they're always there, lurking."

"I guess we should take care of it. Let's call them out, shall we?"

Vanian nodded. Paul rose and crossed over to his altar, pulling out another candle and a brown leather bag from underneath. Lighting the candle with the flames from one on the altar, he placed it on the coffee table. He tilted the bag, pouring out salt in a large circle and made a clockwise trail to the candle.

"We'll summon them and ask why they're trailing you. When we get answers, we'll lead them through this spiral, trapping them in this candle. After catching them, we'll bury the candle and plant roses on top of them. When the flowers bloom, they'll have the chance to find peace."

"What if they don't want peace?" Vanian asked.

"Then they'll remain in the candle with their anguish." Paul stretched, his energy flowing through the room. "Please, meditate with me."

"Aren't we going to cast a circle first?"

"You entered the circle when you came inside my home. This house is charmed."

Vanian took a deep breath and began meditating, his heartbeat keeping time.

"By moon and sun, night and day, in this circle I do pray, with the power of three by three, we summon creatures haunting thee."

The temperature dropped and the candle's flame turned blue. Three forms appeared, hovering in the center of the room.

The shadow people hissed as they swirled around the ceiling, their pointed fingers clawing at the candle's blue flame.

"Why do you trouble this man?" Paul asked, his words fogged in the icy air.

"Life. We want life," one said, its ethereal voice spilling from waves of black smoke.

"Astro could not channel us," another said. "He found madness in our arms."

Another one whipped in front of Vanian's face. "He was not strong enough. He killed Patricia before we attempted her vessel."

"But now we have two powerful witches."

"You are in my circle," Paul said. "We're protected from your advances. We are here to help. Follow my spiral, and you will have a chance at rest."

One of the shadow people lunged for Paul, but he pulled out the silver pentagram from his shirt and held it up. The creature froze, screaming.

"Go to the spiral. All of you. Leave this man alone. I command you to follow the spiral so you may find peace."

The blue flame burned brighter. The three shadows lengthened, being pulled into the salt spiral. They grappled with the air, straining to swim free, but Paul's spell was strong. He chanted, faster and faster. The shadow people were sucked into the spiral, around and around, their howls increasing in pitch until they vanished into the candle. The flame returned to its normal color. Calm fell over the room.

"So be it mote," Paul said.

"How did they get here?" Vanian asked.

"There are many cracks between realms. They found one and slipped through. You were right, evil was at play in the deaths of your friends. Unfortunately, they illustrate my point about how dangerous the other side is."

Vanian thought a moment. Was his desire any more a fool's errand than trying to start a rock band in the first place? He understood and respected the natural order of life and death, but what had happened was supernatural. He had to try.

"I still want to go. If I must search the world for one of those cracks, Patricia and I will be reunited."

Paul lowered his head.

"How can you deter a man in love? I never took another lover after Cali left me. I clung to the hope she would return one day, that the three of us would be a family. It is too late for that now, though you and I will always be in each other's lives. Withholding the spell from you is an effort to protect you as much as it is selfish. I don't want to lose you. I see you're determined, that's there no stopping you. As a mentor, all I can do is try and prepare you for the worst."

"So, you'll give me the spell?"

"I love you. How can I deny you from path you'll venture down with or without my blessing? There's one thing."

"What's that?"

"I can't see you off on Charon's ferry. If something happens, I don't want that realm swallowing you up to be my last memory of you."

"I understand."

"I have an elixir you will need. Concocting it will take time, but it will give strength to your best defense in the Otherworld."

"What's that?"

Paul leaned back in his chair and steepled his fingers. "Your voice."

# DISC IV

# THE OTHERWORLD

# ♫ TRACK 1 ♫

Vanian was scarce. Bad Apple postponed another tour, releasing *You Can't Escape the Fly* over their webpage. Their first single, "Ocean Girl," was getting rotation, and numbers were strong. Dar and Carter didn't chase down Vanian, giving him time to mourn. It was best letting a bleeding heart mend. He would come around when ready.

It happened just before Valentine's Day.

Dar was reading Bukowski's *Women* when the familiar knock came. He rubbed Kitty's swollen tummy and answered the door, embracing Vanian in a bear hug.

"You old beatnik," he said, not wanting to draw attention to how weathered, how worn his friend looked. "How are ya, Van? Come on in."

Vanian entered and sat on the couch across from Kitty.

"I can get her back," he said.

Kitty and Dar exchanged a glance. She rose, slipping into the back bedroom.

Dar frowned. This sounded more like Astro towards the end of his life.

"Van, this isn't healthy. Patricia was awesome, no one denies that. But you have to let her go, cat. We have another hot song, and no tour to back it up. We need to get our asses back on the road and selling t-shirts and bumper stickers, man. Strike while the iron is hot, right? I know you're fighting major demons, but don't let them take you down."

"Hear me out, Dar," Vanian said. "You know that I...that I dabble in the occult."

Dar couldn't believe Vanian felt he had to point it out. He normally didn't state the obvious. "Fuck, that's no secret. It's your mystique. Fans love that shit."

"I've been studying knowledge some might consider questionable." Vanian bit his lower lip.

"Questionable?" Dar braced himself for the worst.

"Let's just say Carter would call an exorcist if he knew the company I've been keeping."

"You're scaring me," Dar said. Had Van lost it, too?

"I practice a magic that is neither white nor black. Each spell I cast brings forth change. It isn't benevolent or malevolent, but merely the result of my will. Good or evil, it is a matter of perception."

"I don't follow," Dar said.

"For example: if I cast a spell for rain, it may cool off a hot afternoon, or it might drown my flower garden. Either way, it just is. Things are beyond good and evil. One man's wickedness is another's righteousness. It's balance."

Dar sighed. Religion was a personal thing. Vanian always kept his beliefs quiet, and this was the most serious conversation they'd ever shared on the subject. Dar was a humanist with a set of morals he deemed adequate for proper living. Following no set of written rules, no unseen deity, he followed his gut. Once or twice his relaxed attitude got him into trouble, but normally tough times worked out.

Vanian spoke slow. "I found a way I can cross over. To the Otherworld or whatever death is."

"This isn't some *Flatliners* crap where I kill you and then bring you back is it?"

"No," Vanian laughed. "Nothing that theatrical. I learned a spell to call Charon."

"Charon?" Dar didn't like where this was heading.

"The ferryman who ushers the dead to the other side."

Dar looked at his friend. Had Vanian had lost his mind? He wasn't prone to flights of fancy, but this revelation was out there. Should enable his friend or shoot him down? Deep down, he knew there would be no stopping Vanian. Once he began rolling, it was like an alcohol bender or an acid trip. The only thing you could do was hold on and enjoy the ride. That's why they were so close—they were exactly alike. A long silence followed.

"I've been working new riffs," Dar said, starting to reach for an acoustic bass he kept near the couch. "Pretty gloomy stuff, Van. You'd dig them."

"You're not listening. I'm going to summon Charon, Dar. I've been spending time with Paul. There were a lot of lessons I had to learn, but I've mastered them."

Vanian reached into his pocket, pulling out two old coins.

"He gave me these. Paul is the embodiment of music. He's shared the gift with me, and I'm using it to save Patricia."

"Dude, we're musicians because we've practiced over the years. Hard work made us better."

"Yes," Vanian said, "it was us. But I had help. I had magic. Do you know what these are?"

Vanian held out his hand, showing off the two silver coins. Dar didn't recognize the worn head on one side, but when Vanian flipped it over he saw an owl.

"Looks like something from a pirate movie. Hell, I don't know what they are."

"They're called tetradrachm. They're ancient Greek coins for paying Charon's fare. They placed them under the tongue or over the eyes of the deceased. If you don't have the tariff, your soul wanders this side of the river for years."

"Sounds shitty."

"It is." Vanian returned the coins to his pocket and cracked his knuckles. "I need your help."

"My help? Have you thought this through?"

"Seriously, cat. I want you to go with me. I want you to witness me crossing over so if I don't come back you can tell Paul I at least made it through."

"Are we going to Greece for this little adventure, good buddy?"

"Not that far." Vanian smiled. "How does New Orleans sound?"

# ♫ TRACK 2 ♫

Vanian, Dar, Carter, and Kitty began the five-and-a-half hour car ride from Panama City Beach to New Orleans. A straight shot, Dar steered the car onto I-10 West as soon as they hit Pensacola. In the passenger seat, Vanian stared at the road ahead, his expression offering nothing.

"How's the book, honey?" he asked. He couldn't believe Kitty, sitting in the back seat and reading *The Dharma Bums*, agreed to a spontaneous road trip to the Crescent City on Valentine's Day morning.

"It's difficult to follow," she said, "but the words are nicely arranged and filling the time."

"It's a religious text," Vanian said.

"Sure it is," Carter said, keeping his eyes on the video game in his hands. The handheld machine beeped and blipped.

"I booked us a room at our usual spot on Canal," Vanian said.

"Lot of memories there," Dar said. "Remember getting hammered with those old black bluesmen in the atrium?"

"Shit, we were singing and playing guitars all damned night. I thought the front desk girl was going to call the cops on us," Vanian said.

"You guys are lucky I only had hand drums with me," said Carter, still immersed in his game. "That would have done it for sure."

"That city is a musical one. Even while walking through the streets, the conversations you strike up with the colorful characters are songs." Vanian started to sing one of their newest tunes.

*Late one night, it's dark and cool*

*Creeping form, a graveyard ghoul*

Carter drummed on the back of Dar's seat.

*Silhouette, he strikes the earth*
*Fog rolls in, so hard at work*

Dar began humming the bassline. Kitty put down her book.

*Not far down, a hallow sound*
*Hands and knees, on sacred ground*
*Open lid, look deep inside*
*Old and dry, all mummified*
*Hands and skull, that is his prize*
*So damned glad you had to die*

A moment passed before Dar cleared his throat. He didn't need a song about death to remind him of the plan.

"Yeah," he said, "it doesn't matter what time it is, somewhere in the quarter a sax is blowing."

"I can't wait to eat at Coop's," Kitty said. "Cajun fried chicken...mmm."

"I like their rabbit jambalaya," Vanian said. "I could eat that shit for the rest of my life."

Carter groaned. "Stop it, you guys are making me hungry."

They barreled through the Mobile tunnel, honking the car horn to hear the reverberation on the arched white walls.

The passing landscape shifted from trees to swamp as they neared their destination.

"You know," Vanian began, "I watched *Close Encounters of the Third Kind* the other day, and I realized I had never seen it before."

"Never seen it?" Dar asked. "How did you miss that one?"

"No, I've sat through the movie, yes, but I've never *seen* it."

"What do you mean?" Carter asked.

"What is that film about?" Vanian asked, twisting around and looking in the back seat.

"It's about aliens," Carter said. "They've abducted people over time and finally bring them back. It's them making first contact with us, with humans."

"Yeah," Dar added, "and we can only communicate with them through music. It's the language that transcends our species' differences."

"I saw something different," Vanian said. "That movie is not about aliens at all."

"I've seen it, Van," Kitty said. "I remember it's about aliens. Scared the hell out of me when I was little."

"*Close Encounters* is about the dissolution of the American family. You're right, Kitty, it's a scary movie, but the aliens are not frightening. Well, they abduct a boy, and that shit was bloodcurdling. But what terrified me most was a scene when Richard Dreyfuss is fighting with his wife, played by Teri Garr. They are in this screaming match, and their kids are flipping out, crying and shit, but they keep on. It is intense, man. What we are really seeing is this family falling apart, and they don't even know why it's happening. By the end of the movie, Dreyfuss is scaling a mountain with another woman—a woman, I must add, who understands him and what he's going through better than his own wife—and then he takes off with the spaceship. Who knows if his family ever sees him again? Now we have this broken family, and when asked what happened to daddy, all we can say is that he flew off into outer space."

"That's pretty wild," Dar said.

"Also, backtracking, when the kid is abducted, he is pulled from his mother's arms. She runs outside and this dark cloud is pulling away, her son in tow. This can be symbolic for growing up, as her child is no longer innocent, like the American family. There's a lot more than aliens going on in that flick."

Kitty sighed. "Aliens are still terrifying."

"Yes," Dar said, "we know. Don't we, Vanian?"

Vanian swallowed and nodded. "The film really hit me hard. It reminded me of Mom running off Paul and then going away. Maybe the aliens took her years ago."

They fell in silence, crossing the Louisiana state line.

No one mentioned the trip's purpose the entire way to New Orleans, and when they approached the towering buildings overlooking the Mississippi River, Kitty snapped photos.

"She's come a long ways since that last hurricane." Vanian craned his head to look down Canal Street. "I wonder if it will fall to the waters again, become America's first great ruins."

"Only time will tell," Dar said.

# ♫ TRACK 3 ♫

They pulled off the Canal Street exit and landed in their hotel's parking garage. After paying for two rooms, they pulled Kitty's car to the top of the parking garage and parked beside the pool. Taking an hour to settle into their rooms, they met back down in the lobby and walked to the French Quarter, Vanian carrying along his coffin-shaped guitar case.

As they approached the river, Vanian saw the graffiti splattered across the top of several Canal Street buildings. He wished he could watch Patricia paint again.

"How did they even get up there?" he asked, pointing.

"Look, man," Dar said. "I hope you don't plan on scaling some damned building. This trip is crazy enough without any daredevil acrobatics."

"I'm not climbing up anything," Vanian said. "I was just thinking aloud."

A streetcar passed in the median, and Carter waved at the riders.

"I love the clatter of the wheels rolling on the tracks," he said. "We should sample that for the next record."

"What about a noise record featuring only sampled sounds?" Dar asked. "Astro would have loved that."

Vanian stopped and shot his friend a glance.

They fell silent, continuing down Canal Street as yellow cabs honked and weaved between slack-jawed tourists, impatient commuters, and white buses decorated with Mardi Gras colors. Vanian lowered his gaze to the cement cracks, avoiding stepping on them.

Dar tugged his arm, pointing towards a couple smoking reefer in a storefront entrance. The fruity smell gave way to the rich aroma of

Cajun cooking as they approached the Quarter. They crossed Canal in front of Dauphine Street, resting at the statue of Ignatius J. Reilly, holding a shopping bag and staring at the sidewalk.

Vanian reached out and ran his hand along the statue's scarf, pausing at his chest. No heartbeat inside the bronze man.

"What's he looking at?" Kitty asked.

"At Hell," Carter said.

Passing Bourbon Street, the city's Great Neon Way, crowds were already spilling out of the sex shops and restaurants. Several children banged beats on plastic, upside down paint buckets. A Mardi Gras Indian posed for a snapshot with some tourists as Christians passed out tracts and told visitors they'd entered hell. Brass band music and alcohol tempted his senses.

"Let's get a Hand Grenade," Dar said.

"Let's eat first," Vanian said. Although his instincts longed for drink, keeping his head clear for the ritual was essential. "We can have fun in the den of vice later, after I grab supplies."

They turned on Decatur Street, into the Quarter.

The steamboat *Natchez*'s calliope bounced through the cobblestone streets as they passed tourists carrying bags filled with Mardi Gras beads and painted ceramic masks, gutter punks looking for loose change, locals rushing to work, and conmen looking for their next easy mark. They passed Jax Brewery and Jackson Square, browsing the French Market before hitting Coop's Place for a good meal.

"So, why here, Van?" Dar asked. "You can't do this in Panama City?"

"This place is magical," Vanian said. "The tarot card readers gather in Jackson Square because they know its power. There's a belief that when the world ends, the initial tear in the fabric of reality will occur there. Can you imagine monsters and demons crawling out of that little park?"

Dar and Kitty exchanged a glance.

"The Mississippi culminates here. All the pollution from this country's heart gathers momentum upstream and travels here before dispersing in the Gulf. All that energy…here. This place embraces the darkness. Voodoo, vampires, ghosts—New Orleans worships its dark side and brags about it to the rest of world. If not here, where else?"

"I need to say something," Carter said.

"Go ahead, man." Vanian sipped his beer, suspecting what the drummer was about to say.

"I know you have your own beliefs, I respect that. But what you're doing, it goes against God."

Dar coughed, reaching for his beer. Kitty peeled at a hot sauce label.

Vanian knew he had to proceed with caution. "How do you figure?"

"Patricia's death sucked," Carter said. "But what happens is all part of God's grand design. Rearranging His plan isn't natural. It's just not right. Maybe Patricia is supposed to be dead."

Carter leaned back, drumming his fingers on the table.

Expressionless, Vanian's hand guarded his beer. The time for bandmate diplomacy over, polite frankness was that remained.

"I dig where you're coming from," he said. "I knew my intentions on this trip would bother you. It was only a matter of time before you spoke up."

"I'm not sitting here and quoting scripture at you, Van. But you're going too far. I'm worried I'll go to Hell just knowing what you're about to do, let alone being a part of it."

"Thanks for your concern. It means a lot, really. I you don't want to watch, beat it. no hard feelings. But I have to do this. I have to try. My entire belief system is based on the idea that my will can send enough ripples through the universe to affect change. My religion puts me in charge of the elements, and I believe that death is simply that, an element I can manipulate."

"I have no doubt you can control it," Carter said. "The real question is if it is the right thing to do?"

The waiter returned with their feast. Carter fell silent and distant.

"So," Kitty said, "you climb on this boat, or whatever, and go off with death—how long before you come back?"

"Paul believed that my departure and return will be simultaneous, that time doesn't work the same way beyond the grave as it does in this reality."

"What happens if you don't come back?" Kitty asked. "I mean, what are we supposed to do?"

"If I don't make it back, I'll be with her," Vanian said, never breaking eye contact.

The waiter returned with two baskets of warm bread.

"Need another beer?" the waiter asked.

Dar and Vanian nodded, and the waiter vanished behind the bar again.

"What were the last lessons Paul taught you?" Dar asked.

"He channeled not only his power, but pure music into me. I woke up brimming with song ideas. Beautiful music the world needs. He also gave me a failsafe, an elixir. The essence of music."

"And what if Charon doesn't show?" Kitty asked as the waiter brought fresh beers, setting them on the table. "What if you cast your spell and nothing happens?"

"Then I go back living my life," Vanian said. He wondered if he even could.

"I don't want to piss you off, but can't you do that now?" Dar asked.

"No. I have to find her. There's something in here," Vanian said, patting his chest, "that insists that this is the right way. It's like a torch, burning bright blue. It screams *find her, find her.*"

The waiter returned with more beer as the setting sun turned the Louisiana sky orange, yellow, and pink.

# ♫ TRACK 4 ♫

After dinner, they wandered the Quarter, looking at wrought iron balconies and galleries decorated with Mardi Gras flags and ferns. On Bourbon Street, Dar ordered a Hand Grenade in a long green plastic cup called a yard from Tropical Isle. Kitty browsed the leather shop, buying a box of spaghetti with penis-shaped noodles and a book of erotic poetry. Vanian hit Marie Laveau's House of Voodoo to gather magical supplies. At the register, the hippie clerk ringing him up wrapped the candles in tissue so their energies didn't mingle.

"These are serious lights, my friend," the clerk said, tossing his dreadlocks over his shoulder. "I'm tempted to ask what you plan on doing with this stuff."

"It's probably best you don't," Vanian said.

"Nightshade oil, dragon's blood, skeleton key, nutria bones… From the looks of it, you're dabbling in necromancy," the clerk said. "Summon yourself a ghost, huh?"

Vanian didn't answer.

"Just remember: whoever fights monsters should see to it he does not become a monster, and when looking long into the abyss, the abyss is also looking into you."

"Nietzsche," Vanian said.

"A learned man," the clerk smiled, flashing two front gold teeth. "This is a wicked city. There are those who swear this place is the official city of the damned. Those storms we get, the murders—they're a dress rehearsal for end times. You're dabbling with the dead here, and they don't usually take too kindly to intruders. Many will suck your soul dry to taste life again. Be careful, man."

"Thanks," Vanian said as he took the bag and left the store. He hoped he knew what he was doing.

## ♫ TRACK 5 ♫

Carter paced outside of the voodoo shop, a fire of his own burning in his chest. As Vanian picked out candles and oils for his witchcraft, Carter knew what he was about to witness was sacrilege. He'd always been patient with the band. It was his ticket out of Panama City Beach, and he understood that image sold records. When the other guys got too intoxicated or took the Lord's name in vain, he figured his soul was safe and secure because of his faith. God would protect him even in the face of darkness.

He watched Vanian talk to the clerk and a new calm entered his soul. His friend was verging on an unforgivable violation. What had to be done was clear.

As they headed towards the Moonwalk, the promenade overlooking the mighty Mississippi, Carter knew it was time to live a blessed life, for better or worse.

## ♬ TRACK 6 ♬

They waited until the celebratory sounds of the Quarter ebbed into a low, drunken murmur. As the street's merrymakers thinned, a thick fog rolled in over the city, bringing the bayou's dank fingers over the Quarter. The sky was soup green, forbidding stars from shining down.

Vanian, Dar, Kitty, and Carter relaxed on the levee, in the kinetic structure, *Ocean Song*. Constructed by John T. Scott, the work of art consisted of several stainless steel mirrored pyramids crowned with moving spiral tubes noting the direction of the winds, said to evoke patterns found in New Orleans jazz as well as the music omnipresent in nature. Vanian meditated in the center of the structure, soaking up the vibrations.

From the murky haze, a bald, bearded street performer wearing camouflage pants and a torn jean jacket approached. Smoking a joint and hauling a bottle of whiskey, the performer sang to himself and the river.

"You're that G. G. Allin impersonator putting cigarettes out on himself on Bourbon, right?" Dar asked.

"Howdy, good citizens," the performer said. "If you can't sleep tonight, and if a fever grips you tight, there's a place we must explore, open wide the door."

"Hello." Kitty said. "You doing good tonight?"

"Fantastic, my lady," he said, bowing. "The sky is a poisonous garden, ain't it folks?"

"You have no idea," Dar said.

The performer nodded. "Now I was wondering."

"What's that," Dar asked, suspicious of the gutter punk's motives.

"Does anybody else in here feel the way I do? Really, folks, is there any way I can spange a few ducats so I can get totally shit faced on this, such a joyous day?"

"I'm sorry, dude," Dar said, "but we're busy."

"No one's busy in the Big Easy," he said. "Hey, I can do something to make it worth your time. I'll puke on the floor here and then suck it up with a straw for three dollars. You guys can spit in my mouth for a dollar an emission, or I'll drink from the Mississippi for a Hamilton. That's the Valentine's Day special, people. You won't get this kind of entertainment anywhere else."

"Here," said Vanian, holding out a twenty. "Get fucked up, man."

"Thanks, mister," the performer said. "You sure you don't want me to drink the river? I can keep it down. You know there's a legend that says anyone who drinks from the Mississippi will always return."

"Can't say I've ever heard that before," Vanian said. "Now, if you don't mind…"

"Didn't mean to be any bother," the performer said.

"You're fine," Vanian said. "Just be safe out there."

The performer nodded and vanished into the swirling haze.

"People pay for crazy entertainment," Dar said.

"Vanian," Carter said, "before you do this…"

"Speak your peace," Vanian said, brushing hair from his eyes.

"I'm Christian. I know this without a doubt in my mind, even though I battle some of the things my church teaches. I admit I walk the line, with the band and the life."

Dar cocked his head at the drummer.

Kitty nodded.

Carter sighed. "You have no idea how much it tears me apart when you guys call each other names. How much it sucks when you call *me* names. That shit hurts, but I didn't have the balls to be honest about it."

Vanian stepped forward. "Man, I—"

"No," Carter said. "I have to find the strength to do this on my own. I'm not afraid of being who I am anymore."

"No one ever asked you not to be yourself," Dar said.

"I know," Carter said. "Now here's the thing you are not going to like. Vanian, this is going too far. This isn't lighting candles and chanting or selling an image, this is blasphemy."

Vanian lifted a hand. "Carter, I—"

"You are messing with things…things I don't want any part of. I hope you find what you're looking for. And I will be praying to God that you make it back safe. But I am out of the band. I'm playing music for God. I want to spread the word about His love, and how that love doesn't stop because you're gay, purple, or, hell, even pagan. I want to throw in my hand at ending hate and moving forward as a species. It's how I have to be true to myself."

"So be it mote," Vanian said.

Dar's shoulders slumped.

Kitty bit her lower lip, tears welling up in her eyes.

Vanian looked to the fog-swept river. "I have to do this. It's time."

"Get back to us, man," Carter said.

Vanian nodded. He reached into his pocket and pulled out the ruby engagement ring and a folded sketch Patricia had drawn of them together, handing them to Kitty.

Dar and Kitty exited the silver structure and took a park bench. Carter opened a bottle of chartreuse and wandered onto a grassy knoll overlooking the Mississippi.

Vanian opened the bag filled with the voodoo shop's wares. He anointed the candles with the proper oil for each corner, placing the candles in position—north, south, east, west. He scattered the nutria bones in the structure's center, placing the skeleton key in the center of the remains. Striking a green-tipped match, he lit the candles in proper order. No wind allowed the candles to glow strong. From his guitar case, he pulled out his athame, opening the circle and calling to the elements—earth, air, fire, water. The fog became heavier, and Vanian called into the night.

"Charon, I call you. Come to this shore. I bring two tetradrachm and a heavy heart. Charon, I call to you and demand safe passage to the Otherworld."

Vanian chanted the incantation as instructed by Paul. Carter, Kitty, and Dar watched. Vanian sent his energy towards the riverbank, calling the ferryman.

"Look at that," whispered Kitty. Through the thick haze, a green light appeared in the distance, slowly approaching from the Algiers Point. "Is that one of the paddleboats?"

"No," Dar said. "It's him."

Vanian stepped off the mirrored structure, removed up his guitar from its case, and walked down the Moonwalk towards Jackson Square. Vanian saw groups of forlorn people waiting by the shore, hanging off the levee wall, and calling out to the ferryman. Amazed by the number of wretched souls lacking fare, sorrow filled his heart.

As he passed Woldenberg Park's sprawling green lawns, Vanian lost sight of the light as it passed behind the sternwheeler Steamboat *Natchez*. Hurrying past the pavilion and the paddleboat's loading dock, he rounded the slight bend and saw the light approaching the dock across from Jackson Square and Washington Artillery Park. The thick fog consumed St. Louis Cathedral's three spires pointing towards heaven, watching over the Quarter. He looked back at Dar, Kitty, and Carter, still following but keeping their distance.

The green light grew closer. In the dark, Vanian made out the shape of the ship, long and narrow like a Venice gondola and propelled by a cloaked figure. The craft hit shore, and Charon stepped to the bow, oar in hand. The howls of the stranded created an unholy cacophony as Vanian approached the boat.

"Who summons the ferry?" Charon called in a raspy voice. Vanian, thankful he couldn't make out Charon's features in the shadows, stepped forward.

"I have," Vanian answered, holding up the two coins.

Charon hissed. "You are forbidden to cross. You are still living."

Vanian slid on the guitar, finger picking A minor. The haunting forced Charon to lean forward. He'd never played so vulnerable, so honest. And then he sang, his voice dripping with loss and hope:

> *We could swim to Saturn on our way to the moon*
> *Pass aside the misery and heal the old scabbed wounds*
> *Float off into space, watch the earth grow small*
> *We can help each other break gravitational law*
>
> *Together we can drift into infinite perfect night*
> *Leave behind the worry, turn away from every plight*
> *Pulling each other close near the cool red shores of mars*
> *We can burn it bright and become a brand new star*

The song drew tears from Dar and Kitty. Carter took a few steps closer.

Charon's poise relaxed. "Though shuttling you across the river is prohibited, your music is a gift. I cannot deny the divine."

A skeletal hand protruded from the cloak, motioning for Vanian to board.

Vanian glanced back at his companions. They could no longer follow.

Swallowing hard, he stepped onboard. The gondola shifted under his weight. He handed Charon the coins, and they disappeared in his bony fingers before the ferryman shoved off with a beech oar. Vanian took a seat under the swinging green lantern, noticing that the boat was constructed from human bones. Moss clumped around femurs and ribs, and the shattered skull masthead stared off towards nothing.

As the gap between gondola and riverbank widened, Dar, Kitty, and Carter vanished from view. On his left, the string of white lights making up the two arcs of the Crescent City Connection bridge were consumed by hungry, cold mist.

Vanian was alone with the ferryman gently sculling the craft.

Water lapping against the vessel turned darker, thicker. The surrounding air became heavier. Something knocked the boat under his feet, and by the lantern's unnatural glow, Vanian saw serpents slithering through the water's surface. He held the guitar tight, keeping his mind clear of anything but the image of Patricia's smile.

"Why have you come?" Charon asked. "Nothing you want lies beyond these waters."

"That's where you're wrong. I've come for love, and she's somewhere on the other shore. I'm going to find her."

"Love is all you need," Charon said, "in life, that is. Where you're heading no such rules apply. After crossing this river of woe, all hope is gone."

"How do I find my heart in this place?"

"Ah," boomed the ferryman. "You want a chaperone. I will guide your voice, mortal, for I suspect it comes from this place. The Otherworld has three realms along the trail to the king's palace. If a soul is virtuous and heroic, then it passes eternity away at the Elysian Fields. These reed fields are paradise, and only the truly worthy are allowed entrance. Wicked souls, on the other hand, go to a gloomy realm. An abyss used as a dungeon of torment and suffering, hemmed by three layers of night and encompassed by a bronze wall. This dark and wretched pit is Tartarus. Not a compassionate place. The Asphodel Meadows house the indifferent and ordinary souls, near equal lives of good and evil trapped in an even less perfect version of life on Earth. Most people wind up there, for better or worse."

"How will I know where to look for my love?" Vanian asked.

"I'm just a ferryman," Charon said. "Minos, Rhadamanthys, and Aeacus—the judges— determine the fate of souls passing through these parts. You'll find them at the road's trident."

Vanian heard gravel crunch underneath the boat, and he was jerked with the sudden stop.

"Abandon hope, for we are here. The Otherworld. Step lightly, for the king is the unseen one, the rich one who does not take kindly to trespass. When you find your love, be ye lamps unto yourselves."

Vanian stepped from the gondola onto the rocky shore. Mist covered the dark land. As a breeze wafted around the singer, an icy chill ate through his clothes. He turned to thank Charon, but the ferryman was already heading back to gather more souls in the land of the living.

Before disappearing into the fog, Charon called out: "Beware Cerberus. The three-headed beast craves intruder's flesh and will devour you."

Vanian stood at Acheron's shore, unsure where to begin his hunt. Surrounded by death, emptiness crept into his soul.

## ♫ TRACK 7 ♫

Through the darkness, Vanian followed the embankment to higher ground until his footsteps drowned out the gurgling Acheron. The loose, umber soil under his feet gave way, sending rocks tumbling down to the shoreline. With little light and heavy fog, Vanian found his way by instinct more than sight.

Vanian hurried his pace towards a soft red radiance, hoping for another guide. Closer to the illumination, the rocks underfoot shifted into smashed bones. A few fragments resembled animal parts, but most he recognized as human. He kicked an alligator skull, and it crumbled and splintered. Shards bounced away, sending up a cloud from the dusty floor that burned his nostrils.

Seven more paces towards the light, a low growl filled the darkness.

Time stopped in the surrounding stillness. Instincts demanded he flee, but his heart, that persistent glowing blue torch, pushed him forward. He took another step, and three pairs of glowing eyes pierced the mist. From the thick murkiness, a monstrous form emerged.

Cerberus.

Towering over Vanian, its three mismatched heads snarled and snapped at the air. The pit bull's green, bloodshot eyes scanned the rocky cliffs. Vanian recognized the pit bull's intelligence, for it seemed to already know he was there.

The Doberman's ice blue eyes swept ahead of the colossal beast, rising and falling like an unholy sea. It snipped at the pit bull, but the other head ducked before the Doberman made purchase. The

Doberman head went back to bobbing, its neck snaking in the dark sky.

The Labrador's mismatched yellow and brown eyes both focused on the dusty path. Each snarling mouth dripped with drool as nostrils, oozing with thick mucus, flared. Huffing and puffing,

Talon feet digging into the bones and dust supported its muscular body, and a long serpentine tail protruded from Cerberus's backside, swaying to and fro on the ground behind the creature.

The hellhound's stance tensed, all three heads homed in on Vanian. Six angry eyes burned into the singer's soul.

Vanian pulled his guitar tight against his chest.

"Easy, boy," he said, backing up slowly.

Cerberus growled, each head hungry for the singer's flesh and blood. Vanian stepped aside as the beast lunged, its talons reducing a skull pyramid to crumbs. Dropping his guitar, he scrambled away and ducked beside a large jagged rock. His axe moaned when it hit ground. Vanian cringed. Lacking a backup set of strings, he swore at himself for the amateur mistake. Cerberus circled around, the pit bull head smelling his instrument with its mustachioed snout.

*Huff, huff.*

Dust swirled up around his fret board. A dark blue tongue licked the strings.

Vanian tucked his hand into his pocket, fingering the Victorian lachrymatory filled with Paul's elixir. Power radiated from the glass bottle that once captured the tears of mourning lovers, but he resisted the urge to toss it at the monster.

The Doberman head attacked, Vanian barely dodged its sharp teeth. An ear hit him in the face, filling his nose and mouth with an acrid, damp dog taste. He slid underneath the monster, grabbing his guitar and gaining several paces on Cerberus as the lumbering behemoth turned.

He held the guitar up, unsure if it was still tuned. No time for tinkering, the beast began another approach.

Vanian took a deep breath and began strumming, thankful his minor chord was in key. Playing a lullaby to soothe the savage animal, Vanian hummed instead of faking lyrics. The Doberman panted, licking its black lips. Vanian played slower, noticing the canine's muscles relaxing.

"*La, la, la,*" Vanian sang, stepping closer.

Cerberus kneeled before him, resting its three heads on his front paws, chunks of bloody flesh dangling from the sharp talons. The monster yawned. After a few minutes, the massive beast's six eyes shut. Cerberus snored. He continued playing as he stepped over the slumbering dog and headed towards the red light. Vanian avoided Cerberus's reptilian tail as it snaked in the bone-filled rubble.

Rustling came from overhead. The darkness filled with yellow eyes reflecting in the soft red light. He paused, still strumming, and the eyes, belonging to hundreds of bats, swooped down. They darted around Vanian before landing and transforming into black cats. Ignoring Vanian, they gathered around Cerberus, meowing in time with the music.

Vanian pushed on.

# ♫ TRACK 8 ♫

The red light of a flaming river cut across a black landscape. Spider-webbed tributaries fed a fiery lake, spawning burning plumes engulfing the starless night. Orange sparks leapt from the clouds, dancing in the air like bright confetti.

One fell towards Vanian, so he stepped aside to keep from being burned.

As it drifted closer, he realized it was not burning ember, but a tiny winged creature.

Beautiful and petite, its yellow eyes locked with his. The fire fairy sailed past his head, stopping midair and inspecting the singer. Warmth radiated from the sprite. Looking him up and down, the fairy winked before zipping up into the inky darkness.

He pushed closer to the river.

Vanian broke out in a cold sweat. Approaching the blazing stream, the intense heat singed his hair and eye lashes. A broken path ran along the shore, and he followed it until he came upon a crouched figure, dressed in rags and doodling in the black sand.

"Excuse me," Vanian said.

The figure looked up. Burn marks covered his face. Clouded eyes looked through the singer.

Vanian gasped.

"Who goes there?" the blinded ragman asked. "I can't see, but I know you are mortal. I can smell life pouring off of you."

Vanian backed away.

The ragman resumed drawing in the black sand with his uneven limbs. Although Vanian understood some of the magical symbols, most escaped him.

"My name is Vanian. I'm lost, and I need help."

"I can't help you," the ragman said with a raspy voice. Deep wrinkles interrupted by burns creased his forehead. "The king will toss me into Tartarus."

"Can you at least tell me where I'm at?"

"This is Phlegethon, the river of fire." The man coughed viscous black ooze into the crook of his arm. Dangling slime dripped from his elbow. "One of five flowing through this land. If you value your soul, you'll return the way you came."

A fire burst sprang from the lake, burning out with an agonized wail.

More fire fairies broke free from the plume, pirouetting above the volcanic river.

"I must continue," Vanian said. "If I turn back now, I lose what I believe in."

"And that is?" ragman asked.

"The woman I love."

"You've come…for love?" The ragman blinked. His milky eyes sparkled.

"A love unjustly taken from me."

"The Phlegethon was once very much alive, a god whose essence was flame. Styx, the goddess of the river of hate, fell in love with Phlegethon, but his fire was too intense. It consumed her with a light brighter than your sun. Together, they burned to ashes in the mortal world, but King Hades has reunited them here, so they may flow parallel while protecting his world."

"If the king was sympathetic to their love, then he should see the righteousness of my quest," Vanian said, hope feeding the blue flame in his chest.

"I wouldn't count on it. Theirs is a story of gods, not the dream of a man. Hades is unforgiving, his judgment final."

Vanian crossed his arms. "Point me in the right direction, and we'll see about that."

"The hubris of youth."

Ragman's lips pulled into a smile, exposing a toothless mouth with black rotten gums.

"Love," Vanian said. "I believe in the power love."

"Love may be the most powerful thing in the universe, but I'm not sure even it can save you. The king is moody and hateful. Just coming here is reason enough for him to imprison you in Tartarus."

"I have to try. If it costs my life, it's worth it."

"Follow the flames until you come across the River Styx. She separates Tartarus from the land between life and death. You'll know her when you see her. If you continue in that direction, you'll come to a bronze wall, fifteen feet high. Beyond that fortification is a realm of torment no one should gaze upon. Maybe there you'll find answers."

The man cackled, scooting himself towards the fiery shore.

Vanian took a deep breath, thinking about holding Patricia again. The blaze in his chest raged on.

# ♫ TRACK 9 ♫

S weat poured from Vanian's brow.

Along the path, the fiery waters narrowed.

He looked for a place to rest.

Negative energy pulled on the singer.

Dark whirlpools gurgled and churned, plummeting over broken cliffs.

Coughing, Vanian sat down on a jagged point overlooking a drop and watched gravity master the dark waters.

In the extensive pool below, shadow people struggled against the river's grasp. One pulled its slime-covered torso above the roiling waterline. The unforgiving water pulled back, drowning the creature.

Keeping several yards between his feet and the gummy waters, Vanian followed the shore until he stumbled upon a towering bronze wall intersecting the trail. Vanian rested a palm against the wall and remembered Ignatius J. Reilly's chest.

Vanian took a deep breath and coughed into his hand.

Black goo peppered his palm.

His guitar.

The wall.

He followed until, legs aching, he discovered a triangular crack. Vanian stooped, entering the tight gap. The cave's musty interior drowned the outside light.

He ignored the darkness, closed his eyes, and sent out energy, like he'd shown Patricia at the state park.

His psychic radar mapped the cavern's walls, so he pressed on, feeling his way until the cavern's mouth dumped him into a vast, new world.

He opened his eyes and realized he had entered Hell.

Tartarus mixed dusk with dawn, blue and green. The sky blended every sunset he'd ever witnessed. Violets and blues danced into pinks, red, and yellows, never getting dark, but not illuminating either. Layer upon layer of night swirled like olive oil in water. The rocky, desolate path expanded into eternity. Breathing in liquid instead of oxygen, the sulfur-laden air burned his throat. Passing a skeletal tree, bent and oozing with dripping black flowers, he wondered how anything thrived in such an evil place.

"Help me," a strained but familiar voice penetrated the darkness.

Vanian followed the sound, coming across his mother submerged in a murky stream. Naked, her withered breasts floated with the waterline. Above her head, a bush wealthy with jet black berries dangled.

When she saw Vanian, she reached towards him.

"Mom?" he asked.

"Is that you, Vanian?"

"Yes," he said, reaching out.

"Did you bring me cigarettes?" she asked. As soon as the question left her lips, Vanian drew his hand back.

"N-no, mom. I didn't."

"I'm so thirsty. Did you bring me beer? I need beer."

"There's no cigarettes or beer here, Mom. You don't need them anymore."

"Good for nothing louse. You don't understand how cruel life is. How traps are set. How you grow to love them, get attached, and then they leave you."

"Mom…"

"All that's left is a shell of a person."

"I agree with you there." Vanian fought back tears.

"Just bring me some damned cigarettes. Is that too much to ask for?"

Vanian shook his head. "We left so much unsaid. I can't tell you how many nights I wanted to tell you exactly how I felt about what you did to me and how you treated Paul. He's still in love with you. Probably will be until he dies. Mom, there were so many times I wanted to tell you to go to Hell, and now, here you are."

Vanian pitied her, for she was still stuck in the same cycles in death.

The special place for her in his heart broke.

"You really don't have a cigarette for me, boy? What about a shot? Will you pour me a shot of vodka? I'm *so* thirsty."

"I have a drink for you, Mom."

Vanian cupped his hand and dunked it into the water, scooping up the cool liquid. Before he brought it to her lips, he hesitated. He'd already crossed into the Otherworld. This broke another law. Defying her punishment might upset Hades even more. One way or the other, there would be hell to pay.

He poured the water into his mother's mouth. A rivulet ran down her chin.

She swallowed a bit, coughed, and then spit the rest out.

"What the hell is that? I asked for beer or potato juice. I don't want water. Now I am even thirstier. Did you bring me cigarettes?"

"You say I was a trap," he said, "but the only person trapped is you. You can't see beyond yourself. I thought something extraterrestrial snatched you from me, but now I know the truth. You took yourself away from me, away from us."

"Cigarettes, you bring 'em?"

Vanian rose.

"I need full flavors," she said.

"You don't deserve this," he said. "No one does. I forgive you, for what it's worth."

"I'm hungry," she said. "Quit running that gator and find me food."

"I'm sorry, Mom. I have to leave now."

"Maybe just a few berries." Cali struggled to move. She looked up at the branch. "I'm starving."

"I can't." Vanian tore his eyes from her. "I may be heading for a punishment worse than yours. I'm sorry."

Cali frowned, her eyes losing hope. "No cigarettes?"

Vanian hurried away, not looking back. Her cries for cigarettes and beer grew fainter and fainter.

The gloom ate at Vanian.

Love had brought him to this wretched pit, yet there was no trace of his heart. The Otherworld's limitless, horrible corners left him wondering if he'd ever find Patricia. For all he knew, she'd wound up in the Elysian Fields or Asphodel Meadows. No telling where the judges sent her.

The sky rumbled.

The ground shook.

From the blackness, a flaming wheel rolled by.

Attached by red hot chains, a man screamed as the fire scorched his flesh. The unbearable smell filled the air. As the wheel rolled away, Vanian swallowed hard, the reality of his own actions becoming clear.

Still the blue torch burned in his chest. He could not give up.

The landscape turned mountainous. In the distance, another doomed soul pushed a boulder up a crag. Once the rock reached the crest, it rolled back down and rested at the mountain's base. The man grunted and returned to the bottom where he began pushing it upward again.

Vanian pressed on, exhausted from the engulfing dreariness.

"Vanian, over here."

A lump formed in Vanian's throat. Over the years, that voice had expressed itself to the singer with every imaginable emotion, but he'd never heard anything like the anguish now clinging to Astro's words.

He followed the words and found Astro, chained to the side of a mountain. The shackles dug into his wrists, drawing blood. With each movement, more blood spilled, splattering on the dusty ground below.

"Vanian, help me," Astro begged. He pulled his arms away from the boulders locking him down, but the chains did not give much play.

Despair and hurt.

Rage.

Vanian wanted to spit on the guitarist, slap him, tell him what a fucker he was.

Seeing Astro's pain stirred pleasure in a dark part of Vanian's soul, but once he realized the reaction, guilt seized his heart.

Vanian reached toward his friend, but paused.

His fingers trembled.

"I can't," he said. "I'm so sorry you're here, but I've come for Patricia. Maybe in another life, we can talk."

"Dude, remember when we spent all day at the movies, hopping from theater to theater. How many flicks did we see without paying for? Three? You were so scared when the ushers caught us."

Astro chuckled, coughing up blood.

"Those were better days," Vanian said. "For sure."

"Help me get out of these chains. We can cut that new record."

"The new record is out. We finished without you."

A tear the color of blood streaked Astro's cheek. "I'm so sorry, man. I'm sorry."

A vision of Astro holding down Patricia, stabbing and raping her again and again, flashed through Vanian's mind. Her unheard screams echoed through the darkness of the Underworld. Hatred boiled over.

"Fuck you, Astro."

Vanian stepped away.

"No, you can't go." Astro tried to reach out. More blood spilled from his wounds. He groaned. "We're brothers."

Astro tried to pull free of the shackles, but they snapped his arms back to rock.

"You and I—we're like one-half of the same person."

"Maybe we were one day," Vanian said, clenching his teeth. "But that day has passed. We now stand here under three layers of night as enemies. Goodbye, old friend."

"Wait," Astro called. "Van, please. Don't...don't go. Please."

Vanian didn't look back.

He walked, timeless and lost, until he crossed another bronze wall extending from a rocky precipice.

Climbing it would take no time at all...

## ♫ TRACK 10 ♫

Daylight.

White flowers swaying in a gentle breeze.

Hot?

White flowers underneath Vanian's palms.

Cold?

The rocks crumbled, but with a little effort, a foothold

White flowers.

Sticky.

Vanian saw people standing in the flowers.

"Have you seen Patricia?" Vanian asked a woman as she frowned at her fingernails.

"Why would it matter?" the woman replied, never taking her gaze from her hands. "Nothing matters anymore."

A man sitting crossed-legged and staring at his bare feet while chewing on an Asphodel root blinked twice when Vanian asked about Patricia. When asked again, the man offered him a flower.

Coughing.

Vanian wouldn't find her.

These souls were useless.

They were caught up in despair and self-loathing, their apathy weighed on Vanian's heart.

Their energy infected him.

He rushed to the edge of the flowers.

## ♫ TRACK 11 ♫

Vanian stepped into a dreamlike world, drenched with cold sweat. Sunshine poured down. Clouds floated through a pale sky, reed fields surrounding green pastures—paradise. The parasitic sorrow peeled back as his lungs filled with clean air. Vanian heard a few laughing souls and headed towards their blissful and content vibrations. Approaching a naked couple holding hands, he prayed the lovers might be of assistance.

He cleared his throat, coughing more black gobs on his palm. "Excuse me. I'm looking for a woman that might have passed through here. Her name is Patricia, and I need to speak with her."

"So you're the mortal that searches the Otherworld for love," the man said. Rolling over, his flaccid penis flopped across his leg. Vanian forced eye contact.

"Word of your journey has spread fast here." The woman mussed the man's hair, her ample bosom sparkling in the light.

"So brave," the man said. "There may be room here for you yet."

"Have you seen her?" Vanian asked.

"No, but many do not pass through here. The judges will know where she's being kept," the woman said. "They are the ones who decide such things."

The man yawned. "We were a lucky pair."

"The last life, this one, and the next," she said. "We belong together."

The exchange, though off-topic, warmed Vanian. Their snuggling reminded of his quest, of Patricia. After the darkness and indifference, their love replenished hope.

"Where do I find the judges," Vanian asked, hating to interrupt their bliss.

"The next land is Erebus," he said. "It lies just beyond those hills. There you'll find two pools. One is called Lethe, and that's where common souls flock to erase memories. It makes what they held onto in life easier to deal with here. One drop, and it's all gone."

"And the other pool?" Vanian asked.

"The other pool is Mnemosyne," she answered. "Initiates of the mysteries bathe from this pool. It is the path to enlightenment."

"How will I know the difference?" Vanian asked.

"You'll know," he said, caressing the woman's long golden hair. "After crossing the pools, you'll fine to three merging paths, the trident of the road. There you'll come to the judges."

She nodded, adding, "Minos, Rhadamanthys, and Aeacus. They will know where your Patricia is located."

"Thank you, both," Vanian said. "Maybe our paths will cross again someday."

"I hope so," he said.

Vanian left the lovers, heading towards the hills.

# ♫ TRACK 12 ♫

Paradise ended the moment he entered Erebus, giving way to swampy, rolling hills. In a fold overgrown with cypress and pines, Vanian found the two mirror-like pools, impossible to distinguish one from the other. Vanian paused. Treading through the wrong pool would erase all he'd ever known, including the memory of his beloved.

He sat between their shores, gazing into his reflection. Attempting a scrying spell, the pools did not betray their secrets. The reflections remained anchored on the flat surfaces. He closed his eyes and sent out energy, trying his psychic radar, but that also failed. Both pools were exactly alike.

Vanian strummed his guitar, clearing his mind. The sad song lamented Patricia's sudden death. He sang, imagining making love with her, their bodies pressed together on the Elysian Fields.

*Her love I long for everyday*
*Though she's no longer here*
*To god and goddess I both pray*
*To cleanse away my tears*

*Now, wherever you may be*
*To you I sing this tune*
*So I may hold you eternally*
*Under cycling moon*

"Beautiful," a winged creature said, stepping from the mossy shadows of an old cypress. A young, diminutive man carrying a bow stood before Vanian. Shaggy blonde hair fell in his eyes in loose spiral curls. A burlap quiver filled with long arrows hung over his bare chest. "Simply beautiful."

"Thanks," Vanian told the cherub.

"I knew when I struck you with one of my arrows your union would be tragic."

This was Eros, the god of love, and remembering Paul's warning, Vanian raised his guard.

"My loss?" Vanian asked. "I haven't lost her yet."

"My arrow must have plunged deep within your chest," Eros said. "Such bravery, such foolishness. To come here to rescue a loved soul from a king as unmoving as Hades...what a passionate man you are, Vanian. Paul was wise to grant you his power, his music."

"How did you know about that?" Vanian asked.

"I have eyes, loverboy."

"So, can you help me?" Vanian asked. "I need to cross and see the judges, but I don't want to touch the Lethe. Unless you can show me Patricia, I need to know which of these pools is the Mnemosyne."

"Mortals," Eros said, "always need and want, want and need."

"How do I get to her?"

"Hades would sink me next to your mother without a thought." He looked over his shoulder, offering a mischievous grin. "But I will show you which pool is the Mnemosyne. I owe you. I'll have to answer to Hades, but sometimes a song is worth the trouble."

He motioned with his left hand, pointing to the pool on the right with his bow.

"Be quick, mortal" Eros said. "The king knows you are among his subjects."

"Thanks," Vanian said as Eros extended his large wings.

"Anything for talent like yours."

The god flew off, vanishing into the darkness overhead.

Vanian took a deep breath. Paul had mentioned Eros was a trickster, and Vanian suspected deception. Something about his wicked grin didn't settle with him. The wrong choice and he would forget Bad Apple—even worse, Patricia. Would it totally erase his memories, his first cat, Mickey, those long afternoons learning chords in Binjo's with Paul?

He'd come so far.

Against the cherub's suggestion and kneeled before the left-hand pool and brought his lips to the water.

Was he drinking the reflection, or was the reflection was drinking him?

Taking a sip, the crisp liquid cooled his throat.    He waited. Forgetting nothing, Vanian waded through the Mnemosyne, eager to meet the three judges.

## ♫ TRACK 13 ♫

The trail was easy to follow, extending out of the swamps and high into the hills. Two other roads approached either side of the brae, but he pressed on until they met at a grassy crossroads. There, three thrones seating the three judges rested upon the crown of the tallest hill in the valley.

Vanian bowed. Their vibrations, ancient and powerful, surrounded him. If not for the gentle heaving of their chests, Vanian would have assumed they were regal statues cloaked with fancy robes. He thumbed the lachrymatory. Fearless, the burning fire in his chest gave him enough strength to make eye contact. Their gaze pierced his soul, and unseen hand gripping his aura.

"You have no business here," the center judge said. "Turn back and go."

Vanian studied his expressionless features. The judge's eyes were deep and cold. Infinity unfolded in those dark marbles. His white hair fell in twisted locks framing his square, ashen face, his hands hidden within flowing purple robes.

"I must pass," Vanian said. "Where is Patricia?"

The other two remained silent, staring him down with the same fierce glare as the center judge.

Vanian sang, a cappella.

*Goodbye, sweet princess*
*I must sail west*

*Goodbye, sweet homeland*
*I leave your breast*

*Goodbye, cold cruel world*
*I'll take the test*
*This is not the end*
*We'll meet again*

"You love this woman?" the center judge asked, shifting in his throne. The other two remained silent. A warm breeze passed through the hills.

"Yes," Vanian said.

"What makes you believe that is enough? You think you are the first man to love? Many have loved fortunes and empires and people, yet lost them faster than a tear falls from a cloud. You selfishly chase a life that was not yours to command."

The judge leaned forward, his bones creaking at the shifting weight.

"Death is part of life," he said, "acceptance of this loss makes humans cherish the moments they have on Earth. If Hades started giving back lives loved and lost, then no one would respect life. If you find earth indifferent, it's only because people are indifferent.

"Vanian, Paul has given a gift you can use to influence the world. Perhaps it was too much too soon. Or maybe holding onto things is human nature. I'll never know. What I am certain of is that I can't send you to Patricia. You are brave and foolish, but you have no business being here. I, Minos, find you guilty of trespass. Stand before the king."

The world swirled, and Vanian lost track of reality.

# ♫ TRACK 14 ♫

Over the years, Vanian had watched a lot of horror movies; however, no onscreen image packed as much fright as Hades' ominous palace. The edifice rose from cooled, bent lava. Flowing, dark purple igneous rock shifted into the brickwork forming the castle's misshapen walls. Light flickered behind a complex rose window. Thorny spokes radiating from the window's center separated blue, red, and green panes of glass.

Winged beasts, screeching and growling, circled black and purple spires soaring into the starless Otherworld night. Their horrible cawing intensified as the singer approached. The creatures left the spires, encircling him.

Vanian clenched his sweaty hand around the fret board and coughed up more black ooze. How much of his own life was he leaving in the realm of the dead?

He'd lived a full life. Playing music with Bad Apple had broken the vicious cycle, allowing the chance to travel and meet interesting people. Though he wouldn't meet Dar and Kitty's child, he'd made peace with Paul. Leaving behind great friends and few loose ends, he laughed at the unfinished novel's pages in his notebook. Things weren't bad, but nonetheless incomplete without Patricia.

He did not regret his quest.

He did not regret anything.

The cobblestone trail extended to a large, gothic-arched entrance. Rows of torches illuminated the rusted gate lining the walkway. He followed the path, passing limp, bent trees that wailed as the wind passed through their bony branches.

A thin mist blew in, and Vanian plucked his strings, keeping his mind free from the creeping terror threating the fire guiding his heart.

The flying monsters circled closer, their hungry shark-like eyes lifeless and empty. One dove at his head, and Vanian ducked, narrowly avoiding the fiend.

He sang.

*He brings her flowers*
*He sings her songs*
*He shows her dead things*
*He writes her poems*

*And he will do anything for her*
*Anything for her*
*Anything for her*

They circled lower. Sharp fangs gleamed in the torchlight. He smelled death as their hot breath brushed his neck. The rancid blasts of heat from their jaws chilled him inside, as if they were draining a part of him, stealing his life. Before he could react, one scratched his face with its jagged talons. Warm blood trickled his cheek. The creatures squawked and squealed. He closed his eyes, singing louder.

*Bring petals to my lips*
*Sip the tears they caught*
*How can so much pain exist?*
*When nothing's real at all*

*You are gone and I am here*
*I push my way to you*
*Through the pain, through the fear*
*My quest is brave and true*

He reopened his eyes and found the beasts perched on the skeletal trees lining the path. Their birdlike heads leaned forward. One squawked. The mist thickened, freezing the air as Vanian entered Hades' castle through two tall doors.

# ♫ TRACK 15 ♫

Stained glass murals filled the courtyard beyond the wooden doors. Purple, green, blue, and black glass shards joined together, depicting scenes of torture and anguish, crushed dreams and fallen stars. One illustrated a giant offering a torch to a frail figure while the skies wept. Another showed two men with wings, one soaring while the other plummeted into an unforgiving ocean. Still another portrayed a beautiful but emaciated woman hiding behind a rock and eating six pomegranate seeds.

Horrors aside, the beautiful art captivated him. Painting the boxcar's walls felt like a lifetime away. If he was successful and won Patricia back, they would spend more time painting. He would buy all the oils and spray cans her heart desired, and together, they would cover the cottage's walls.

He coughed. Larger globs of black ooze dripped from his fingers. The glop was settling in his lungs, making it harder for him to breathe.

Vanian pressed on.

The castle's galleries were huge. More murals adorned the crooked walls. Sagging moss dangled from the ceiling, occasionally rubbing across his shoulders and neck as he passed cracked buttresses.

Wary, Vanian whispered a poem into the darkness, one he'd written as a dirge for the new album's liner notes.

*Epicurean feast;*
*Red wine waterfalls*
*Chase rum cakes and ham*
*Dim*
*flickering candles*

*light large, round tables*
*mood swings as we reminisce faded times*
*accordion player invokes old Italian melodies*
*hot suites inside*
*a foot of snow outside*
*cousins I don't know crying*
*nibbling carrot sticks and cookies*
*doily's freckled with crumbs*
*flowers—*
*Lilies—*
*Everywhere...*
*Grandma's not eating much today*
*Uncles having cigarettes*

*Dining at the funeral party*

He passed torches, their flames alive with brilliant blue fire before an arched entrance leading to King Hades' majestic hall.

# ♫ TRACK 16 ♫

C onstructed from layers of cooled lava, the Great Hall's walls piled to an arched ceiling where bats nuzzling their wings hung upside down from serrated, black stalactites. The blue flames cast eerie shadows over the room. Hanging silver silken tapestries caught the blue light, creating moving images upon their folds, horrible scenes of agonized men and animals succumbing to death.

Vanian entered, his footsteps bouncing off the tunnel.

In back of the long hall between towering ebony ionic pillars, the King and Queen of the Otherworld watched from two golden thrones.

Hades, expressionless, sat holding a jeweled scepter topped with a crow's head, dressed in the fanciest purple, blue, and black robes Vanian had ever seen. His short hair spiked from his skull like shark's teeth, and his combed beard dangled over his chest in a neat cropped point. Surprised, Vanian expected a monster, not a wise sage.

His wife was beautiful. Her long, brown hair fell to the floor beside the throne. She slid her delicate hands into a blue dress that looked as if it was sewn from twilight itself. Stars flickered in its countless folds. Her piercing green eyes locked with his.

Vanian stepped forward and kneeled.

"Hades, he who enriches himself with our sighs and tears, I come with humble respect and pure intention. I enter your kingdom peacefully to retrieve my heart, for it was stolen."

Hades motioned for him to rise. Vanian marveled at how such a frail hand wielded so much power.

"Not many seek me here. I am aware of your plight, Vanian. My kingdom has been teeming ever since Charon ferried you across the Acheron. Let me ask, mortal, why go through all this trouble? You've seen things men aren't to see. Horrible things. Indifferent things. Wonderful things. And you pressed on, fearless. Driven by your heart. At what point is your mind going to step in? At what point are you going to realize she belongs to me?"

"Great Hades," Vanian said, "I respect your decision to take her. I understand things must pass on, however, I have to wonder why?"

"Taking her was not my decision. That choice belongs to my servant." Raising a shrunken hand, Hades gazed into the darkness above them. "Thantos, come forth."

A dark shadow stirred from one of the volcanic walls, descending from the darkness and stopping between the King and Queen's thrones. Hovering three feet above the ground, it lacked defined form, only shifting tentacles surrounding a smoky core. Vanian could not see through the fog's dense shape. Its presence lowered the hall's temperature.

"Thantos," Hades said, "was it time for the mortal artist Patricia, lover of Vanian, to enter my domain?"

"*Yes*." Thantos' waiflike voice raised goose bumps on Vanian's arms.

"There was no mistake in her acquisition or delivery?"

"*None*."

"See, Vanian," Hades, said. "It was written. It was her time. Nothing more. Nothing less. Her presence here is not a punishment for you. It's the balance of things. Don't mistake my stance for apathy; your undying compassion has…moved me."

"I've looked my entire life for someone so fair, so wondrous. It killed me to lose her."

"Funny," Hades said, "you don't appear dead to me."

"That was merely a figure of speech. If you'd humor me, I'd like to play a song."

"Amuse me, Vanian. Let's hear what Paul has given you. So many whispers about your gift have reached my chamber. Let's hear if the rumors hold weight."

He reached into his pocket, fumbling the elixir to enhance his voice. It would give his voice an edge, but looking at the King and Queen, he remembered Paul's lesson about less being more. In his heart, he knew love was stronger than any mortal's spell.

He released the elixir and raised his guitar.

Vanian bowed and finger picked his guitar. Closed-eyed, fingers in G major, he could not hash out a Bad Apple tune for the king—that would not convey his case. What he played instead came from the very fiber of his soul.

*I can't say I believe in an honest man*
*But, every day I do the best I can*
*I know sometimes my heart's too big*
*While other times I can't forgive*
*There's something that I must show*
*Clear and blue like above*
*Cool and dark like below*
*It is love. It is love*

The King and Queen watched the singer, unblinking. Vanian's voice bounced of the chamber's walls. The natural reverb shimmered with ethereal resonance.

*I can't say I believe in a tone-deaf man*
*But, every day I sing the best I can*
*I sometimes hear my words too sharp*
*While other times I sing too dark*
*There's something that I must say*
*Black and blue like space above*
*Bright and loud like the day*
*It is love. It is love.*

Hades leaned closer. Vanian's energy rose from his heart, extending outward until it joined his voice until both echoed rhythmically within the Great Hall.

*I can't say I believe in an indifferent man*
*Every day I give the best I can*
*I know sometimes my life's way too brief*
*While other times it just won't cease*
*There's something I must do*
*Warm and fire like the sun*
*Ice and snow like the moon*
*It is love. It is love.*

He looked at Hades, needing critical approval like never before. Everything hung on the King. What would he do if Hades denied his love?

Hades remained motionless, his unflinching stare sliced Vanian in two.

Vanian bowed again, resting his guitar before the thrones. Vanian's axe, a magical tool from Paul and his constant companion, was his most prized possession. If song wouldn't work alone, maybe heart-felt tribute would help. "A gift, my lord."

"My King," the Queen said. "I cannot remember when I have heard such a voice."

"This is true, Persephone." Hades leaned back in his throne. "He is talented. Paul spared no lesson with the lad. That song—so hauntingly sad."

Vanian looked up at the King. "I stand by my beliefs, that's all."

"Wise," Hades said. "Your beliefs are all you have in the end."

"My husband," Persephone said, "may I appeal to you? May I appeal to your heart you hide so well?"

Hades looked at his wife then nodded once.

She took a deep breath. "You stole me away from my mother's green earth, dragging me to this dark place so long ago, yet I love you. It was not agony I felt when Zeus decreed that I remain here for six months because of the pomegranate seeds I ate, but joy. You were unlike anything else in all the worlds I'd ever known. So withdrawn. I had fallen for you, my lord. And I know you abducted me because you had fallen in love with me.

"A tragic misconception is that you take the mortals for personal amusement. I know this is not so. You maintain balance. A heavy job effortlessly handled by your deft hands. Still, they are frightened. The order you preserve is beyond their fragile consciousness. If you were to show mercy, my love, even just once, then perhaps humanity may understand. Show mercy for love, for what better reason for mercy than love? Show mercy, and they will be forced to forgive death. For all the love on earth. For our love. For me. Please, mighty Hades. I beg you."

He'd reached the Queen. Hope swelled, and the darkness festering in Vanian's heart since Patricia's death cracked, spilling light into his soul.

Hades looked at Persephone. He still couldn't read the King's eyes.

"It would be untrue if I claimed to be unmoved," said Hades. "This is a special case. Not many have the ability or the will to cross the Acheron. I am impressed with your convictions and your voice. Persephone, my love, it will be so that Vanian may have Patricia back. It is not so mortals will forgive me, but because I also believe love is the most imperative thing in existence. Should it come pass that I lose you, Persephone, mortal and god alike would tremble at my unrelenting wrath. My queen, this is as much a gift for you as it is to the mortal. Thantos, bring Patricia."

As the shape floated through the walls, the darkness in Vanian's heart was swallowed by joy. He couldn't wait to see her again. The flames burned brighter than ever in his chest. He'd won.

"Thank you, Hades."

"She's not yours yet," Hades said. "Your will has brought you far. However, sometimes faith must be placed in something larger than what you can see or feel. As a lesson in humility, you must put your faith in my word and leave the Otherworld on your own. Patricia will be following, but since she is still dead, she remains mine. While in my kingdom, you may not look back nor hear her voice until you both return to your realm. Return without violating my terms, and she's yours. One peek, one sideways glance, and she remains with me forever. This is another chance at life, and it will not happen again."

Persephone reached over and clasped her husband's hand. Vanian thought he detected a smile pull on the King's lips.

"Thank you, kind Hades," Vanian said. "And thank you, Persephone. May I see her before I begin my walk?"

Hades thought a moment. "Yes."

Thantos appeared through the wall. Ghostlike, Patricia followed. Though pale and transparent, Vanian couldn't remember her ever looking more beautiful. The Otherworld stood still. Her sunken, lifeless eyes sparkled. Vanian longed for her. He almost reached out and pulled her in his arms to cover her face with kisses, but he held his ground, saving face before the merciful king.

"Now go," the king said. "Leave my realm until it's your time. Eternity awaits."

Vanian bowed, taking one last look at Patricia before heading towards the adjoining hall.

# ♫ TRACK 17 ♫

Knowing she was following and not looking back killed Vanian. By the time he reached the mossy corridors, his fear vanished, replaced with a sense of security missing since Bad Apple left the Pensacola airport for New York. Now a lifetime away, the months of subsequent pain dissolved as the throne room became a memory.

He stopped and heard Patricia's footsteps echoing in the hall behind him.

*Tap, tap, tap...*

She sounded nearby, but how close was an uncertainty. He imagined her only a few paces back. Closing his eyes, he swore he discerned dragon's blood, her favorite perfume.

In the stained glass courtyard, Vanian still heard her following. The stained glass windows towered overhead. Would a pane one day observe his Otherworld visit? No artisan could properly capture Patricia's beauty. He wished he could look at her again, at those red braids framing her oval face. He wished he could see her eyes—oh, how he missed her playful winks.

Coughing, his lungs still expelled black ooze. He pressed on, through the tall wooden doors opening to the outside.

*Tap, tap, tap...*

Past the gothic-arced entrance leading into the foggy path where the winged beasts remained perched on skeletal trees. The creatures shook their wings and howled into the darkness, their oscillating heads followed the couple's passing. Were they cheering or threatening? It didn't matter, he had what he'd come for. Vanian kept his gaze forward, heading down the dusty mountain path in search of someplace familiar.

*Crunch, crunch, crunch...*

Her soft footsteps squeaked in the sand, like they had the first night they kissed on the beach. They would have to go back to that kiosk and add more art to her logo. Maybe he'd help Kitty and Patricia design t-shirts for the next tour.

From time to time, he heard her breathing, so he slowed down hoping her breath would brush against his neck. Standing still, he no longer heard her footfalls, so he continued, never looking back.

As the mountains grew taller, more jagged, Vanian came across the point where the three roads met. Vanian wanted to ask the judges how Patricia was doing, but he bit his tongue out of respect. The judges said nothing as he passed. In the distance, thunder ripped through the mountains.

Vanian led Patricia through the Mnemosyne, taking another long pull from its cool waters. The sip soothed his burning throat. The lovers claimed the pool granted enlightenment and omniscience, but he didn't feel any different. Maybe things will change in the land of the living.

*Splash, splash, splash...*

He heard her wading through, and the urge to kiss her in the mystical waters pulled at his heart.

"I kissed you in the water, and made those dry lips sing," he said.

He waited a minute, but she gave no reply. He stepped on the shores of Erebus. A moment of guilt pained him. He thought about Cali, how her suffering would cease with one drink from the Lithe. One day Hades might fill the position and release her, but where would she go?

He fought temptation to look back at Patricia. His stomach twisted with anticipation, burning as blue as the torches outside Hades' Great Hall. Dar, during a long stretch on the wagon, once told him that falling asleep without alcohol was painful, that the every molecule in his body screamed for drink. For the first time, Vanian knew where the bassist was coming from.

Entering the Elysian Fields, the change separating the two lands lifted Vanian's spirits. The lovers tangled in the reeds, wrestling as one. He left them to their passions, eagerly awaiting his first moment alone with her.

He imagined taking Patricia on a horse and carriage ride through the French Quarter, catching her up on what had happened the past few weeks while holding hands. Spend time in the French Market, looking at the trinkets and taxidermy alligator heads. They would eat dinner, crawfish étouffée and oysters, on a gallery while revelers drank and sang on the street below. Maybe he'd propose to her all over again.

Vanian's heart jumped. He was so wrapped up in his daydream he wasn't sure if he still heard Patricia following. He stopped a second, and from behind, her feet shuffled.

She was still there.

Still following.

He hurried his pace, ready to leave the realm and return to the living.

*Crunch, crunch, crunch...*

Entering the Asphodel Meadows, Vanian remembered why it was his least favorite part of the Otherworld. The mediocre souls wandered around as if nothing mattered, waiting for something or someone to take them away and show them life's real essence. Many people were heading towards this callous fate. He needed to write a song pleading out to the apathetic masses. He didn't talk to the passing souls, and before long, he was standing in front of the mountain interrupting the bronze wall.

He climbed over with ease, keeping his back turned while he heard Patricia scramble over. Tumbling rocks and footfalls said she made it over the edge, her feet *plopping* on the Tartarus side.

"Come on, honey," he said, "this place is scary. I'm here, so don't worry. Just keep following. We'll be home soon."

He wished she could reply but was thankful that he would hear her voice soon.

They walked a ways before he heard Astro's familiar cries.

"Vanian... Patricia... Help me," he called. Shackles rubbed his flash raw, their clinking symphony accompanied Astro's wailing. Vanian ignored the spilling blood. "Please, for the love of God, help me."

"Just ignore him," Vanian said. "He won't hurt you again."

"Help me," Astro yelled again. "Set me free. *Please*."

"I'll sing to you. Just ignore him."

He cleared his throat, coughing up more black tar.

*The universe is on time*

*And everything's all right*
*Sunrise, sunset everyday*
*Cloud in, cloud out, all the same*
*Thunderstorm here and there*
*A little rain but I'm not scared*
*From the east the glowing orb*
*Rise and fall just like before*
*Everything shall work out fine*
*The universe keeps perfect time*

The flaming wheel rolled by, its prisoner screaming. Vanian passed the man still hauling up the rock, and followed the trail where Cali floated.

"Hey, buddy," Cali said. "Did you bring me a cigarette?"

She'd already forgotten the last time he'd passed through. Now, he fought the urge to look at two women.

"Vanian, I need a drink." Her voice turned angry. Years of heavy smoking nipped the edges of her condescending words. "Oh, I see how it is. You chose that whore over me. You'll be sorry. She'll trap you, son. You'll see."

At first, Vanian felt the darkness returning to his heart. Could he save his mother, too?

"If you don't get me a drink, I'll never speak to you again."

He almost looked back at Patricia to ask for advice, but caught himself before glimpsing her. The moment stole his breath, and adrenaline surged through his body. Vanian always drew comfort from his bandmates and, more recently, his love. Their combined support made decision-making easy—there was nothing he couldn't conquer without them. Now, for the first time in his life, Vanian was alone.

Fear rippled across his soul. Vanian centered himself.

"You're not listening, boy," Cali said. The more she prattled on, the easier it became for Vanian to ignore her. That special place he held for her hardened, and a twinge of remorse blossomed like a thorny weed in his garden. They walked on, her moans growing fainter and fainter.

They reached the bronze wall's triangular crack.

"It's dark in here," he explained. "But a wise ferryman gave me good advice about this place. Just stay close, and we'll be on the other side in no time."

He sent out psychic energy into the cave, feeling his way through the darkness. Absent echoes alarmed the singer. Vanian didn't hear his beloved following. Stopping twice, the only sound was his now raspy breathing, the gunk taking over his lungs. Holding his breath and focusing his radar, the cavern walls were clear, but there was no trace of Patricia. Turning around in the dark fissure voided his contract with Hades, so he resisted looking back, pushing ahead.

*Sometimes, faith is all you have*, he thought.

Emerging from the cave, the Styx churned on his left. He walked a few more feet, but he still didn't hear Patricia. Heart pounding, he wondered if she was lost in the darkness, searching for a way out.

"Patricia, I'm out already. Don't stop walking."

He thought he heard footsteps, but he wasn't sure. After a few feet, he stopped to listen, hearing nothing over the restless Styx. Nausea and fear swept over him, but he knew he could not look back.

He could not look back.

"Damn," he said. "We're...we'll keep moving. You and I. We're going to get out of here. Together."

Clenching his fists, his fingernails dug into his sweaty palm. The pain momentarily masked the throbbing in his legs, the exhaustion washing over his body. The Underworld's atmosphere gelled in his lungs, clumping in the back of his throat like cheap whiskey with no chaser.

He'd come too far to lose her now.

On the trail leading to the flaming Phlegethon, his head began swimming. As the river's heat intensified, he felt sick. Coughing regularly, chunks of sticky black goo covered his hands. Not knowing if Patricia still followed ate at his brain. If only they could converse while traveling, he'd have no worries, but Hades' rules were clear. He pushed onward, hopeful he wasn't leaving her behind.

He remembered the spell he carried. Bringing it back to the land of the living was too risky. Such powerful magic in the wrong hands would be disastrous.

Hoping that the molten river would be hot enough to neutralize the potion, he reached the shore and pulled the elixir from his pocket, draining the lachrymatory in the burning water. As the fire swallowed the liquid, a plume spat out several of the fire fairies, and they flew around singing, their voices charmed with Paul's spell. Hearing them, Vanian wondered how the winged sprites would use their voices.

He came across the blind man sipping blazing water from the fiery shore, and Vanian wished he could tell him if she was still trailing behind. The Phlegethon unleashed another molten plume, and Vanian swore he saw two shadows cast on the path.

Further along the way, Cerberus still slept in the same position Vanian left him. A black tongue fell from the Labrador's agape mouth, the pit bull's head was tucked under one leg, and the Doberman's left eye was cracked revealing solid black. Its long serpent tail wrapped around his body as the beast's three heads snored out of synch. Vanian tiptoed by the monstrosity, not wanting to arouse the fiend.

Gloom overtook the Phlegethon's fading light, and ahead the Acheron's waves crashed. The path dropped into the thick, humid mist, and Vanian took the drop slowly, not wanting to slide down the embankment. Struggling not to fall, Vanian heard rocks tumble from behind him.

Patricia was still near.

Charon's green lantern illuminated the Acheron's coast, rocking in the inky haze. By the time Vanian reached the gondola, he wanted to kiss the skeletal ferryman.

"I have another passenger," Vanian said.

Charon chuckled. "I see I underestimated the power of music. Climb aboard. I shall take you both back where you belong."

Vanian climbed on the gondola, making sure to sit in the bow so he couldn't look back. The vessel shifted as Patricia boarded the ship. Sweat poured down his back. Tired and anxious to return home, he planned on sleeping two days away in the Canal Street hotel room, holding her tight.

Charon shoved off, sending the trio into the whirling miasma hovering over the River of Sorrow.

The lantern's green glow revealed sea snakes nipping at each other underneath the dark water's surface. Their fighting sent out ripples that jolted the craft, swinging the lantern. Uncanny shadows danced across Vanian's black-speckled knuckles as he clenched the mossy, boney boat. He looked ahead where only swirling green mist separated the bow from infinity. Charon's sculling came from behind but not Patricia's breathing.

Had she really boarded the ship?

Fighting the fire, the blue torch in his chest, he kept his gaze forward. Sweat poured into his eyes and down his back. Something bumped the bottom of the boat, rocking it from side to side.

Lights sprinkled the distance. Drawing closer, the yellow lights lining the Crescent City Connection took shape. The cantilever linking the Central Business District to the West Bank came into view. Another moment, and the New Orleans skyline became visible.

Charon returned them to where they had shoved off.

Wails from the unlucky souls lining the river overcame the sounds of Charon's paddle, the noise drowning any sign of Patricia's presence. The fog thinned. Onshore, the hopeless begged the approaching boat for passage into the Otherworld. Dar and Kitty appeared waiting arm-in-arm on the levee. A few feet away, Carter stood open-mouthed.

Vanian's hands trembled. He couldn't wait to hold Patricia again.

So close.

The *Natchez's* silhouette appeared. The three spires of St. Louis Cathedral stood sentinel over the Quarter.

The gondola struck the dock, and Vanian leapt off, turning around and offering Patricia his hand.

Although Vanian stood on mortal land, Patricia was still on the skeletal gondola. The air chilled, roaring around them. Her mouth opened as if to scream before she flickered like a dying candle and began fading. She looked at her palms, slowly erasing from view. Though her lips moved, Vanian heard no words.

Panic struck Vanian. His heart pounded out of time, trying to leap out of his chest and smash itself on the Riverwalk.

"Patricia," he said, coughing.

He reached out for her—his hands never seemed so small before. Grabbing just below her elbow, his fingers passed through her, leaving only wafting smoke where they had touched. The fading quickened around her chest—as if Hades was sucking her back into the Otherworld heart-first—funneling her now smoky form into the swirling mist over the river. They locked gazes, a tear spilled from her eye. She reached out with her remaining arm before her features blended into the thin fog hanging in the air.

He'd lost her.

Everything splintered. Vanian's insides came to a crashing halt as a cold numbness crept over him. His mouth filled with bile, but he felt nothing. Would he ever feel anything again?

Speechless, he looked at Charon. The ferryman lowered his cloaked head. The lost souls on the riverbank howled in the Louisiana night as Charon shoved off, heading back across the Acheron.

Vanian fell to his knees. Wet heat blurred his vision as his heart beat became as empty as the starless Louisiana night.

No anger.

No pain.

An unforgiving disappointment came down in time with his tears.

Dar and Kitty rushed to his side, wrapping their arms around him.

"Fuck," Dar said, flipping a cigarette in the dark water. "I saw her. I saw Patricia. What happened?"

"I—" Vanian sobbed, choking back the lump in his throat. The Underworld still filled his nostrils. "I looked back. I wasn't supposed to look back."

Charon's Lantern was now a green speck in the New Orleans fog, shrinking with each passing second. With him, Vanian's hope dwindled.

"We need to close the circle," Vanian said. "Before anything we can't handle comes through."

Vanian, shoulders bent, rose and walked slowly down the Moonwalk to the silver structure. The stone in his chest continued drumming, useless and crippled. Starting with the blue candle, he closed the circle, bitterly thanking the goddess and god for his safe passage through the Otherworld. After picking up the nutria bones, skeleton key, and candles, Vanian looked down to the riverbank.

He wasn't sure he wanted to ever live in the Crescent City.

The waiting souls had vanished, leaving no clue there was ever a tear between our world and theirs. He tossed the magical tools into the river, thanking the goddess and god again for their blessings. Vanian stared over the water, to a place no one would ever know.

The sky opened up, placing its arms around Vanian and brushing away his tears.

# B-SIDE

♪

Carter and Vanian ate lunch at a downtown café's outdoor table. The late spring Panama City air smelled of magnolia flowers and the Gulf. Early June's promise of a hot summer teased with gusts of breeze.

"So," Carter said, "looking better than I've seen you in a while."

"I feel better, cat. Been helping Paul out at the shop a lot. Man, it's good to be around him again."

Carter cleared his throat. "Did you hear Henry is selling the Mozzy?"

"Yeah, it's still going to be the club, just new owners."

"I bet they mess it up."

"I heard he's selling it to Steve." They exchanged a smile. "The only constant is change."

Carter watched a car pass. "I thought you were gonna lose it when Patricia vanished."

"In a way I did."

"No shit," he laughed. "You're the only guy I know that would open a doorway to another world for a woman. I've heard about what happed out there, and I was wondering if that's where you're going when you die? Is that your pagan version of the afterlife?"

"I don't think so. The magic I used was from a Greek invocation. What I perceived is just the manifestation of that spell."

"Does that mean you believe in my heaven and hell?"

A dark-haired waitress with an Eastern European accent brought them water. They thanked her, and she slipped back inside.

"Yes, I do," Vanian said. "Faith defines reality. But what the fuck do I know? Hell, when I die, I could find myself in a restaurant eating steak. It's all subjective."

Carter took a long swill of his water. He stirred ice cubes with a straw.

"Do you think she's still out there?"

"Yes. I'll wait until death reunites us this time."

"And Astro? Is he in Hell?"

Vanian sighed. The memory of the shackles digging into his flesh raised goose bumps on his arms. What punishment awaited him?

"His soul is not at peace. Whether he's still shackled in Tartarus or in your Christian Hell is debatable. I don't know if he'll ever find peace. I'd like to think that it's never too late to mend things, but who knows. I've tinkered enough with the universe. Now, I'm letting go and letting be."

"Sounds like you have your head on straight."

Vanian pulled out a flask and took a sip before sliding it back into his pocket.

"I know death," he said. "Cold fingers wake me in the morning and rock me to sleep at night. When I play music, I take an icy hand to dance. Death is inevitable, impossible to play games or bargain with, and I've seen enough. Though I live with death, I going to live. After what I witnessed in the Otherworld, I know pleasure is not sin, but a divine pursuit in this world."

Vanian coughed, cleaning his hands under the table with a cloth napkin.

A breeze blew in salt air from the bay. Bad Apple was defunct, but the music had not stopped. Dar and Vanian were recording a two man act while Carter formed a successful Christian band.

"Congrats on the single. How's it feel being a singer now?"

"It's interesting. I'm getting my message out. We have a tour coming up next month. We're hitting churches all over the South."

"I love the name, too. Did you come up with the True Vines?"

"George did. Jesus called himself that in John 15:1." Carter took a sip of his espresso. "How's the music you and Dar have been working on coming along?"

"Not too bad. It's not for mainstream radio, that's for sure."

"Have you thought of a name yet?"

"We're calling ourselves Fink Asylum, after a tomb we found in an Uptown cemetery in New Orleans when we were teenagers."

"I swear, you and that city." Carter looked at his watch. "I hope Kitty's okay."

"She's tough," Vanian said. "It'll be fine."

"Wanna bet? Girl or boy?"

Vanian smiled. "Five bucks says it's a boy. Dar kept on saying him."

"You're on."

They shook on it.

Birds sang. A car passed.

"Why did you do it, Van?" Carter broke the silence. "Why did you go after her in the first place?"

"You can't escape the fly, my friend."

Vanian's cell phone rang, and he flipped it open.

"Meow?" he said. "Congratulations, old bean. Is it a boy or a girl?"

Carter leaned forward. Vanian raised his eyebrows and pulled five bucks from his pocket, handing it over to the drummer. "Gulf Coast Hospital, right? Cool. I'm with Carter. We'll be there in twenty. Hey, what's her name?" A smile crossed his lips. "That's a good one, cat. See you shortly."

Vanian hung up the phone.

"I'll pay the bill if you get the car. Still calling her the Badmobile?"

"She will always be the Badmobile. No matter where we are in life."

Vanian nodded. "Let's welcome someone to this world, my friend."

The two men stood, ready for new beginnings.

# ABOUT THE AUTHOR

Living and creating in New Orleans, Louisiana, Anthony S. Buoni haunts swamps and bayous along the Gulf of Mexico, writing, editing, producing, and lecturing about his craft. A practicing pagan, he's responsible for the *BETWEEN THERE* anthologies as well as his screenplay-novel, *CONVERSION PARTY*, available through PULPWOOD PRESS. Recently, he's co-edited and co-produced two exciting anthologies with Alisha Costanzo with their independent imprint, TRANSMUNDANE PRESS: *DISTORTED: vol 1* and *UNDERWATER: vol 1*.

In the past, he produced the underground zine *MEOW* and the illustrated horror rag *OUTRÉ* from MEOW PRESS, and his work has appeared in *WATERFRONT LIVING, NORTH FLORIDA NOIR,* and *SMALL HAPPY*. Currently writing a New Orleans monster novel as well as putting the final edits on novels featuring ghosts, zombies, and a café between life and death filled with secrets and philosophy. His next book, a collection of dark short stories, is due for publication in early 2016.

When not writing, Anthony is a Bourbon Street bartender and underground musician and DJ, drawing down the moon with new wave, trance, and melancholy tunes. Other interests include film, gardening, comic books, and playing video games with his son, Fallon.

www.ingramcontent.com/pod-product-compliance
Lightning Source LLC
Chambersburg PA
CBHW051941220626
47052CB00004B/744